VIRGIN HEAT

VIRGIN HEAT

a novel

LAURENCE SHAMES

AN AUTHORS GUILD BACKINPRINT.COM EDITION

Once again, to Marilyn
". . . you're an O'Neill drama, you're Whistler's mama,
you're Camembert . . ."

Acknowledgments

This is the fifth novel I have set in Key West, and I have never publicly thanked the town for being so humid and so strange, such a congenial place to write about. So, thanks to the fronds for rustling; to the compounds for being clothing-optional; to the bars for being serious; to the people for taking pride in their astute peculiarity; and to the island itself, for being a place where things can happen.

If geography has always been an active—no, a crucial—conspirator in the work, then so have my editor, Brian DeFiore, and my agent, Stuart Krichevsky. Thanks, gents, for keeping me productive and for all the good ideas whose provenance I have conveniently allowed to blur.

PART ☀ ONE

1

Paranoia doesn't sleep; a guilty conscience looks over its shoulder forever.

Ziggy Maxx, nearly a decade after he took that name and the new face that went with it, still hated to be photographed, still flinched like a native whenever a camera lens was aimed at him.

Cameras were aimed at him often. A bartender in Key West, he was a prop in a million vacations, an extra in the memories of hordes of strangers. He was scenery, like the scabbed mahogany tree that dominated the courtyard at Raul's, like the purple bougainvillea that rained down from its trellis above the horseshoe bar. The bougainvillea; the beveled glass and polished teak; the burly barkeep in his mostly open shirt with faded palm trees on it—it made a nice picture, a travel poster, almost.

So people shot Ziggy with Nikons, Minoltas, with cardboard disposables that cost ten bucks at any drugstore. They'd raise the camera, futz with it a couple seconds, then they'd harden down and squint, exactly like a guy about to squeeze a trigger. If the barkeep wasn't quick enough to dodge and blink, to wheel discreetly like an indicted businessman, the flash would make green ovals dance before his throbbing eyes.

Every time he was captured on film he felt the same archaic panic; every time, he had to soothe himself, to murmur silently, Hey, it didn't matter, no one would recognize the straightened nose with the dewdrop septum, the chin plumped and stitched out of its former cleft, the scalp clipped and sewn so that the hairline, once a prowlike widow's peak, was now a smooth curve, nondescript. Hell, even nine years after surgery, there were hungover mornings when he himself didn't recognize that fabricated face, thought his bathroom mirror had become a window with a dissipated stranger leering through it, begging for an aspirin.

Still, he hated having his picture taken. The worry of it, on top of the aggravation from his other job, sometimes gave him rashes on his elbows and behind his knees.

The guys with videocams, they were the worst.

Like this guy right here, thought Ziggy, glancing briefly at one of his customers. Typical tourist jerk, fifty-something, with a mango daiquiri in front of him and a Panasonic beside him on the bar. Shiny lime-green shirt. The round red cheeks of a clown, and a sunburned head peeling already under thin hair raked in oily strings across the hairless top. Next to him, his wife—pretty once, with too much makeup, too much perfume, sucking on a frozen margarita, her lips clamped around the straw as though claiming under oath that nothing of larger diameter had ever penetrated there. Tourists. It was early April, the ass-end of the season, and Ziggy Maxx was sick to death of tourists. Sick of being asked where Hemingway really drank. Sick of preparing complex, disgusting cocktails with imbecilic names—Sputnik, Woo Woo, Sex on the Beach. Sick of lighting cigarettes for kindergarten teachers from Ohio, Canadian beauticians; nice women, probably, but temporarily deformed and made ridiculous by an awkward urge to misbehave.

A regular gestured, and Ziggy reached up to the rack

above his head, grabbed a couple beer mugs, drew a couple drafts. His furry back was damp inside his shirt; Key West was just then poised between the wholesome warmth of winter and the overripe, quietly deranging heat of summer. By the thermometer, the change was subtle; still, it was all-transforming. Daytime temperatures went up only a few degrees, but they stayed there even after sunset and straight on through the night. The breeze diminished, the air sat there and congealed, grew freighted like a soggy sheet with remembered excess. Sober winter plants died back, were overwhelmed by the exorbitant rude growths of the tropics—butter-yellow flowers as big and brazen as trombones, the traveler palm whose leaves were taller than a man, weird cactuses that dreamed white blossoms in the middle of the night.

When the wet heat of summer started kicking in, Key West seemed to drift farther out from the familiar mainland, became ever more an island. Ziggy Maxx had lived here six years now, and he'd noticed the same thing every year: less happened in the summer, but what happened was more strange.

Another tourist caught his eye. Ziggy's glance slid off the face like it was a label in the no-frills aisle, fixed instead on the jerky slogan on the tourist's T-shirt: WILL WORK FOR SEX.

The tourist said, "Lemme get a Virgin Heat."

Ziggy stifled a grimace. Of all the idiot drinks he hated to make, Virgin Heats were among the ones he hated most. Fussy, sticky, labor-intensive. Substitutes for conversation, they drew people's attention away from each other and toward the bottles and the bartender. The building of a cocktail like a Virgin Heat sent people groping for their cameras.

And sure enough, as Ziggy was setting up the pony glass and reaching for the Sambuca, he saw out of the corner of his eye that the man with the sunburned head was readying his videocam. Ziggy flinched, turned a few degrees. He poured the thick liqueur, then felt more than saw that the camera was sliding off his manufactured face to focus on his busy hands. An artsy shot, the barkeep thought, with something like relief. Another jerk who'd seen too many movies.

Ziggy made the drink. He made it with riffs and flourishes it never dawned on him were his alone.

Although he wore a short-sleeved shirt, he began by flicking his wrists as if shooting back a pair of cuffs. When he inverted the teaspoon to float the Chartreuse on the 'Buca, he extended a pinky in a gesture that was incongruously dainty, given the furry knuckle and the broad and close-cropped fingernail. Grasping the bottle in his right hand, he let his index finger float free; mangled long ago from an ill-thrown punch, that bent and puffy digit refused to parallel the others. He didn't bring the bottle directly to the glass, he banked and looped it in, like a plane approaching an airport. Slowly, with the pomp of mastery, he poured a layer of purple cassis over yellow Chartreuse, green crème de menthe over purple cassis. He topped the gross rainbow with a membrane of grenadine, then delicately laid in a cherry that sank with a portentous slowness, carrying with it a streaky red lascivious rain.

He slid the drink across the bar to the tourist who had ordered it. "Five dollars, please," he said.

He took cash, glanced around. The videocam had been switched off, for the moment everyone was happy.

A light breeze shook the bougainvillea on its trellis, the papery flowers rattled dryly. A woman, a nice woman probably, from Ohio, Michigan, New Jersey, fumbled in a big purse for a cigarette. She didn't have a match, she looked at Ziggy. Damp inside his faded shirt at the beginning of that season when things got only damper and only stranger, he snapped his lighter and cupped his hands and lit her up. She smiled, then blew twin streams of exhaust through her nose. If she was out to misbehave, and if she could stay awake till closing time, and if she didn't get a better offer in the meanwhile, maybe she would misbehave with him.

2

A week later, in the chill and sniffly north, a tardy spring was still struggling for a toehold.

Confused crocuses poked up through drab gray grass spiky with winter; forsythia strutted its early blooms against a bleak, gnarled backdrop of naked branches, hopeless twigs. In Pelham Manor, a sliver of lower Westchester that had learned its table manners in the Bronx, on an oak-lined street called Hillside Drive, the lawns were squishy with unseen thaw, yet patches of crusty snow still lingered under boulders; the early evening streetlamps made them blue.

Louie Amaro drove to the street's highest point, parked his car at one end of his brother Paulie's grandly curving driveway, which was glutted with vehicles newer, bigger, sleeker than his own. He switched off his ignition, said fretfully, "Everybody's here already."

"So everybody's here," said his wife Rose. "So what?" She flipped down her sunshade. It had a lighted mirror on the back, she checked her thick red lipstick.

"Why are we always last?" said Louie.

"Plenty a times we've been first," said Rose. "You don't like that either."

"First I like," he said. "First shows respect."

"Your big-shot family, they always make you nervous."

"They don't make me nervous," Louie said. "You make me nervous. D'ya bring the cassette?"

"It's right here in my bag." She blotted on a Kleenex. He watched her. Maybe they bickered, maybe she picked on him, but he still took pleasure, felt a thrill of intimacy, watching Rose do things like that. "Big shots," she went on. "Big shots when they're not in jail somewhere."

Louie raised a cautioning finger. "We don't talk about that, Rose."

"Don't talk about it? How do we not talk about it? The man's been in prison nine years, he's been out for a week. Whadda we talk about, the lottery?"

"He's been away. He's back. End of story."

Rose shook her head, emphatically buffed her makeup.

Louie's unsure pride swelled in the silence. "And lemme tell ya somethin'. My brother Paulie, he's a big shot even when he is in jail. Don't kid yourself. My tan—I'm still tan, right? I look relaxed, ya can tell we took vacation?"

The house was an enormous Tudor, with tall chimneys sticking up like organ pipes and a cluster of different-height brown roofs bunched together like a field of mushrooms. Security cameras panned across the pathway leading to the door. Louie rang the bell, then watched his breath until a buzzer let them in.

In the entryway they hung their cloth coats on top of the furs and cashmeres already piled on the racks. Louie took his hat off; he stood before a huge smoked mirror and raked his sparse hair left to right; translucent flakes of skin drifted off his sunburned head. Then they walked down the long hall with its armoires and its torch lamps, to the living room.

The living room was brightly lit and very big and noisy.

From hidden speakers came the aged rasp of Frank Sinatra, the ravaged voice buoyed up by brass and strings. In one corner, a huge television set was blaring; half a dozen fat children watched it, tickling each other's ribs. In the middle of the room, three overstuffed gold couches defined a conversation nook; Amaro blood relations and in-laws sat back against the yielding cushions and perched on the pillowed arms.

Louie's brother Al was the first to notice the new arrivals.

"Louie, Rose!" he bellowed, standing up and shoving a shirttail underneath his belt. "Look at yuhs! Those tans! I hate yuhs, ya pineapples!"

He came lumbering around an end table topped with nut bowls and alabaster eggs, hugged his younger brother, coolly kissed the wife. "Great ta see ya, great ta see ya," he went on. "Ya seen Paulie yet?"

That had always been the first question, Louie thought. *Did you pay your respects to Paulie?* Not just because, tonight, Paulie happened to be the guest of honor and the host. No. Because Paulie was the oldest, the big shot, the money man. "Hey," said Louie nervously, "I just walked in."

Al looked over his shoulder; the torsion pulling his shirt out of his pants again. "Where's Paulie? Louie wantsta say hello."

"Must be onna phone or somethin'," shouted back the other brother, Joe.

"Get comfortable," said Maria, Paulie's wife. She was handsome, stern, gracious by custom though her heart was all dried up. "Please, you'll have a drink."

Al led them through an archway to the dining room. Bottles were arrayed on a sideboard that small planes could have landed on. On the prairie of the mahogany table a vast buffet had been laid out—a bleeding beef, a turkey hacked and reassembled, wedges of cheese the size of splitting mauls.

Al made Rose a Manhattan, poured Louie a glass of Bardolino. Then he patted Louie's cheek, the bulbous place just below the cheekbone that gave Louie the look of a clown. Apropos of nothing, he said, "Louie, kid, you're still my favorite."

That's the kind of family it was. Everybody had a favorite, but the feelings were seldom symmetrical. What did Al see in Louie? A jumpy sweetness, maybe, a comparative innocence. Louie was the only brother who didn't hurt people for a living, who had never been to jail. To Al, those things made him lovable. As for Louie, he thought Al was a buffoon and a slob who spit when he talked and couldn't keep his shirt tucked in. His own favorite was his niece, Angelina, Paulie's only child. He loved her for her strangeness, her distracted gentleness, a certain feeling she gave off, like she was only partly where she was. What did Angelina think of him? With Angelina it was impossible to tell, though Louie strongly suspected she viewed him as a harmless fool, a smiling nobody.

They went back to the living room, staked out places on a couch. A heated conversation was underway, Louie gradually realized it was about salami. One brand, the pepper was too coarse, it hit that thing at the back of your throat and made you cough. Another label, the rind stuck, yanked off half the meat with it. Then there was mozzarella.

"Ya want mozzarell'," Joe was saying, "ya go ta Arthur Avenue."

"Ya don't think it's the exact same mozzarell' they got up here?" somebody challenged.

"No," said Joe, "I don't."

"Come on," somebody said, "ya see the signs in every deli: Bronx Bread. Ya think they bring the bread but the cheese they don't bring?"

"I am telling you," Joe said, "that me, my opinion, okay, the way it tastes when it's in *my* mouth, not yours, big shot, the mozzarell' tastes better if I go to Arthur Avenue and see it wit' my own eyes sittin' inna . . ."

Joe fell silent. Louie twisted his sunburned neck and saw his brother Paul returning from the bedroom wing.

Prison seemed not to have disagreed with him, though the truth was that, beneath the robust exterior, tubes were silting up, pumps growing sluggish, filters clogging. But he still had his mane of wavy silver hair, the dramatic upswept eyebrows, the power to stop conversation when he walked into a room. His shoulders were still broad and square, the stomach ample but not fat—imposing rather, imperial. The skin was ruddy beneath the careful shave, the strong nose Greek in profile, bridgeless. His pearl-gray suit hung as timeless as the drapery on a statue.

Louie felt himself rising, moving in a kind of trance to greet his brother. Was it love or obligation, awe or fear or just a quailing habit from a lifetime of being the youngest, the weakest, the least important? He let Paulie hug him, smelled the clove and citrus of his aftershave.

"Louie."

"Paulie, ya look great."

"I feel okay. And how's the plumbing business?"

The younger brother flushed, shrank within himself. In a family of big shots, he sold elbow joints and toilet snakes and plungers. Paulie's question—was it concern or an old need to keep him down, humiliate? With family it was hard to tell the two apart.

"Business is fine," said Louie softly. "We took vacation."

"I see the tan," his brother said, looking at his peeling head.

"Key West. I shot some tape. I brought it."

Louie waited, wondered if his brother would ask to see the video, would offer him his moment. He didn't.

Louie said, "Ya like, I thought we'd stick it in the VCR."

Paulie blinked, ran his tongue between his front teeth and his lip. "Sure, Louie. Sure. Later on. For now how 'bout we eat? Anybody hungry?"

3

Angelina was upstairs in her room, marshaling her forbearance and her good cheer for the inevitable moment when she would join the party, be kissed and petted and fussed over by the gathered relatives.

Not that she didn't love her family. In her way she loved them a lot—the men with their rough cheeks and loud laughs and crazy nicknames for each other, the women with their scents of roses and powder, their stunning, modest endurance, her mother presiding over the sacred confabs in the kitchen. She liked them fine, some she even admired.

But it was the constant questions that wore her down, that made her want to hide out in her room for as long as she could get away with.

It was the same at every family party. Aunts and uncles would seek her out, hunt her like hungry lions cutting a single gazelle from the herd. They had gotten incredibly skilled at cornering her. They backed her up against blank walls, ambushed her in the pantry, shanghaied her while heading to or returning from the bathroom. One by one, they'd get her alone, put their faces so close that their pores become as prominent as the pits on strawberries. They'd look at her with a soupy caring that soon dribbled over into condescension, pity. Their voices would drop to a funeral home murmur, and they'd say—

So Angelina, ya met anyone?

You going out much, Angel?

Tell me, Angie, is there somebody you're dating?

Ange, ya found a fella?

Angelina, in turn, had gotten pretty deft at giving evasive answers. She met plenty of people—checkers in the supermarket, toll collectors on the Throgs Neck Bridge. She went out a lot—to the movies with her girlfriends, to bars in groups of bachelorettes whose personnel would shift and dwindle as more of the women stumbled onto mates. And the fact was, she did date now and then. A friend would line her up. Or a guy at another table would send over a drink, and if he didn't seem like a total jerk, she'd talk to him, see him for dinner on the weekend.

But those dates went nowhere, and the rueful glances her relatives fixed on her seemed to suggest that they thought her dates would always go nowhere.

Why did they think that? Angelina wondered. Did they think something was wrong with her, that her insides were faulty, the nerves withered or disconnected? Did they imagine she was frigid? Did they somehow *enjoy* imagining she was frigid, picturing avid hands laboring to rouse her unresponding body?

Well, she wasn't frigid and there was nothing wrong with her equipment, thank you very much. The truth was she had a secret. She was twenty-seven years old and had a secret that had simmered inside her for a decade now, that had burned as unremittingly as one of those red bulbs they use to keep food hot in diners. The secret had given her patience and a kind of anchoring wisdom it might have seemed she had no claim to. But wisdom didn't come from experience alone; it also came from yearning, and waiting, and appraising and dismissing all those many things and people that did not measure up to the thing that one was waiting for.

She thought about her secret and got ready to join the party. She stepped into stretch pants with stirrups, pants that made uncontoured tubes of her calves and thighs. She pulled on a cabled mohair sweater that made her chest into a vague fuzzy nothing. Pulling on the sweater mussed her jet black hair; she restored its arch with a lift of the handle of the teasing brush, pinned it into place with a black velvet headband, made sure the flip at the nape of her neck came free of the woolly collar. She looked at herself in the mirror, thinned mascara on the lashes that shaded her wide-spaced violet eyes. She looked archaic, but what no one realized was that she knew she looked archaic, she wanted it that way, it was a private emblem of her cherished distance.

A virgin with a passionate secret, she slipped into her loafers and went downstairs to face her family's questions and their pity.

✳ ✳ ✳

People were eating.

They sat on sofas, love seats, plates on their knees, the men with napkins stuffed into their collars. They talked as they ate, pointing at each other with their forks. The women cautiously chased oily artichokes across the china, exactingly cut roast beef with silent knives. The fat kids ate in front of television, dropped meatballs and hunks of sausage on their disheveled clothes.

Angelina approached the picked-over buffet, took some raw vegetables, a slice of crumbly cheese, made herself a white wine spritzer, weak. She took a deep breath and stepped through the archway that led on to the living room, hoping to be not just archaic but very small, invisible.

"Angelina, hon!" bellowed Uncle Al, his voice like the wet

tongue of a large and unkempt dog. "And how's the beauty of the family?"

Before she could answer, Aunt Rose, Louie's wife, said, "She *is* beautiful," as though someone had denied it.

"Come sit by your Uncle Joe," said her father's other brother.

"She sits by me," said Paulie Amaro, softly.

Obediently, she did. Her father kissed her cheek, stroked her unyielding hair. She picked up a ring of raw red pepper, took a tiny bite, and chewed it slowly, giving her throat some time to open.

The conversation resumed around her.

"So like I was saying," rasped Uncle Al. "Florida don't show me nothin'."

"Key West isn't like the rest of Florida," Uncle Louie said.

Al ignored him. "Florida. *Ptui.* The beaches, they all got whaddyacallit, men-a-war. Ninety-year-old Jews in baggy shorts. No casinos, no big acts. Everywhere ya go, spicks."

"Not spicks," said Aunt Rose. "Spicks are Puerto Ricans. These are Cubans."

Al said, "So what're Cubans, Eskimos?"

"Key West is different," Louie said.

Joe said, "Aruba. Aruba is different."

"Who's talking about Aruba?" said Aunt Rose.

"Black sand," Joe went on. "How many places, ya see black sand?"

"Jersey, right in Jersey," Al said.

"Key West," said Louie, a little desperately, "it's not about sand, it's about—"

"About what, Uncle Louie?" Angelina asked.

He gestured feebly, his plate wobbled on his nervous knees. "About . . . about, like, the way people are down there. Easy. Funny. It's hard t'explain, that's why I brought the tape."

"Oh jeez," groaned Uncle Joe. "Home movies."

Uncle Louie flushed, his peeling sunburned scalp grew

redder beneath his wisps of hair, his clownish cheeks grew scarlet.

"That's not nice," said Angelina. "After Uncle Louie went through all the trouble."

She said it gently, but she was Paulie's daughter, she was sitting at his right. Joe squirmed against the brocade cushion.

Paul Amaro took a sip of wine, washed his teeth with it. He'd been away nine years, a third of Angelina's life. He was remorseful for having left her; ashamed, he wouldn't let her attend his trial or visit him in jail. He remembered her goodbye kiss better than he remembered his wife's, he wanted to indulge her now in every way he could. "We'll watch the tape," he said, as he stroked her hair again. "We'll have coffee, cake, we'll watch the tape with coffee."

✳ ✳ ✳

Fat, spoiled Allie Junior had red sauce on his bright blue shirt and olive oil on the placket of his fly and he didn't want to watch the tape. "It's playoffs," he whined. "I wanna watch hockey."

"There's another TV in my bedroom," said Maria, Angelina's mother.

"But this is the good TV," the child griped.

"Here we're watching Uncle Louie's tape," said Paul.

"Uncle Louie's stupid tape," muttered the child.

Al made an operatic reach toward his belt buckle. "The strap? You want the strap?"

The fat kid sulked. Buttons were pushed and the tape began to roll. Uncle Louie cleared his throat and launched into his narration, but his heart wasn't in it. "This is the airport—"

"Who wants to see a stupid airport?" said Little Allie, and his father smacked him on his chubby arm.

". . . Open-air, lizards running around, they still got DC-3s parked on the runway . . . And look at this—right across the road, the ocean. How many places, ya rent your car, the first stop sign is the ocean?"

People drank coffee, nibbled cake. Louie did his travelogue and wondered why he wasn't happier about it. He was showing off his vacation, he'd told himself if he got to do that it would be a successful evening. But somehow his triumph had been tarnished in advance, it was always like that with his family.

"Funny names they got for things down there," he rambled on, as unsteady pictures chased each other across the screen. "This is Duds'n'Suds, combination bar and laundromat. Or this place, onna corner of Truman Avenue and Margaret Street, they call it the Margaret Truman Launderette."

"Ya took vacation," said his brother Joe, "or ya did the wash?"

Louie ignored the comment. "Look that sunset," he soldiered on. "The way the harbor faces, the sun slips right into the water."

Angelina was sitting on the carpet, her back against an ottoman. She watched the red disk slide beneath the surface of the barely rippling Gulf, serene and stately as a king entering his bath. "It's beautiful," she murmured. Her face seemed far away, she imagined herself someplace warm as August and foreign as the sea.

Louie remembered why she was his favorite, he felt his sunburned head grow flushed with kinship and with gratitude. He went on, his voice a little stronger now that he believed there was at least one person interested in what he said.

"And the bars, the crazy bars they got there. Live music all day long. Tequila and eggs for breakfast . . . This here's Sloppy Joe's, world famous, look the big picture a Hemingway . . . And this one, Hog's Breath Saloon, big pig for a trademark . . . Oh yeah, and this one—what the heck's the name a this one, Rose?"

His wife was bored. It showed. "How should I remember, Louie?"

"Well anyway," he said, "weird place. Look: Fancy bar, fancy mirror, but hardly has a roof. Just vines. Vines with flowers. All kindsa fancy drinks. Mango this, papaya that. Old-fashioned fruit squeezer . . . Oh yeah, this I got a kick outa . . ."

On the screen, a stranger's blurry and averted face blinked past and then a thick and eccentric pair of hands began concocting a Virgin Heat.

"Playoffs, we gotta watch some jerk makin' a drink?" said Little Allie.

"A craftsman," said Uncle Louie. "A builder. Layer after layer. Look the colors."

The family watched the hands. But no one watched like Angelina did. She watched the bartender flick his thick but supple wrists, watched him arch his pinky as he grasped a spoon. She watched the bent index finger, wounded, independent, that would not fall into line with all the others, and as she watched, her body warmed in its cocoon of shapeless clothing.

She knew it was impossible, unthinkable, but she also knew that she knew those hands, she was sure she did.

She watched them bring the bottle to the glass, slowly, roundly, the strong arm doubling back as though softly to enfold a shoulder, to stake out the small space of a caress. She watched the hands, and, watching them, she heard a voice made more tender by its very gruffness, saying *you and me, Angelina, you and me.* At the edges of her vision, the walls of the room stopped meeting at the corners, the floor got wavy underneath her. It couldn't be, it was fantasy, delusion, but she knew the hands on the screen were the hands she had felt on her hair, on her neck, on the tender place just below the ear, every day and every night for what already seemed a lifetime.

The cocktail was made, the cherry drifted downward toward the bottom of the glass, trailing its red curtain of grenadine. Angelina tried to speak, tried to sound casual. Her throat was dry, the words came out tentative and childish. "The name of that place, you can't remember?"

Uncle Louie pursed his lips, clicked his tongue, shook his head, defeated. Angelina tried not to pout, not to squirm.

The video rolled on, moved in no special order to schooners on the horizon, parasailors against a flawless sky, drag queens on pink mopeds. Angelina pressed her back hard against the couch, let the fibers of her sweater rasp against her skin; locking in the image of the hands, she squeezed her eyes so tightly shut that she could feel the lashes interlace. The Amaro family sipped coffee, nibbled cake.

The tape ended in a dappled glare. Allie Junior put on the hockey game. Chitchat moved to other subjects and after awhile people said good night, walked down the long hallway to gather up their furs and cashmere overcoats.

As Uncle Louie was putting on his hat, Angelina, her eyes too bright, the skin mottled on her throat, hugged him hard and said, "Thank you, Uncle Louie, thank you."

Surprised at her enthusiasm, surprised to be embraced, he smiled shyly, his clownish cheeks bunched up.

As he was walking past the thinning ranks of good cars to his own, his wife said, "She's a strange one, your niece."

Louie, wrung out from the evening, didn't answer.

And by morning, Angelina, without a word to anyone, was on her way.

4

That same morning, having no idea that anything was wrong, Paul Amaro left his house, to be driven through the Bronx to his headquarters in Manhattan.

Almost before he had settled into the backseat of his Lincoln, quiet streets had given onto glutted boulevards, stately homes had yielded to boarded stores and warehouses with smashed windows. Across the city line, sooty high-rises were smeared against the damp gray sky; the highway crumbled under the smoking, rusted, veering cars of the uninsured and reckless poor.

With it crumbled the thin crust of gentility that Paulie had affected since moving to Westchester. Mile by mile, the well-dressed commuter devolved back to the thug, the suburban businessman became once more the bully, the threatener, the felon. His posture changed, he skulked low and coiled against the window; his eyes became more vigilant and furtive. Ahead, the skyline loomed; buildings climbed up one another's backs like jungle trees clawing for a little swath of open sky. The appalling density put tension in Paulie's forehead; the city seemed to him a clot of greed, a boil throbbing with frustrations and thwarted drives and ten million interlocking fibers of aggression.

By the time he stirred his espresso in the back room of the Gatto Bianco Social Club on Prince Street, he had been subsumed entirely into his urban persona, his professional stance; he was angry, snarling, crude, and obsessed with honor in a shrill and sullen sort of way.

"Nine fuckin' years," he said to his old friend Funzie Gallo. "More like ten. All that fuckin' time, we can't find the mizzable fuck that ratted me out?"

Funzie was eating a pastry with powdered sugar on it; these days he was always eating pastry, as though to mask the souring of the life he knew with syrups, glazes, oils from nuts, reductions of fruit. The pastry was making him fat in odd places. His ankles hung over his shoes and little pads of blubber were narrowing his eyes. Now he licked his stubby fingers almost daintily before he answered. "We tried, Paulie," he said. "We put the word out everywhere. But the Feds, that program they got, they want a guy to disappear, they can make him disappear."

Paulie slowly, resolutely shook his head. "No one disappears except he's dead. People get new faces. Fuckin' government can give 'em histories, all the papers. But disappear? No. Ya know why? They don't disappear 'cause they never stop being who they are. Who they are, sooner or later it's gonna show."

Funzie licked his gums, tugged lightly on some extra flesh that hung down beneath his chin. Outside, trucks clattered past, music to smash things by was pumped out of people's radios. Cautiously, he said, "Paulie, what happened to you was a long time ago."

Amaro just stewed. Funzie knew he should leave it there but he didn't leave it there.

"Life goes on, Paul. We got businesses to run. Deals to consider. Opportunities, like this thing down south—"

Paulie wasn't listening. He didn't want to think about business; he wanted to think about revenge. "I want that scumbag dead."

"Dead, not dead," said Funzie. "It's not worth losing sleep. This grudge, Paul—for your own sake, why don't you let it go?"

Paulie's big knuckles were white against his tiny abused espresso spoon, blood pressure made his ears turn red. His voice was pinched, quietly furious. "We didn't get where we are today by letting grudges go."

Yeah? thought Funzie. And where were they today? Hiding behind metal roll-down shutters that some nigger kid had had the balls to paint grafitti on, drinking coffee at a stained card table in a dim outpost that smelled of roach spray and anisette. Gray, unhealthy men who each day mattered a little less to the world outside than they had the day before. Paulie didn't realize; he'd been away too long. He'd seen the headlines, sure—the indictments, the betrayals, the defections—but the guts of their decline he didn't grasp. He, Funzie, had wolfed biscotti and run the *brugad* while Paulie was in the can; he understood the slippage all too well.

"But Paul—" he began.

The other man cut him off. "Funzie, I'm sixty-three years old. That fuck stole nine years a my life. Took me away from my home, my daughter."

"I know, Paul. I know. But that's over now. It's over and the world has changed."

"You telling me it's changed so much that shit like that goes unpunished?"

❋ ❋ ❋

Angelina had never in her life been guileful, had never had to be. She'd never snitched candy, because candy had always been pressed on her. She'd seldom fibbed as to her whereabouts, because all in all her whereabouts had been contentedly licit; it hadn't cramped her to stay in the neighborhood, because she lived mainly in the precinct of her thoughts, and for the most part she'd been happiest in her room, the nursery of her imaginings.

But now, as she was abandoning her home and her family to seek out the treasonous man she loved, she discovered, with surprise and an exciting shame, that an instinctual cunning seemed to exist in her, as ripe and fully formed as a baby on the day of birth, that had been waiting only for a purpose. Once the purpose had been revealed, she shocked herself by being rather shrewd and as outwardly calm as a veteran spy.

Noiselessly, carrying only a large handbag, she'd stepped out of her parents' sleeping house—the house that, with breathtaking suddenness, no longer seemed her own. She never once looked back at the shrubs still struggling to awake from winter, the brooding chimneys stacked up on the roof. Under swift clouds racing through an undecided sky, she'd strolled down Hillside Drive to the intersection with busy Maple Avenue. She'd called a cab to take her to LaGuardia, where she paid cash for an airline ticket.

On the flight south, she'd sat silently among chintzy end-of-season tourists, watching with no real curiosity as they left their seats in brown sweaters and returned from the bathroom wearing shirts of pink and acid green. Through a gap in the jetway at Miami airport she caught her first real whiff of Florida, the smell of salted mildew colonizing damp carpets and the foam inside of vinyl chairs. She'd walked in a daze past promotional pyramids of plastic oranges and listened as lost travelers were paged in Spanish.

Now she was looking out the window of the small clattering propeller plane that made the short hop to Key West.

Below her gleamed the Everglades, a weird inverted patchwork of wet and dry, puddles of grass standing in a desert of hot water. Then the mainland ended, just petered out—no bluffs, no surf, just the flattest of lands dissolving like a dunked cookie into the shallowest of seas. When the imprecise and arcing line of Keys appeared, it looked to Angelina like a spoiled necklace, irretrievable beads rolling off a broken string. Suddenly she was lonely, burdened for the first time by the enormity of what she had begun, rattled by an understanding that, whatever happened, her life had already been changed.

She needed to talk with someone.

She glanced at the man sitting next to her, thumbing with utter lack of interest through a magazine. He wore a lavender tank top that showed strong freckled arms and a stomach from the gym; his light brown hair was just barely longer than a crewcut, and in his right ear, not the lobe but along the edge, were three stud earrings—diamond, ruby, sapphire.

She caught the corner of his eye and said, "I've never been to Key West before. Have you?"

He closed the magazine and faced her. His teeth were small and even, his eyes a disarming green; the sandy eyebrows had an enthusiastic arch. "A few times," he said. "It's heaven."

"You on vacation?"

"Vacation," he said, and he gave the word some thought. "Actually, I've just been fired. Retail. Just as well. I'm looking for romance. Looking for love. That's my real career, my calling. I'm Michael."

"I'm Jane," said Angelina, and in the next heartbeat she regretted it. Maybe she wasn't such a good liar after all. Besides, the problem with lying was that it was just too lonely, it created a floating world where no one could be trusted, where it would be much too easy to lose one's bearings altogether. "No," she said, "I'm Angelina."

Her seatmate gave a casual shrug. "Hey, it's Key West. Jane, Angelina, Liza Minnelli—what's the difference?"

"No, really. I'm Angelina. Jane—I was just being stupid."

Michael turned up his palms, smiled. There was mischief in the smile, and unbounded acceptance. Angelina felt she had to atone for her first deception with a headlong candor.

"And I'm looking for love, too," she went on.

He gave her a comradely look, the comprehending glance of one pilgrim to another. "Careful, hon," he said. "Remember: safe sex, maybe; safe love, no such thing."

"You don't know the half of it."

He looked intrigued, ready to hear and be nourished by some gossip of the heart. But Angelina went no further, and soon the plane began to bank, leaned against the thick and rubbery resistance of the air.

"Do you know where you're staying?" she asked him at last.

"Coral Shores."

"Nice?"

"Fabulous," he said. "Big private garden. Pool. Jacuzzi. Balconies draped with palms."

"Maybe I'll stay there too."

They were over the harbor now; below them, sails stretched back from masts, foamy chevrons spread out from the sterns of tiny boats. Michael toyed with his three stud earrings. "Not a great place for you to look for love," he said.

"Gay place," she said. It was not a question.

"To the n-th," said Michael.

"You're saying I wouldn't be welcome?"

The plane sank lower, scudded over tin roofs throwing back the sun and over cool blue squares and rectangles of swimming pools. Michael looked at Angelina—the Annette Funicello hairdo, the stretch pants out of some other age. Was she simply clueless, or was there some screwball moxie there, some retro originality? "You'd be welcome," he said. "Of course you'd be welcome."

"Well, then—"

"The question is . . . well, the question . . . I'll be blunt: It's how comfortable you'd be around a bunch of naked queers."

The landing gear clicked down; palms came up so close that one could see the slow dance of their swaying fronds.

"Is that all?" Angelina said. "I got no problem with that."

5

For Ziggy it had not been a terrific day.

He'd awakened in a damp, stale bed with a slightly over-weight redhead on his arm and a familiar wish in his mind—the wish that, starfish-like, he could simply shed the limb that was pinned under the heat and bulk of this wheezy stranger, and slink away, returning only after she'd smoked a cigarette and had the decency to vanish from the face of the earth. It hadn't always been this way for Ziggy; dimly, he remembered a time when appetite was not so stubbornly separate from emotion, when passion was not ashamed in daylight. But somewhere along the line some connection had been broken. Lately, night was night and day was day, and once the itch of sex had been briefly relieved, Ziggy craved to be alone, to think and scheme.

Though, after the redhead was gone, Ziggy had to admit that he didn't have that much to scheme about. He had his straight job; he had his action; they had both become routine. Was that good or bad? Pacing, he briefly pondered the question till he started to sweat, then forgot about it and blotted his back on the faded cushions of the droopy old couch. He felt muzzyheaded, logy. Maybe it was just the weather, the spongy heat that made vines hang discouraged against the crooked shutters of his bungalow, gave a narcotic heaviness to the smells of frangipani and jasmine that wafted through the ragged screens.

Or maybe it wasn't the weather.

He was anything but introspective; for the most part his inner life was as hidden from him as his asshole. Still, he'd lived thirty-six years, long enough for certain inner terrain to begin to look familiar, for certain signs to register as signs he'd seen before. And one of the few things he'd learned about himself was that, when he had a hard time concentrating, it might just be a tip-off that an upheaval was in the works, that he was nearing the end of something he was used to and approaching the start of something new and weird.

That's what had happened a decade ago, when he wasn't Ziggy Maxx but Sal Martucci. It happened in the weeks before he'd gotten arrested.

Things had been going swimmingly. He was an up-and-coming soldier in the Fabretti family, a trusted hand and a good earner in the crew of capo Paulie Amaro. He was at that intoxicating age when every week he felt a little more confident, a little more established. He'd muscled in on a couple of downtown restaurants; he had guys who owed him favors at the fish market. He'd just recently started buying custom suits; his loins twinged with importance when the tailor tugged the buttery wool to measure cuffs. He got laid at will, and he had started to tarry with his boss's pretty teenage daughter. He didn't dare to pop her cherry, but he liked her, was moved somehow by the chewing-gum taste of her mouth, the delicious unease with which she let his fingertips trace out the lace of her bra. It would not be a sacrifice, he felt, to marry into an alliance through her someday.

Then, in a way that seemed abrupt and mysterious even in retrospect, Ziggy/Sal lost his concentration and it all went down the tubes. Did things fall apart because his attention faltered, or was his attention overwhelmed by the droning approach of unstoppable disaster? Even now he didn't know. He only knew he'd begun to make mistakes. Here he missed an opportunity, there he made an enemy. His mind wandered, he didn't always notice when he was being observed or followed.

And in the midst of his floundering, something crazy, something ridiculous was going on. He was falling for Angelina. Not just toying. Falling. Getting all gooey and gentle, making promises he truly meant to keep. Absurdly, he found himself preferring Angelina's inexpert kisses and circumscribed caresses to the virtuosic strokes and mouth-play of his other girlfriends; to his shock, he came to shun the others. Angelina filled hollows he hadn't known were there. There was something in her violet eyes that would either redeem him or destroy him altogether; the weight of her head on his shoulder was either an insupportable burden or an insupportable hope, he was damned if he knew which.

Had he been thinking about her when he got nabbed? He couldn't recall; the shock of the arrest, its blinding quickness, obliterated everything.

He'd been delivering a hot BMW to the docks in Jersey City, where it would be discreetly loaded onto a ship whose official manifest listed as its cargo cigarettes and medical supplies. The Beemer—like many others, along with Jags and Benzes and Audis—was on its way to pre–Gulf War Kuwait, where it would be landed free of tariffs, stamped with a new serial number, and sold for lots of the same dollars the former owners had paid for gasoline.

Except this car wasn't making it to Weehawken, let alone Kuwait.

This car was ambushed at the Lincoln Tunnel tollbooth, locked in bow and stern by FBI guys in dented Plymouths. There were eight of them, and their dully gleaming pistols were pointed at Sal Martucci's head. For good measure, the toll taker had a bead on him as well.

And that was basically the end of Sal Martucci. They took him in, promised him Attica and not some cushy Federal establishment, and painted him a lurid and highly detailed picture of what happened to handsome young white guys who went to prison without their protectors. Whereupon he turned. It was a much longer story, of course, but, bottom line, he turned, traded in his former life at discount, said a distant goodbye to everyone and everything he knew. Including Angelina, who he never got to see.

The case, from the Feds' perspective, proved to be a disappointment. It didn't lead all the way to the top of the Fabretti family. It didn't bring indictments for murder, just the usual racketeering charges. Paul Amaro and two other capos got sentenced twelve-to-twenty.

Sal Martucci signed over his destiny to the Witness Protection Program. He ate steaks at the taxpayers' expense, stayed for awhile in nice apartments, had cops picking up his dry cleaning. Then he got his nose cracked like a walnut, the pieces rearranged. He got his scalp sliced open, his hairline reshaped like a refinement on a paper doll. For the loss of his young face he felt only minor regret. But when they told him that his new name would be Robert Clark, he rebelled. He would not accept such a white-bread name, a name like an ad for a credit card. His new name would be Ziggy Maxx—a jaunty moniker that just occurred to him one day.

Look, they told him, the whole idea was camouflage, you didn't want to draw attention.

Tough shit, Ziggy/Sal had said, it was still his life—a point the Feds thought arguable. But in the end he had mostly prevailed, his official name being logged as Sigmund. Sigmund Maxx.

They sent this new-created Sigmund to Ohio, got him a union card and a job in a tire factory. Like everyone else who worked there, he detested it. The stink of sulfur. The hiss of exploding steam. After two years he couldn't stand it anymore—

the headaches, the boredom, the annoying paychecks with taxes taken out. He bolted in darkness and made a point of not staying in touch. He was through with the Program and, at least as far as he could figure, the Program was through with him.

But that was a long time ago, a tale from an existence long aborted, and Ziggy, wasting another Key West morning, mocked his own brain for lingering on it.

He stalled in his slow pacing, mopped sweat from his furry stomach. He went to the greasy stove, took a cup of lukewarm coffee into the bathroom. Coffee, a shower, maybe a fast belt of tequila. He had to get himself started, ease into his day now that it was afternoon. In a few hours he had an appointment with Carmen Salazar, the man who linked him to the world of crooks and fibs and ill-gotten cash, and thereby kept him interested in life.

✽ ✽ ✽

Having registered under an alias, hit some stores for the rudiments of a tropical wardrobe, and had a nap under the ceiling fan, Angelina stood now on her tree-shaded balcony with its wicker settee and whitewashed gingerbread, and surveyed the postage-stamp paradise that was the courtyard of the Coral Shores resort.

Palms arched up from patches of white gravel, brown-tipped fronds scratched like hordes of crickets at the slightest breeze; hibiscus hedges squeezed out hot pink flowers from tangles of pale green leaves. Wooden lounges were arrayed around a pool shaped like a lima bean, and Angelina discovered that not everyone went around entirely unclothed. It was true that, here and there, a pair of pinkened buttocks saluted the sky, a blur of genitals spilled out from a nest of pubic hair. But most of the men wore tiny pastel bathing suits or kept their towels wrapped around them until they stepped into the pool or slipped into the sudsing and redundant warmth of the hot tub.

Angelina leaned across her balcony railing and sighed. These undressed men neither titillated her nor put her off, and she wondered if this was normal, if maybe something was wrong with her, after all. She had that simmer deep inside, she knew she did—but the warmth did not come out, nor did fresh heat apparently seep in to stoke it. Like an old crystal radio, she was locked on just one channel, thrummed to just one frequency. Or maybe she was being titillated all the time and had just stopped knowing it, maybe desire was always slowly accruing, like airborne toxins or like money in the bank.

She locked her room and went downstairs.

Crossing the courtyard, pretending not to be looking for him, pretending not to be lonely and afraid, she spotted Michael. Draped in a towel, he was catching late yellow sun and looking at promotional brochures. It surprised her that he was sitting alone. She'd imagined that he would move very easily, if not into romantic escapades, at least into some sort of breezy and congenial social life.

"Hello again," she said. "How are you?"

He must have seen something in her face, some comment on his solitude, because his answer sounded a little forced. "Great," he said. "Just relaxing. Settling in. And you?"

"Terrific," she said, though the truth was her stomach was in a knot at the thought of moving her yearning for Sal Martucci out of the realm of pristine fantasy and into smoky taverns and steamy crowded streets where she might conceivably find him in the flesh.

"Off to sightsee?" Michael asked her.

"Happy hour," said Angelina, and could not hold back a cockeyed smile at the perverseness of the phrase. "Gonna check out a couple bars."

Michael's sandy eyebrows moved the slightest bit closer together; he fingered his three stud earrings; he looked at her. Her imperfectly pouffed-up hair was translucent behind the passé headband; her bra strap showed haphazardly under a sleeveless blouse that was not quite red and not quite pink; she was wearing brand-new sandals that would surely hurt her feet after a few hundred yards of sidewalk. She did not look to Michael like a person who started doing bars at five P.M.

"Have fun," was all he said.

"You too," said Angelina.

6

But Ziggy wasn't working happy hour that evening.

As Angelina was heading out into the libidinous tourist clutter of Duval Street, he was half a mile away, driving slowly through a locals' precinct that tested the line between tropical funk and simple squalor. His archaic hulking Oldsmobile passed squat cinder-block houses that were painted pink and green, and through whose open doorways babies wailed and televisions blared. Plastic tricycles and cracked coolers stood in weedy yards strewn with the husks of fallen fronds; unseen chickens burbled behind a fence of woven reeds.

Ziggy parked on Bertha Street and climbed the single cracked step to the candy store from whose hidden garden Carmen Salazar ran his operation.

The store itself was gloomy and a mess, a graveyard for soggy pretzels and stale chocolate. Cobwebs fluttered in the corners; flies circled and sometimes stuck to gooey bottles of brightly colored Cuban syrups. The guy whose job it was to look like he was running a business sat behind the counter in a yellowed undershirt, baring his wet armpits to an oscillating fan matted with beards of dust.

Ziggy silently went through to the open doorway at the rear.

Carmen Salazar, as always, was sitting, alert but not tense, in a lawn chair. His back was to the door, he was gazing past tangled shrubbery to a light-blotting curtain of vines, yet as always he knew who had arrived. Without turning his head, he said, "So Bigtime, how goes it?"

Ziggy sort of liked it when Salazar called him Bigtime. He vaguely knew it was sarcastic, but a sarcastic compliment was better than none at all. He moved around so that he faced his boss, and said, "Goes fine."

"Goes fine," Salazar repeated. He was small and elegant, with hollow cheeks, a sharp chin, and thick black hair so short and glossy, it looked like it was painted on. On an island of damp skins, he never seemed to sweat; in a town of sloppy dressers, his sky-blue and mint-green guayaberas were always crisp, their pleated fronts immaculate. "You northern guys," he went on. "With you it always goes fine. Why? Because once you're in the south, you assume you're overqualified, smarter than the locals. This ignorance, it makes you confident."

Ziggy chewed his gums a moment but couldn't swallow back the words. " 'Cept I am overqualified," he said.

"Of course you are," Salazar agreed. "Much too smart to be just a bagman in a little numbers racket. Far too sophisticated to be an errand boy for a whorehouse. I only wish my humble enterprise offered greater scope for your talents."

Ziggy said nothing, just looked around the garden at monstrous flowers and bulbous fruits he didn't know the names of.

"Then again," Salazar went on, "if I was into bigger things, I would have to deal with bigger people, and they in turn would be doing business with bigger people still, and soon it might involve the kind of people I don't think you want to work with anymore. Isn't that right, my friend?"

Ziggy didn't answer, tried with limited success to keep his face as smugly placid as his boss's. He couldn't figure exactly how much Salazar knew of his past, but it was clearly more than he ought to; and that, Ziggy realized, was his own damn fault, the result of certain ill-advised boasting—references to New York friends, associates with broad connections, that kind of thing. Had Ziggy imagined it, or did Salazar stare a little too closely at his altered hairline the first time the two had met in private?

"But Ziggy, hey," the little boss resumed, and his voice seemed very abrupt as it bit through the other man's thoughts. "I'm a small-time guy, I'm gonna stay a small-time guy, so what's the problem? Pablo, bring the bag."

With only the slightest rustling, the vine-curtain parted, and Salazar's bodyguard appeared. He was always there, Ziggy knew he was there, and yet it never stopped surprising him that someone so big could hide so totally behind those slender vines. Pablo reached out an enormous hairy hand and passed along a briefcase.

"The usual place," said Carmen Salazar. "Gordo counts it, gives you a thousand. I'll call you in a few days."

✳ ✳ ✳

So Ziggy headed up the Keys.

Long before he reached his destination, Angelina had had two margaritas and a glass of Chardonnay and was feeling very blue.

In each bar men had approached her; the wrong men, always—obnoxious, leering, or just plain wrong. Sunburned vacationers had imposed on her their noisy, trivial, and irritating fun. She'd had smoke blown in her face, her breast had been elbowed, someone had stepped on her foot as he lumbered toward the bathroom.

Through it all, she had tried to smile as she dragged herself from tavern to tavern and carried on an intimate study of bartenders' hands, an exercise perversely delicious in its secrecy, sadly exquisite in the singularity of its goal. As cocktails were assembled, she examined palms and wrists, her eyes measured the weight and warmth of them against her shoulders. As beers were drawn, she studied fingernails, felt them lightly scratching at her neck. She scrutinized forearms for antic, looping, roundly ardent gestures. She contemplated knuckles, imagined their wisps of down tickling her lips.

But she did not see Sal Martucci's hands, nor, following arms upward to shoulders, faces, hair, did she see even the remotest recognizable trace of the man who'd stamped her with his image—an image gone forever except in her recalling. It was strange to think that his solid flesh could be altered, reinvented so much more easily than the ethereal impression he had made on her.

After three bars—not even the beginnings of a dent in the number Key West offered—she was ready for her room, and darkness, and quiet. She pushed her way past elbows and glowing cigarettes toward the door; unwelcome bodies surged against her as she sought the open evening.

But the street she emerged onto was, at that just-past-sunset hour, as loud and jostly as the saloons—was, in fact, a long extension of them. Neon mixed with dusk to produce a grainy, unnatural, and vaguely nauseating light. Drunks weaved and belched in strangers' faces. Motorcycles rumbled, brain-stunning bass thumped forth from convertibles. On feet that were chafed and blistered by the straps of her brand-new sandals, Angelina struggled back toward the quiet end of town. By the time she pushed open the picket gate of Coral Shores and slipped into the relative tranquility of its courtyard, all she wanted was a bath, some Band-Aids, and a pair of earplugs.

She took a deep breath that smelled of jasmine and chlorine, and headed for the outside staircase that led up to her room.

On the way, she once again saw Michael, now sitting on the little private patio that attached to his poolside cottage. He was dressed for evening, wearing a green silk shirt that shimmered softly in the failing light. His face gleamed too, seemed to give back some of the heat of the day.

He said hello, and Angelina said, "I figured you'd be going out."

"Nothing starts for me till ten, eleven," he said.

Angelina nodded, tried to smile, then felt oddly incapable of continuing the conversation. Words wouldn't come, but nor did her feet want to carry her away.

After a moment Michael said, "Are you all right?"

Alcohol and emotional exhaustion converged on Angelina, moved together like big dark knobby clouds closing in from different quarters of the sky. Feeling safe behind the picket gate, feeling safe with Michael, she gave in and let the clouds roll over her. She shook her head.

"Are you ill?"

She shook her head again. Then she hiccuped.

"Have you eaten?"

"No," she said. "I haven't."

"Would you like to? Shall we grab something?"

She raised her head then, got her eyes to focus. Michael's sandy brows were drawn together, his chest leaned forward and his arms were poised as though to catch someone who was falling. "Why are you so kind?" she asked him.

He blinked, he didn't answer. Though the answer, had he been able to frame it for himself, would have been that he was kind because in his deepest heart he hoped that it would be his kindness and not his green eyes and his stomach from the gym that would win him romance, that would make somebody love him.

"Let me change my shoes," said Angelina.

7

Paul Amaro got back home around nine o'clock that evening, and the first thing he felt upon opening the door was a small sharp hurt that his daughter hadn't run down to the entryway to greet him, that it was no longer the way it was when she was small, when the sight of her violet eyes and feel of her cool and carefree forehead would cleanse him of the rage and filth of the day and remind him what he was living for.

Now the entryway was dim and silent. Paulie hung his hat on a peg, draped his topcoat over the rack, walked slowly toward the living room. No TV was on, no stereo. The quiet might have been serene but that wasn't how it felt. It felt sepulchral and chilling, it made Paulie want a bourbon and some noise—clattering dishes, distant sirens, anything.

But before he could get his drink, his wife approached him. She stood in the semidarkness of the living room; behind her, the doorway to the kitchen was jarringly bright with a flat and cold white glow. She had a shawl wrapped around her shoulders. She looked old and tired—was *he* that old and tired?—and she didn't kiss him. She said, "Angelina didn't go to work today. She hasn't come home."

Paulie said nothing. This was an old habit, an old technique. First you listened, then you thought, and only then you answered.

"I called," continued Angelina's mother. "I called, she wasn't there. She hadn't told them, they didn't know she wasn't coming in."

You listened so you would learn; you thought so that your answer would not return to humiliate or harm you, because, in Paulie's world, once something was said it could not be called back or explained away.

"She's not like this," his wife went on. "If she's going to be late, she calls. She always calls."

Paulie thought, choked back the clammy taste that was the beginning of fear, said evenly, "She's a grown woman, Maria."

The comment, the unearned certainty with which it was said, made Maria angry. Her hands went to her hips. The kitchen light behind her made her outline look ferocious. "Who knows that better than me? Who was here with her, seeing it happen? I know her, Paul. She's considerate, she calls."

He sighed without a sound, walked right past his wife, moved through the dimness toward the dining-room sideboard with its stash of liquor. Maria followed, harrying him like a sparrow chasing off a crow.

"Animals!" she said. "People are animals. The people you deal with, Paul. Your friends. Your enemies. They'll do anything. You think your family's safe? You think your daughter's safe?"

With the bourbon bottle in his hand, he said, "No one would dare to touch my daughter." He said it faster than he wanted to, without a pause for thought. But some things, you could no more hold back an answer than stop a nerve from twitching at a shock. "She's out," he said, more softly. "She's at the movies, she's having dinner. She'll be home right away."

"Animals," Angelina's mother said again, and Paulie understood that the insult was meant to hit him first, before it went spattering outward to soil others.

He drank deep of the whisky, shut out his wife's voice but heard instead the voice of Funzie Gallo. The world had changed. The rules had changed, and people broke them now without shame or fear. Was it conceivable that someone had done something to Angelina? Why? Who were his enemies now? What would they want of him? He swallowed bourbon, thought as best he could, and in his silent, bitter way, he prayed.

✳ ✳ ✳

When Angelina had told him the story, had revealed, in her tipsy loneliness, far more than she'd intended to, Michael said, "Jesus. And I thought I stuck it to *my* father."

"Whaddya mean?" she asked.

They were sitting at a beachside restaurant on flimsy plastic chairs. Lingering nighttime heat pulled salt vapor out of the surfless ocean, smells of garlic and parsley wafted up from plates of seafood. Michael sipped beer, studied her a moment for some sign of the coy or the facetious. Finding none, he said, "What do I mean? I mean, all I did, ten, twelve years ago, was come out at Thanksgiving dinner. My old man, military, Air Force, he about choked on chestnut stuffing. But loving the guy that sent your father to the slammer—"

Angelina interrupted with a slight impatience, as though what she was explaining should be obvious. "Yeah," she said, "but that was *after.*"

"After what?" said Michael.

Angelina put down her fork, drank some water. Food was settling her tummy; talk was easing her mind; she felt the fragile well-being of a second wind. "After I was already in love with him," she explained.

Michael thought the comment over, watched a moonlit

pelican do a brain-first dive into the shallows. Then he folded his hands, put his elbows on the table, and leaned close to his companion. "And once you were in love with him, it didn't matter what he did?"

To Angelina the question seemed rhetorical, she didn't see the point of answering. Michael thrilled at the realization that he'd met someone even more desperately romantic than himself.

"It didn't matter that he betrayed your father?" he pressed.

Angelina said nothing, her expression didn't change.

"It didn't matter that he abandoned you?"

"What else could he do?" she said. "It was that, or die."

"Die for love," Michael murmured.

"If he loves me," Angelina said.

"You don't know that he loves you?"

"He did before. At least I think he did. The only thing I know for sure is I love him."

"God almighty!" Michael said. "And what'll happen when you meet?"

Angelina shrugged. "Maybe fireworks. Maybe nothing. Nothing at all. That's what I have to find out."

Michael put his beer down, reached out with a cool damp hand and clutched his new friend's wrist. "Of course you have to, dear," he said. "Of course you do."

8

Typically, Uncle Louie was the last to hear of Angelina's disappearance.

Her mother and father, after a night bereft of both sleep and conversation, had set about contacting the people they looked to for help and solace, and Louie was on neither of their lists. Paul spoke to his other brothers, Joe and Al, grilled them as to whether they'd been party to anything that might end in a vendetta. He spoke with Funzie Gallo, he spoke with whatever members of his ragtag *brugad* he could roust from their slovenly beds. As for Maria, she called Angelina's girlfriends, she called her own relations; when there was no one else to call, she called her sisters-in-law. No one thought to call Louie, stuck in his plumbing supply store in East Harlem, armed with a claw-pole to grab toilet floats from upper shelves, as cut off from importance as a jellyfish cast out above the tide line.

It was not till dinnertime the next evening that he heard a word about it.

His wife Rose was frying pork chops. She was a lousy cook, all she did was salt the pan, put the flame on high, slap the chops in straight from the supermarket plastic so that they sizzled dryly like souls in hell. Fibers of meat always stuck to the pan, when she flipped the chops there were tears in them, pale places like still-knitting scars. Cooking, she smoked a cigarette and sipped a Manhattan with a cherry in the bottom of the glass.

"Your niece Angelina," she said, as she stabbed the pork and tiny fat globules dotted the stove, "she flew the coop."

"What?" said Louie. He was looking out the window. They lived in a big tall building in the Bronx, near the Westchester line but still the wrong side of it, and what he saw out the window were other big tall buildings in the Bronx.

Rose said, "She didn't come home last night, didn't call. Maria's panicked."

Louie scratched his head. His head was still peeling from vacation, shreds of weightless skin rolled up beneath his fingernails. Angelina was his favorite, he wanted all good things for her. "Maybe she eloped," he said.

His wife sucked her cigarette, gave a short malicious laugh that ended in a cough. "Eloped with who? Who's she gonna 'lope with?" She sipped her cocktail, poked absently at the hissing meat. "Maybe she got picked up in a bar. That'd be a start at least."

Louie kept looking out the window. There wasn't much to see, but the familiar geometry was soothing, there was a kind of peace in the shifting patterns of lights turned off and lights turned on, shades pulled up and shades pulled down. "Paulie's worried?"

"How should I know, Paulie's worried? I talked to Maria. Maria's worried. Y'ask me, I don't see what the big worry is. Y'ask me, Angelina, for once that oddball kid is acting normal for her age."

"Maybe she's in trouble," Louie said.

Rose didn't answer. She put her cigarette in the corner of her mouth and stabbed the pork chops, flicked them off on plates.

Louie thought a minute, watched the frying pan, still sizzling and steaming.

* * *

"How many bars in this town?" Michael said. "How many would you guess?"

"I don't know," said Angelina. "Hundreds."

"At least they're close together," Michael said, as they ducked into another one, their fourth or fifth that evening.

It was in a courtyard off Duval Street. A mostly outdoor place, Caribbean. Cockeyed tables, their legs sunk in white and dusty stones, leaned against the trunks of scabby palms. Speckled crotons sprouted up from shallow soil and scratched at the backs of chairs. The bar itself was basically a shed—a seamed and ripply metal roof to siphon off the downpours of the tropics, a set of flaccid shutters for locking up the booze during the brief nondrinking hours between four and eight A.M. Vines clung to the overhang; a smudged mirror stood behind the ranks of bottles.

The place felt familiar, and Angelina wracked her brain to remember the details of Uncle Louie's video. But remembering was difficult. The bar where Sal Martucci worked—before the camera had zoomed in on the longed-for hands, how long had it been on the screen? Three seconds? Four? And, until she'd seen the hands, she'd had no reason to pay particular attention. She thought she remembered vines. She recalled a mirror, a warmly polished slab of wood in a place that was not quite indoors, not quite out.

But in Key West there were lots of places that looked like that, and with a tiny heartbreak Angelina saw that the hands that made their gimlets were long and regular and slender, not the hands she dreamed about. Discouraged and mirthlessly looped, she led her escort to a table under a palm whose deadly coconuts had been snipped away like the testes of some gigantic wild beast.

"Cheers," she said morosely, as they clinked their streaming glasses. Then she added, "This whole thing is crazy, isn't it?"

Michael beamed. "Absolutely."

"I mean," said Angelina, "who knows what he looks like anymore? Who knows what his name is?"

"That's what makes it so romantic," Michael said. "You've got to find him with your heart, there's no one that can help."

"You're helping," Angelina said.

Michael modestly blinked, toyed with his stud earrings.

They sipped their drinks, looked up at the sky. Lumpy clouds were massing, their pillowy bottoms reflected the red of city lights, their tall tops fell away in darkening shades of purple and charcoal and inkiest black.

"And it's really not fair," Angelina went on, "my taking up your time like this. You came here looking for excitement, passion."

"And I found it," Michael said.

Angelina scanned his face, refrained from saying, yes, but what he'd found was someone else's passion, not his own. As that thought rolled through her mind, however, it trailed behind it a hunch about Michael that surprised her. She heard herself saying, "You're really kind of bashful, aren't you?"

He looked away, and she wasn't sure she should have said it. But after a moment he answered. "Meeting people. It's really not so easy."

Angelina dabbed her lips.

"A lot of straights," he said, "they have these wild notions, they think it's all disco dancing and meet me in stall three. But if you're talking about really finding someone . . ."

He broke off, drank, glanced up at the wet, black, spongy clouds.

"Little secret, Angelina?" he went on. "Men talk big. Straight men do. Gay men do. There's a little bit of wishful bullshit in all of us. Or a lot . . . But when you're out there, looking, there's all this insecurity, all this doubt. I'll tell you—you can take a guy with a fabulous body squeezed into six-hundred bucks worth of perfect leather, and inside he's just like a kid at a high school dance."

They drank. Faint orange lightning was pulsing deep inside purple clouds, the glow came through like a candle on an egg. Angelina felt it was only fair that she answer confidence with confidence. "That dating stuff," she said. "I've spared myself a lot of that." She ran a finger over the rim of her glass. "You know—by being strange."

Michael looked at her briefly, then his eyes slid off her face.

"It's okay," she said. "I know I'm strange. I don't feel bad about it."

It started raining. It wasn't gradual; from the first instant it was a hammering downpour, the way it happens in the tropics. Angelina sat there in the rain, her pouffed hair flattening as she waited for Michael's eyes to lift back to her own. "Hey," she said, "it's really okay. You're queer, I'm strange. You don't know I know I'm strange?"

* * *

" 'S'raining," slurred a tourist at the bar where Ziggy worked, as drops the size of grapes slammed through yielding foliage and clattered like BB shots on metal roofs.

Brilliant deduction, asshole, thought the bartender, as he threw the man a small tight smile.

The evening had been even steamier than usual, the air was like some fat guy's underpants. The weather, and on top of it the endless parade of jerks, made Ziggy feel even grumpier than normal. He let off some private huff the safest way he knew: he stood there amid the clamor of the teeming rain and he thought about quitting. A job, a love affair, sometimes life itself—a big part of what made them bearable was knowing you could quit, reminding yourself. When you stopped believing that, that was when you got a bellyache.

This job, thought Ziggy—could he afford to blow it off? He made okay money with Salazar. But who knew how long Salazar would keep him on? Then too, it was a good idea to have a legitimate source of income, something to point to in case people got curious as to how you paid the rent. Besides, tending bar at Raul's wasn't all bad; like a savvy trout behind its rock, he could linger behind his arc of varnished teak, and the endless current of the tavern brought him sporadic amusement and sometimes business opportunities.

But then again, always, in unending supply, there were the assholes.

Like the guy coming in right now, motioning for a drink before he'd even got his butt up on the barstool. He was soaking wet from the rain, and plastered to his chest was a shirt that said I'M SHY—BUT I'VE GOT A BIG DICK.

Wrong on both counts, douche bag, Ziggy thought. What kind of fucking idiot would wear something like that? He was so disgusted that he barely looked at the guy as he took his order for a Virgin Heat.

Which was exactly how the man in the unspeakable shirt, whose name was Keith McCullough, wanted it. When you were working undercover, your goal was to distract your quarry, cause him to look away or to notice nonessentials, to focus on anything except your face.

9

"Maria, this is Louie."

"You want Paul? He's in the shower."

"No, Maria. I wanna talk to you. About Angelina. Have you heard anything? Is she back?"

It was around eight the next morning. Maria, in a quilted robe, was making coffee, telling herself her movements around the kitchen were purposeful, productive, not just aimless pacing. She hesitated a second before she answered Louie's question. She was surprised that her shriveled heart warmed a little toward her husband's youngest brother.

"No Louie, she isn't back, I haven't heard a thing."

"I hardly slept last night," said Angelina's uncle.

For this there was no answer, so Maria nestled the phone against her ear and resumed her shuffling across the cold tiles of the kitchen floor.

"She didn't say anything?" Louie went on. "She seemed okay?"

"She seemed," her mother began—"she seemed like

Angelina. It was right after the evening we were all together, Louie. You saw her same as me. How'd she seem to you?"

"To me?" he murmured. But he could not put into words how Angelina seemed to him. "I guess she seemed fine."

There was a helpless pause.

"Look," he resumed, "if she comes home, if you hear from her, will you call me, please, Maria? I really wanna know."

She said fine, she would. They hung up. Louie poured himself a few more sips of coffee, stared out his Bronx window at the next building's mystic pattern of shades pulled up and shades pulled down. He went to the bedroom, looked in on his sleeping wife. A lousy cook, a grouchy and critical companion, he yet doted on her, when she let him; he stole a moment of a lover's secret joy, seeing her head half off the pillow, faded lipstick still visible beyond the natural outline of her slightly parted lips. Then he went downstairs, started his car, got on the highway and headed for the plumbing store in East Harlem.

He turned the radio on, but he could not get Angelina off his mind.

How did she *seem?* She seemed like a dear sweet kid with something missing, or maybe she was just still waiting for her life to begin, her youth leaking away as she moonily listened for the starter's gun that everybody else had heard a long time before. She seemed like one of those polite untested children who stayed too long in the nest, getting softer, odder, nerve eroding day by day until the normal fright of flying off became an overwhelming terror.

Except that now she *had* flown off, thought Louie. Either that, or something unthinkable had happened.

Why had she flown off? he wondered. Why now? Where to? He drove; he thought; he was oblivious to the people who cut around him and gave him dirty looks for going slow.

He tried to recollect the other evening at his brother Paul's. In all, it had been for him a painful evening, but for the sake of his niece he tried to reconstruct it. They'd had drinks; they'd eaten. Thanks to Angelina's quiet intercession with her father, he'd gotten to show his video. He recalled the faces of his relatives—uninterested, impatient, condescending. Among them, one wide-eyed and attentive face, one person who asked questions, who seemed to share his fascination with this place that was different and loose and new.

A horn honked; Louie slid over a lane.

Then there was the weird intensity of the way she'd said goodbye. *Thank you, Uncle Louie, thank you.* She'd said it twice, her eyes a little glassy, her voice a little breathless, like he'd given her some wildly extravagant and unexpected gift. When she hugged him, it was not a normal good-night hug, it was the kind of hug you give someone at a wedding or a funeral, a hug that marks, and eases someone through, a passage.

Louie drove. Ahead, Manhattan poked up at the sky, cloud shadows put gloom on unlucky buildings, left misty sunshine on others. A hunch was growing in him, simmering: Angelina was a kindred spirit after all, was seduced by the Keys as he had been seduced, but she was nuttier and younger and therefore readier to act.

His meekness tried not to notice the hunch; his unconfident mind shushed what his heart was making bold to whisper. He didn't know where his niece had gone, he told himself; he didn't know, and in any case it was not his place to track her down.

But she had always been his favorite.

He drove. Above the cluttered, crumbling roadway hung a huge sign that offered monumental choices in the form of big white arrows. To the left, New England. Manhattan, straight ahead. To the right, the George Washington Bridge, New Jersey, and points south.

Louie's car was in the center lane and he had no intention of turning the steering wheel; he held his long-accustomed course. But then the steering wheel seemed to turn itself, he could swear he didn't do it, but was only carried helplessly past dashed lines and honking commuters by some freakish whim of rods and gears and tires.

His heart thumped as the runaway vehicle wound around the cloverleaf that put him on a strange new road that was not the highway he took to work each day. His balding head was burning, not from sunburn now but inside, as he veered from home and habit, as the bridge stanchions loomed up in the distance, high above the old brick buildings of the Bronx.

Then he was crossing the river, making the leap from the skyline to the Palisades. Vertiginous and giddy, he let himself imagine that he would find his niece, rescue her, and call up Paulie, call up everybody, with the epic news. Imagining that, his eyes smarting, he remembered an archaic fantasy, a fantasy so old and unweeded and unwatered that until that moment he was sure that it had died. The fantasy was that there would come a time when he would be a hero to his brothers, when he, Louie, would show himself as brave and wise, would be the one who saved the day.

10

Angelina sat at poolside, writing postcards then tearing them in little pieces.

She couldn't send them, clearly. But it was noon, she was faced with a chasm of empty hours before she could resume her quest, and she needed something to occupy her mind.

What did people *do* when they were on vacation? she wondered, glancing absently at towel-clad and naked men, late risers, as they straggled to the pool for their wake-up dips. Vacationers went sight-seeing, she supposed. But that seemed like a lot of work when the temperature was ninety-three and the relentless sun caromed off the pavements and tripped you up behind the knees.

Maybe couples stayed in their air-conditioned rooms and made love through the heat of the day. Angelina could imagine that, sort of; and did. The details of the act itself remained teasingly hazy behind a curtain put up by her mind and the nuns and her mother; but the accoutrements of the moment she saw very clearly: the champagne chilling in its water-beaded bucket, a single perfect flower in its cut-glass vase; under silver domes, fancy eggs nestled in a warm and creamy sauce. Lovemaking became linked in her mind with toast points.

Or maybe what people did on vacation, Angelina thought, was wonder what *other* people on vacation were doing.

Like Michael. What did he do after eleven at night, by which time Angelina had had it, and he seemed just to be coming awake? Did he go off and have the kind of adventures that Angelina would and wouldn't want to hear about? Or did he stand around at clubs, ankles crossed and an elbow on the bar, too shy to ask someone to dance?

Angelina tore up another postcard, let her bare legs flop down against her lounge. Who knew what anybody else thought, or felt, or wanted? She sighed, watched with imperfect detachment the forms of undressed men, swimming, sunning, toweling dry. It was challenge enough in this life to have a clear idea of what oneself was thinking or wanting or trembling in the face of. It was enough to feel, once in life, the pure unceasing gravity of a fierce and undeflectable desire.

✳ ✳ ✳

At the Gatto Bianco Social Club on Prince Street, Paul Amaro had called a meeting.

His brothers Joe and Al were there, Al with his wrinkled shirttail hanging out. Funzie Gallo was there, his fat eyes pinching closed, his fingers sticky with strawberry glaze. Attending as well were seven or eight of the young and unreliable and half-the-time-on-drugs soldiers left in Paulie's *brugad*. As a token of respect and in recognition of the seriousness of the occasion, Benno Galuppi, the Fabretti family underboss and Paulie's direct superior, stopped by, wearing his amber-tinted glasses that changed to opaque brown when he turned away his gaze.

The Paulie Amaro they saw there was not the man that they were used to. The past few days seemed to have chastened him in ways that nine years in the can had not. His alert dark eyes looked flat and sluggish. Something tentative had crept into his raspy voice. The proud chest had caved in a little; for all his bulk, he seemed to be cowering under the soft wool of his dark blue suit.

He rose now at the front of the room; to mask a moment's lightheadedness, he leaned an elbow on the old Formica counter that held the espresso machine. He put down his coffee cup and began. "Most of you already know that my daughter Angelina is miss—"

His voice broke and he was ashamed. He drank some water and summoned rage to bully out the humiliating fear. Rage came easily as he looked out at his colleagues, sitting at card tables on ill-assorted chairs or leaning against the pool table where no one ever shot pool. These men were his allies, the closest thing he had to friends, but he would be ready in a heartbeat mortally to hate any of them, even his brothers, if it turned out that anything they'd done had led to Angelina's disappearance.

". . . Missing," he resumed, his voice edgier, louder. "We're here today to see if anyone has any idea where she is or how she got there."

His eyes panned accusingly, his mouth twitched, showing teeth. No one spoke. A few of the men had espresso cups in front of them, but they didn't pick them up, they didn't want to draw attention by even the softest rattling against the saucer. In the silence Paulie's anger and frustration swelled like mushrooms in the dark.

"Pete!" he spat out after a pause, and a thin young man whose nerves were chafed red on amphetamines jerked in his chair like a yanked marionette. "You still fuckin' with Pugliese unions?"

"No, Paul. No," said the wild-eyed soldier. "Funzie tol' me back off on that, I backed off months ago, I swear."

Paul sucked his gums, drank more water, turned on another of his minions.

"Butch, your Florida stuff—you makin' enemies wit' that?"

Butch was calm, well-dressed, and businesslike. "Every-thing's been divvied up," he said, "negotiated. I don't see that there's a problem."

Paulie paced. He didn't have much room, it was mostly just shifting weight from one foot to the other, turning his head from side to side. Noise of trucks and honking taxis came in from the street, people walked past the iron shutters talking loudly, heedless of these obsolete men with their quaint rituals and vio-lent sorrows. Paul suddenly slapped the counter, slapped it hard enough so that tiny spoons did somersaults and attention was riveted as at the crack of a gun.

"Goddammit!" he said through a hard throat behind clamped teeth. "God fucking dammit!"

He leaned forward now, a thick hand raised as though to slap and pummel. Veins stood out in his forehead. His shoulders bunched up like the shoulders of a bear, his squat neck billowed with forced hot blood. "If any of you fuckers have been fucking up out there, if any of you have been using my name, turning people against me, I swear to Christ I'll have your fucking—"

A soft voice interrupted him. "Paul," it said. "Be fair."

It was Benno Galuppi talking. He was the only one who would have dared break in on Paulie's rant, the only one who could talk so softly and be sure that he'd be heard.

"You don't make accusations," the underboss continued. "You don't make threats like that."

Paulie Amaro was breathing hard, his arms and legs were pumped and nervous, like the limbs of a man pulled away from a fight that's just begun. He stared at Galuppi from underneath a blur of tangled, knitted brows. He didn't speak.

"We sympathize, Paul," Galuppi said. "We all do. We know how you must feel."

Bullshit, Paulie thought. Not a man alive knew how he felt, to contemplate with horror and self-hate the possibility that his own hoarded sins had crashed down and destroyed his child.

"But Paul," the underboss went on, "her disappearing, there's no reason to assume—"

"Then where is she?" her father almost whispered, his rage suddenly melted to undisguised desperation, grief.

People breathed shallow, tried not to move their feet against the scratched linoleum. To Paulie's men, to his brothers, it was as fearsome seeing him brought low as seeing him enraged.

Benno Galuppi softly cleared his throat. In the instant before he spoke again, he flicked his eyes behind the amber glasses toward Joe and Al and Funzie, and this, maybe, was a mistake, or maybe not; but either way it sent Paulie a message, told him they had talked, conspired, come up with something they thought needed saying, that only the underboss could say.

"Paul," he began, "there's something—I just want to ask if you've even thought about . . . Sal Martucci."

The capo tightened at the name. Galuppi went on, pitiless as a surgeon.

"I know you'd like to find him. I also know—we all do, it wasn't any secret—that your daughter Angelina was very taken with him. Infatuated. So what I'm asking—has it occurred to you, Paul, have you considered, that just maybe, if you find either one of them, you'll find them both?"

Paul Amaro didn't answer, couldn't answer; his mouth hung slack at the outlandish suggestion, he was acutely aware of the weight of his jaw. His daughter run off with his betrayer? Unthinkable. Beyond insulting. If anyone but Galuppi had mentioned it, Paul would have gone for him, seized his lapels, spit in his face. As it was, he stood there dumbfounded, humiliated, stripped bare and foolish in his beautiful expensive clothes, eating the shame of the idea like it was rancid food forced down his gullet.

Outside, trucks went past, rattling the metal shutters. A chair leg squeaked on the linoleum. When Paul could finally lift his head, he saw that his brothers Joe and Al didn't really want to meet his eyes and Benno Galuppi's amber glasses had turned an opaque brown.

11

A day and a half later, achy and discombobulated, Uncle Louie dropped his car keys in an ashtray, kicked off his northern shoes, fell back on his motel bed, and soupily gazed up at the ceiling fan.

The fan was turning very slowly, the canted blades seemed to be swimming through the air. The ceiling, like the walls, was a coral color, sickened by time and damp toward orange. The carpet was a shaggy beige, thinned and darkened by the tourists' treading between the door and the bathroom, the bathroom and the bed; and it held a smell—of sandy feet, and contented mold, and a tang like that of sun-dried seashells—that, more than anything, reminded Louie he was back in Key West.

Back in Key West! The bare illicit fact, now that he was fifteen hundred miles too far along to ignore it, made him giddy. He was quite pleased with himself, no doubt about it. He was also terrified, beset by the secret dread of the meek, who fear that even the smallest detour from routine could be the end of order forever, that even the mildest act of daring could call down monstrous consequences. Louie, in his mind, was risking all.

What would Rose say? Would she be furious? Furious enough to throw him out? Awful to contemplate, because, no matter how it looked to others, Louie deeply loved his wife.

Viewed through different eyes, their marriage might have seemed like one more joyless habit, one more self-imposed diminishment, but to Louie it was something else, a remembered exaltation that he cherished all the more because nothing but his cherishing was keeping it alive. There was a time when they were young and Rose was beautiful, more beautiful, with her full lips and arching eyebrows and terrific shape, than any woman he ever thought would be attracted to his bumbling manner and clownish cheeks and uncontoured arms and shoulders. He loved being out with her, could hardly believe the way she clung to his arm, laughed at his ill-told jokes. Even then he realized in some part of himself that she was drawn to him because she knew his brothers were big shots and imagined he would be a big shot too. It didn't turn out that way, and Rose had made him pay every day for thirty-two years.

But Louie didn't blame her; in fact, he blamed himself. He knew he wouldn't end up like his brothers, he'd known it all along; he should have set her straight. But he didn't. By omission, he'd made himself a fraud for the pleasure of her company, a fake for the flash of her eyes. Even now he didn't want to lose her, because he knew there was nothing to replace the pride he used to feel in being her man, a pride that, on his side, had ripened into stubborn love.

Then there was the store. The plumbing store. An embarrassing secret: Louie kind of liked the place. Other people hated it on his behalf, but he was fond of it—the cool fluorescent lights that buzzed, the perforated metal shelves, the joints and valves in their dusty cardboard boxes stamped with codes and sizes. It was peaceful, and it was the only place he was the boss. He got a kick out of the Dominican kid who worked for him. His name was Eduardo, but he was an American now, you could only call him Eddie. Eddie's eyes looked off in different directions, he wasn't very mechanical, but he was honest and willing, sweet-natured. He leaned on the counter and worked on his English by reading newspaper horoscopes and doing those puzzles where you find words hidden up, down, backward, and diagonal. Louie liked when Eddie asked him what auspicious meant.

Truth was, he liked the whole crumbling East Harlem neighborhood, where what seemed decline to some, was the next poor bastard's promised land. He liked seeing the domino games on the stoops; he liked hearing the women shout down from windows, exactly like old-time Italian mamas back when Italians were the immigrants, the underdogs, the losers waiting for their turn at being winners. His brothers wanted to forget all about that, they couldn't grasp Louie's affection for the marginal. A marginal neighborhood, a marginal store, its remaining clientele a few stooped and white-haired plumbers with arthritis, a smattering of Puerto Rican supers with the enterprise to turn a wrench.

Then there was . . . what? What else did Louie have to lose? He looked up at the slow mesmeric turning of the ceiling fan, sniffed the ripe and complicated air, and concluded there was nothing else. His life's entire wealth consisted of a very so-so marriage and a crummy business on its last legs anyway. Maybe it wasn't much to wager; what mattered, though, was not the size of the bet, but its completeness.

And now that Louie was back in Florida, now that he'd taken the unprecedented and irrevocable veer away from custom and reliability, the thing that he was betting on—that his niece Angelina was in Key West—suddenly seemed a ridiculous long shot, the baseless hunch of a lunatic. Out of all the places she might be? Out of all the things that might have happened to her?

Louie exhaled, let his soft and stumpy body settle deeper into the motel bed. He felt heavy, daunted, slightly suspicious of his sanity. But then he almost giggled. He'd been keeping a secret from himself, and now, between one breath and the next, the secret stood revealed: He had no idea if his niece was here. He hoped she was but he had no idea. He'd come to find her, but finding her fell into that vast gray zone between reason and excuse. Lying there, smelling tropic air, feeling his pores grow lush with the beginnings of candid sweat, he realized that his hunch hadn't been about Angelina. It had been about himself.

He'd been waiting a long time to take that first calamitous or saving veer, to let the steering wheel turn itself for once and put him on a different path, one with a whiff of recklessness.

✳ ✳ ✳

Paul Amaro had never learned the tender art of looking to his wife for comfort, and now that he needed her he was clumsy and ungracious, his questions soured into accusations, and the kindness he was asking for was smothered before it could speak.

It was early evening and they were standing in their cold white kitchen. Dinner stood uncooked on the counter. A cadaverous steak; broccoli still pinched in its wire tie. Paul drank bourbon from a big glass, Maria absently sipped at coffee that had long been cold.

"Is it possible, Maria? Is it possible she ran off with that scum?"

Angelina's mother didn't answer. Her daughter's disappearance had made her less sad than irretrievably bitter, grimly vindicated in her ready sorrow. Her husband's violent life would fold back someday and destroy them all—that was a bleak belief she'd lived with for decades. Now that the bill was coming due, she was unsurprised and strangely calm, as helplessly resigned as though the devil himself had appeared on her doorstep to claim his half of the bargain.

"I'd almost rather believe . . ." her husband said, and then he fell silent. What he was thinking was unspeakable, and the part of him that was beyond the death grip of his pride knew he didn't mean it anyway. He stoppered his mouth with the glass of liquor, then tried again. "Was there any contact, Maria? Were they in touch?"

"I told you, Paul. I don't know. Do I know everyone she talked to for nine years? Did I look at every piece of mail?"

"You say no boyfriends all that—?"

The phone rang. It was bolted to a tiled wall; the tiles made the ring sound very crisp and cold and loud.

Husband and wife stared at each other a long second, there was hope and a pale conciliation in the look. Then Paul Amaro squared his shoulders and went to the phone, hearing in his mind his daughter's quiet hello.

It was not his daughter. It was his sister-in-law Rose. She sounded drunk and she was crying.

"It's Louie," she sniffled. "Louie, he's not here. Last night he didn't come home. I called the store, it rang and rang. Today, no Louie. Again no Louie. I'm calling the police."

"You don't call the police," said Paul. He said it by reflex though his head was spinning. "Now pull yourself together, Rose, and tell me what happened."

"What happened? I don't know what happened. He left the house, he didn't come back. That's what happened."

Paul Amaro leaned against the counter, closed his eyes, held the phone a few inches from his ear. His chest hurt and his bowels burned. His whole life had been a crude campaign against ever feeling helpless, ever being the sucker, and now helplessness was ripping up his insides like a fast disease. Was someone out to get him, out to get his family? And if they were, what kind of craziness made them start with the few relations who were innocent?

"He'll come back, Rose," said Paul, his voice not feeling like his own. "We'll find him."

"We won't find him," snuffled Louie's wife. "He's dead. I know he's dead."

For a moment Paul stared at the telephone, then he quietly

hung up. He took a pull of bourbon and looked down at his shoes. He needed to think. He'd been weak and foolish to imagine he'd get any solace from Maria; a silly sloppy broad like Rose just complicated things. He needed to think the way he always thought, alone.

"Louie's missing," he said to his wife, and then he turned his back on her and headed for the door.

12

Even in Key West, people's schedules sometimes got cluttered, and the next time Ziggy was summoned to meet with Carmen Salazar, the appointment made him late for work. The meeting, fortunately, was routine and brief, dealing with the distribution of certain bribes to assure the smooth operation of Salazar's lap-dance joint on Stock Island. Still, Ziggy was in a big hurry when he left, and as he barreled through the dim and narrow chute of the candy store, he almost collided with a short and stocky man on his way in. He noticed a broken nose and beautiful shoes and almost nothing else.

By the time he reached Raul's he was in a lather, his shirt splotched before he'd even gone around to the professional side of the bar. He endured a snide look from the guy he was late relieving, and then he started making drinks for the early crowd already edgy to get their sunburned hands on some alcohol.

What happened to the years, he wondered, when season had a beginning and an end, when places got mobbed in mid-December but relative sanity returned by April? Now it was non-stop; month after month the desperate hordes flocked in, hungover, blistered, crudely raucous, acting like they'd never act where the neighbors might see. Their boobs showed; they laughed at their own ill-told dirty jokes. Was there anything less dignified on earth than a human being on vacation?

He made drinks. He hustled for twenty minutes, half an hour, then, when there was finally a lull, his mind flicked briefly back to the guy he'd almost run into at Salazar's. Something had been bothering him about the guy, and only now did what it was come into focus: He didn't seem local. His pants had a crease down the front, and Key West pants lacked creases. His hair was neatly combed, something about him smelled expensive. Plus which, Ziggy now remembered that when he'd retrieved his ancient Oldsmobile, he'd noticed a big car, dark and shiny new, parked nearby, probably a Lincoln. Unease tweaked him; just below the threshold of conscious wondering, he wondered if Salazar was as small-time and small-town as he claimed.

But the fret ended almost before it registered. Two guys rattled empty mugs and Ziggy, a good bartender and even, sometimes, a charming one in spite of himself, sprang forth to refill them, dowsing the worries of his other life in a foamy spray of someone else's beer.

* * *

"Michael? Michael, you ready yet?"

"Just a second, hon," he said from behind his door at Coral Shores.

Angelina was standing on his tiny patio, cowering in the crosshatched shade of an oleander. The sun, though very low, was just barely relenting in its heat, slipping from broil to bake; it threw purple shadows in distended shapes of languid palms and overhanging roofs. Angelina tapped her foot.

Then the door opened, and Michael stood there in shorts and a tank top and sandals.

"I don't understand it," Angelina said. She herself wore a

pearl-gray camisole, a blue blouse chastely buttoned over it. Her hair was neatly poufed, her eyes were on, pale lipstick smoothed the shallow crevices of her slightly sunburned lips.

"Understand what?"

"I wear all this stuff," she said. "You put on a couple shreds of clothes. You have like half an inch of hair. And I'm always waiting for you."

Michael closed his door, pocketed the key. "Attention to detail," he said.

"Like what details?"

"Like teeth, okay? I don't go out until I floss."

"Flossing doesn't take that long. What else?"

"Sweetheart, you don't have to know everything."

They wove through the courtyard, around scraps of hedge and groups of lounging men, past the Jacuzzi where naked people sipped champagne from plastic cups. At the gate, they turned left, toward the noise, the crowds, the bars.

It was a ritual by now, the kind of thing that old friends did without having to make plans. They convened at six or so, they drank and talked till nine or ten. They watched men's hands together, analyzed them. They'd been served by gay hands and straight hands, lean hands and pudgy hands, hairy hands and smooth hands, hands whose fingernails were dirty and one hand that was missing a pinky, ended in a shiny stub. They'd drunk margaritas and frozen daiquiris and Mai Tais—drinks that were sometimes a little sickening, but that gave them a chance to appraise the bartender's style. They'd been in bars with guitar players, bars with pianos, bars with karaoke and bars with giant speakers hanging from the ceiling. Maybe thirty bars so far, with no sign of the hands Angelina had come to find.

Leaving Coral Shores behind them, Michael said, "I have a good feeling about tonight."

"You say that every night," said Angelina.

He toyed with his stud earrings. "And every night I do."

"Perennial optimist."

He didn't deny it. They walked. Slanting sunlight skidded off the pavement, sapped strength from their legs.

After a moment Angelina went on. "Me, I'm kind of nervous tonight. I don't know why."

Michael didn't answer, just watched reddened tourists walking past.

"Really nervous all of a sudden," Angelina said. "Like jumpy. I feel it in my throat."

They crossed a street, dodged pink rented scooters.

"On edge," she said.

They crossed Truman Avenue; the crowd began to thicken. She said, "Michael, would it be okay, I mean, would you think it's really stupid, if we held hands?"

He stopped a second, looked at her. Then he held out his hand, she took it, and they moved on toward the crush.

* * *

Uncle Louie sucked like a kid at a mango-flavored sno-cone that was melting as fast as he could eat it.

He wove through the sunset crowds at Mallory Square, among guitarists and magicians and a flag-draped man on stilts, and admitted to himself, a little guiltily, that he hadn't felt so alive in many years. He'd enjoyed his vacation with Rose, sure, but that was different. That was . . . *vacation*, an allowed and strictly bordered break between vast tracts of duty and routine. Besides, being with Rose—well, she made him nervous. Little things—was his hair messed up, his bald spot showing? Did he sound wimpy, unsophisticated, asking for a table in a restaurant? It was a nervousness he put on himself, he knew that, but still, it was nicer not to feel it. And it was strange—now, in the face of the overriding dread that he was ruining his entire life, all small nattering worries vanished and he felt marvelously light and unconstrained; the relief was like the profound and secret pleasure of reaching under the table and undoing the top button on a too-tight pair of pants.

So he strolled among the musicians and performers, and he lapped his liquefying sno-cone, and everything delighted him. He held the paper cone between his teeth and clapped as house cats leaped like miniature tigers through flaming hoops. He dipped and swayed in communion with the tightrope walker silhouetted against the setting sun. He dropped dollars into the hats of jugglers and bagpipe players.

Then the sun slipped into the Gulf, slow and stately as a king entering his bath. People applauded. The sky behind Tank Island went striped with jagged slabs of pink and purple that every moment compromised toward bluish gray. The colors faded; the show was over; the tourists left the pier.

Louie lingered a while, watched the dimming sky, walked in aimless little circles among discarded rinds of fruit, pieces of waxed paper smeared with mustard. Freedom tickled him, but with the noise gone and the light going, the beginnings of loneliness whispered gloom in his ear. But he would not be gloomy. No! He would smile, he would stroll, he would revisit places that amused him. And he wouldn't worry about a table for dinner! He would eat as he walked, and he would eat what he wanted. Ice cream. Pie. Conch fritters and Italian sausage if he felt like it. Just why the hell not? Could anyone tell him, could he tell himself, just why he should not for once do exactly as he pleased?

He left the pier, headed for the crowded streets with their colliding bodies, their winking signs, their carnival smells of beer and grease and perfume. He would walk and smile and maybe even talk to strangers; he would remember what it was like to be a person with fewer worries, without responsibilites.

As for finding Angelina, that high goal hadn't left his mind, but had for now become invisible. It was something he would think about tomorrow. Tonight, he thought, was just for Louie.

13

"I've gotta get out of here," said Angelina, already shouldering her purse and sliding off her barstool as she said it.

It was the third place they'd hit that evening, and before the after-sunset throng had been added to the happy-hour contingent, it hadn't been too bad. But now butane and phosphorous and cigarette smoke were fouling the air already turbid with the vapors of skin cream and libido; management had seen fit to crank up the music with its jackhammer bass. The bartender's hands had been futilely examined, and it was time to leave.

On the bustling sidewalk, with flashing neon throwing unflattering washes of orange, then blue, across her face, Angelina bit her lip and said, "I don't know how much more I can take of this."

Michael cinched his brows together, grabbed her gently by the wrists, tried with his gaze to lift her downcast eyes. "Look," he said, "do you want to find your prince, your stallion, your perfect love, or not?"

"The truth?" said Angelina. "Right at the moment I don't even know."

Michael frowned. He understood discouragement, recognized the dispiriting cycle of wanting too much and trying too hard, then plummeting down to a numbness where you ceased utterly to understand why you were bothering. Discouragement might yield briefly to serenity, which would be defeated in turn by loneliness and boredom, which would open the heavy creaking door to lust, which might cloak itself in the splendid garb of romance; romance would implode, and then the whole damn draining and befuddling thing would start again.

As fazed as Angelina by the relentless and exhausting weight of passion, he said, "Listen, hon, why don't we get off this vulgar street, forget about love, and just find someplace quiet and maybe a little seamy for a nightcap?"

✳ ✳ ✳

Keith McCullough stepped out of his motel shower, patted dry, and thought about which of his crude moronic T-shirts he would wear that evening. He decided on the one that said FREE MOUSTACHE RIDES.

For as long as he'd been working underground, he'd felt the simplest disguises were the best. His favorites weren't disguises at all, really—more like diversionary ploys. That was the beauty of these shirts—they made people dismiss him as a pathetic buffoon, embarrassed people to the point where they wouldn't meet his eyes, so that the smallest alterations—a pair of glasses, some fake sideburns—would make them fail to realize they'd seen his face before.

It helped, too, that his stature was average, his features unremarkable except in their flexibility, with hazel eyes that might appear amiably lax or killingly intent, a chin that could tuck down blandly or jut forth in recklessness. The pliant face was an asset, but more important was pliancy of personality. Disguises only worked if there was some oblique but resonant truth in them, a harmony between the mask and the person being masked. Working underground required, therefore, an un-squeamish knowledge of oneself, of one's alternate selves; and this knowledge was not the least scary thing about pretending not to be a cop while doing the things cops did.

In any case, Keith McCullough felt confident that his incognito was holding up, but he couldn't claim that his sporadic and routine surveillance of one Sigmund Maxx, a.k.a. Ziggy Maxx, a.k.a. Sal Martucci, had as yet turned up anything of interest. The guy had a job. He drove a crummy car and lived in a crummy bungalow whose upkeep seemed to be within the means provided by the job. If Ziggy kept criminal company, McCullough had not so far discovered it.

But the agent enjoyed these occasional postings to Key West, and had his reasons for hoping to prolong them by unearthing evidence of Ziggy backsliding. Backsliding, as everyone in the Program knew, was common as most other sins. People got bored with legitimate life, and who could blame them? They got lonely for old habits, old pals—even old pals who now wanted to kill them. Criminals rarely turned once and for all. They oscillated. And oscillating was something Keith McCullough understood.

Dressed now, he lay down on his bed and called his wife up in Fort Lauderdale. He asked if Keith Jr.'s cold was better, if Jeannie had done well in her soccer game. Then he rose and went to the mirror, where he applied a phony moustache and streaked his temples with gray, and thought with guilty anticipation about the night that would come after the evening's work, when he would slip into a disguise of a different sort and, on his own time, hit a couple bars.

✳ ✳ ✳

"Gimme a slice," said Uncle Louie. He thought a moment, then said, "Extra cheese."

He watched the guy drizzle on the curls of mozzarella.

"While you're at it, pepperoni. Maybe a few mushrooms. Fried onions, ya got 'em. And a Coke. No. Dr. Pepper. Large."

He leaned against a wall as his wedge of pizza was slid into the oven, and he found contentment in the unlikely coolness of the tiles against his moistened clothes.

Back on the street, he soothed his burned mouth with Key Lime sherbet eaten off a wooden spoon with the astringent feel of a doctor's tongue depressor. A little while after, he happened upon a sidewalk stand that offered mango smoothies, and he had one because he could not resist anything with mango. Up and down the street he walked, twirling postcard racks, looking in store windows displaying leather bathing suits and harnesses, discreetly glancing at people with paisley tattoos, ripped denim vests festooned with bits of chain, silver staples through their noses and their eyebrows.

At length his legs got tired, but his mind still had some verve, he wasn't ready to surrender the easy fascination of the streets. So he tapped into his small store of extravagance, and hailed a pedicab, a sort of bicycle rickshaw powered in this case by the muscles of a beautiful young woman with skintight purple shorts, blue hair in a soup-bowl shape, and a rivet through her cheek.

She asked where to, and he told her there's this bar, he couldn't remember the name of it, it was outside sort of, off the main drag, by where the boats were, with like a frame for a roof, flowers hanging down.

The driver smiled pleasantly, didn't mock him, said she thought she knew the place he meant.

Louie settled into the broad and curving rickshaw seat, watched the dimples migrate in the driver's buttocks as her legs pumped up and down, and rolled slowly through the town he already thought of as his own, feeling nothing short of royal.

✱ ✱ ✱

The first thing Angelina noticed was the vines.

They didn't really hang from their trellises; it was more like they were plucking downward, abrupt and greedy like monkey fingers, snatching whatever they could. The vines seized tree limbs, annexed the dark wood columns of the back bar, created by their grasping beauty a sinister impression that time was on their side, that vines and jungle riot would someday soon own all.

She recognized the vines—or thought she did, as she had thought about other things in other bars before. She reached for Michael's arm, twitched as though to hold him back. He felt her hesitation, that discouraged tug away from life and toward the unsatisfied ease of one's quiet room and empty bed. He urged her on, through the dim courtyard open to the sky, nearer to the gleaming horseshoe of well-rubbed wood, the smoky mirror, the celebrated bottles.

They found two stools on the near side of the bar.

At first the place seemed unattended. Then Angelina saw the bartender—saw the back of his dampened shirt as he crouched before an under-counter fridge, taking out lemons and limes. Slowly he stood, still facing away, and cocked his head just slightly as he took an order from a guy whose shirt said FREE MOUSTACHE RIDES.

A hollow burn was set aglow in Angelina's stomach as the barkeep reached back for a bottle, his nubbly index finger arched away from all the others. Her throat clamped down as she noted the small flourish of the heavy wrist that now stretched upward for a glass. And when he poured, pinkies lifted, his arms defining a languorous loop that closed in like a slow embrace, she reached out silently, spasmodically, for Michael and her red nails dug deep into his skin.

There was no mistaking what was powering that grip. Michael felt the glory of the moment in his own empathic loins.

In the next instant, Angelina was twisting off her bar stool, her vision blurry, her thrumming body poised to flee.

Michael held her by the arm. You couldn't rush destiny, he felt, but you couldn't dodge it either. "Steady, kiddo. Steady."

She worked hard for a breath. Her nostrils flared, her forehead flushed, she felt the wet weight of her heart squeezed like a sponge by the hoops of her ribs. She was halfway off her bar stool, one foot was on the floor, the strap of her purse was dangling. Above her, vines plucked downward, seizing, grabbing; somewhere an unfelt breeze was rattling dry fronds. Angelina whispered: "Sal."

That wasn't his name. He'd been trained, he'd trained himself, never to respond to it. It was not his name; it had never been his name, except perhaps in some life so remote and dead that its names had been erased, forgotten. Still, reflex lived even after life was over, and Ziggy could not stop his head from moving toward the sound. It turned a few degrees; he tried to stop it, but then it was the voice and not the word that spun him till his eyes met Angelina's.

His face was blank and false, a stranger's face. His hands were the hands she dreamed of.

For a long moment no one spoke, the noise of the bar rose up in a gibberish crescendo.

Then a voice said, "Angelina." It wasn't Ziggy talking. It wasn't Sal.

Angelina turned her head and saw her Uncle Louie, standing at her elbow. He had pizza on his breath and was looking very happy; a smile made the flesh bunch up beneath his sunburned cheekbones.

PART ☀ TWO

14

Ziggy had a policy. He didn't drink at his own bar, not while he was working.

But as soon as Angelina and her escorts had sipped one highly awkward cocktail and headed for the door, that rule went straight to hell. It was a deviation that Keith McCullough didn't fail to notice, watching discreetly as the bartender took a high-ball glass, filled it half-full with tequila, and fired it down.

With the rasp of sour cactus scratching at his throat, Ziggy leaned against the back bar, steadied his hands against the damp teak, and tried to think. Angelina in Key West. What a fucked-up idea. What a wild mismatch. What the hell was she doing here, and how in Christ had she recognized him when he could barely recognize himself? Thank God she'd had the smarts and the reflexes not to blow his cover when that funny-looking guy showed up. Uncle Louie. He'd distinctly heard her call him Uncle Louie. It was a name he remembered hearing long ago, back when his own name had been Sal. Louie—the black sheep of the family, the guy no one took serious.

But he was still Paul Amaro's brother; Angelina was still

Paul Amaro's daughter; and Ziggy saw no percentage in getting reacquainted with the family.

He gazed absently around his now mostly empty bar, gave muddled but exigent consideration to the question of whether he should spring nimbly off the balls of his ass and get the hell out of there. Charter a plane to the Bahamas. Smuggle himself into Cuba. Go to Mexico, Panama, Belize—someplace he could again molt his soiled identity, peel off the numb dead skin of another weak attempt at a life.

Should he flee? Absently, he drew beers for a couple guys who really didn't need them, and tried to measure the depth of the dung he was standing in. Paulie didn't know his whereabouts, he reasoned: If he did, he would have sent the guys in trench coats, not his daughter. But why, then, was Angelina here? Was it possible that it was just an appalling coincidence? A lot of people, after all, came to Key West for vacation; a lot of them wandered into his bar. And how did Uncle Louie figure in? Now that Ziggy thought about it, the guy looked a little bit familiar. Had he been in here before?

The barkeep reached toward the tequila bottle, but then, midway through the motion, a whole different line of thought stopped his arm and tweaked a memory at the base of his belly. He finally let it register that Angelina looked very, very good to him.

She'd hardly changed. Her skin was not quite as taut as it had been ten years ago, not quite as burstingly translucent. She was a little fuller in the shoulders and the bosom. But in all—not just compared to Ziggy with his lopped-off being, but by any standard—she was remarkably, triumphantly the same. Unmarked; seemingly outside of time; constant as a compass needle though a whole world pivoted beneath her. The violet eyes remained clear and frank. The black hair was as lush and imperfect as it had ever been. Ziggy recalled the smell of her perfume, a little sweet and girlish. He remembered the pulse in her neck, the slight scratchiness of the lacy scalloped edge of her bra . . .

His hand shot out for the tequila bottle, and he quashed his incipient lust as decisively as though he'd slammed a window on his private parts. Was he crazy? Was he out of his mind? This was Paulie's daughter, for Chrissake, and he, Ziggy, was no longer family friend and protégé, but mortal enemy, pariah. He may as well fuck death as lay a finger on her.

He should bolt; in his heart he knew it. But leaning against the bar, his shirt wet against his back, his revamped hairline beaded with oily sweat, he strongly suspected that he wouldn't. Maybe it was just the weather, the soggy sapping air that smothered decisions and nurtured indifference like a mold. Maybe it was the gnaw of something unfinished, an infecting tension passed down from one existence to the next. Or maybe it was something more perilous still. Maybe what kept him from fleeing Angelina was something that could almost stand for love, a mute desire for nearness that was as close as Ziggy or Sal had ever come to caring for a woman.

15

For Angelina the evening had been at least as flabbergasting as it was for her old flame.

When her Uncle Louie had appeared at her side at the bar where she'd found Sal, the abrupt combining of the forbidden with the incongruous had dizzied her, had hit her like a mix of pills and booze. Her eyes had gone unfocussed, the sinews of her knees had briefly caved, but somehow she had bluffed her way through a charade of social niceties. She'd kissed her uncle on the cheek. She'd introduced Michael, realizing in an instant that he—a young man, a date—served naturally as camouflage. The three of them performed a little skit of small talk as Ziggy stood apart, skulking in the shadows of the vines and wondering if he would be unmasked; as Angelina, stealing glances at the barkeep's hands, begged her reeling mind to keep alert; as Uncle Louie thrummed with his chance to be a hero to the family; as Michael fairly swooned with the desperate romance of it all.

But the small talk could not go on forever, there had to be a time when Angelina and her relative would have a heart-to-heart.

It happened not long after they left Raul's to walk in no particular direction through the hot streets with their slinking cats, their sleeping dogs nestled against the tires of parked cars. At a quiet intersection, Michael looked at Angelina, tried to read in her eyes what it was she needed from him, then gave a somewhat theatrical yawn and announced that he was tired, he was going home—which meant, of course, that he wasn't tired and he was going out.

Alone now with his niece, Uncle Louie said, "Cuppa coffee?"

They ducked into a side-street cafe, really just a Cuban grocery with a few tables set up in an alley dimly lit with strings of Christmas lights. They settled into slatted wooden chairs from which hung little curls of peeling varnish, and after they'd ordered, Angelina said, "So Uncle Louie, why are you here?"

"Why are *you* here?" he asked right back.

"I asked you first."

He was fidgeting with a sugar packet, shaking all the sugar to one end. He replied as though the answer was self-evident. "I came to find you."

Angelina had been uneasily proud of her getaway from Pelham Manor, the unpracticed deftness with which she'd sneaked and fibbed. Now all of a sudden she wondered if she'd fooled anyone at all, if there'd been even a moment when she wasn't in the unrelenting bosom of her family. "You knew I was here?"

Uncle Louie didn't answer right away. Instead, he folded his hands, tilted his head, fixed Angelina with a cockeyed smile full of fondness and collusion. Then he said something he would never say to anyone up north, because up north he could not imagine that it might be taken as a compliment. "Angelina, you and me, we're a lot alike, I think. My tape—I saw the way you looked at it. This town—I could tell it struck a chord with you."

"Who else knows?" said Angelina. She couldn't entirely keep panic out of her voice, nor could she wholly banish from her mind a shaming and equivocal hope that her father might yet rescue her and spoil everything, drag her kicking and screaming away from this splendid adventure she shouldn't be having.

Her uncle had hoped for a different kind of reply, some confirmation from his favorite niece that they did in fact have lots in common. Hiding his deflation, he said, "Who else? No one else. Nobody knows I'm here either. And dollars to donuts no one figures it out."

He leaned low across his elbows, his tone turned even more conspiratorial. "Our family, Angelina, I'll tell ya something about our family. They think they're close-knit, they pride themselves on being loyal, but the truth is, no one really pays attention t'each other, no one sees enough to really know what anybody else is feeling, wanting."

The waitress brought the coffees. Steamed milk foamed on top, the bubbles turned blue and red and green beneath the Christmas lights.

"Now it's your turn, Angelina," Louie said. "Why did you come here?"

She drizzled sugar into her coffee, watched the crystals turn translucent, then congeal into a coffee-colored paste, then sink beneath the foam. Finally she said, very softly but with a serene defiance, "I came to find the love of my life. And I have."

Louie did not expect quite so fraught an answer. He settled back against the peeling varnish of his chair to mull it over. He looked at Angelina with wonder and almost shyly, the way a father looks upon his daughter as a bride, and he trembled for her, knowing suddenly that she was grown and he had no wisdom to impart, no advice that could assure her happiness. Still, he hated to see her hurt or disappointed. "Angelina," he said, "maybe it's none of my business, maybe I should keep my mouth shut, I mean, hey, wha' do I know? But okay, lemme say it straight out: Don't'cha think maybe he's gay?"

"What? Who's gay, Uncle Louie?"

"This love of your life you found. This Michael."

"Michael? Of course he's gay. He's a friend."

"Ah," said Louie, and he blushed beneath his sparse bundles of hair. "Then who—"

Angelina reached across the small table, put her hand on top of his. "You can't ask me that, Uncle Louie. I'm sorry, but you can't."

"Why not?"

"And you can't ask why not. Sometime maybe I'll tell you."

They fell silent, sipped their coffee. Farther back in the alley, lizards made furtive scraping sounds as they nosed for bugs in gravel; from high up, tree frogs smugly croaked, nestled under the skirts of palms.

After a moment Angelina smiled, said, "Pretty smart, Uncle Louie, you figuring out I was here."

Louie smiled back, knowing that his favorite niece was being kind, was giving him a gift. But in that moment he was not so sure he'd done right by her. He'd set out in search of a lost child, and found instead a woman with her own desires. He felt like he was meddling, like he was in the way.

Angelina reached for him again, took his wrist this time, pressed it as she fixed him with her violet eyes. "But please don't tell my father, Uncle Louie. Please don't make it so I have to leave."

Louie sighed, blinked, weighed his giddy reborn fantasy of being a big shot, a hero, against Angelina's right to choose herself a life.

"Sometime I'll go back," she said. "But not now, Uncle Louie. I'm not ready to go back."

He slipped out of her grip, pushed back onto his chair's hind legs, and looked up from the confines of the alley, past the strings of Christmas lights, to a narrow swath of sky where tropic stars were nested one by one in cottony and lucent puffs of humid air. He said, "You know what, Angelina? I'm not ready to go back either."

16

The next morning, Ziggy was summoned to the garden of Carmen Salazar.

With not enough sleep behind his eyes and not enough caffeine in his bloodstream, he drove the still streets to the candy store. When he walked through to the bright doorway at the back, he found Salazar in conversation with two men, who fell instantly silent at the arrival of a stranger. Salazar nodded that it was okay to talk, and one of them resumed mid-sentence.

He said ". . . a chance to profit from a patriotic duty." This man was tall, with the rumpled and phlegmatic good looks of a warped aristocrat. He had a prosperous and graying moustache, the wise liquid eyes of a hound, and a Panama hat he held in his lap, slowly and ceaselessly rolling and unrolling its brim.

But his argument wasn't playing well with Salazar. "That Cuban stuff does nothing for me," he said. "My people left Havana in the 1870s. Me, I have as much feeling for Cuba as I have for Lithuania."

Ziggy recognized the other man—short and stocky, his nose so badly broken that you saw his profile when he was looking you right in the eye. He had crisp unlocal creases down his pants legs, and he couldn't sit still, was always plucking at lint or at imagined wrinkles. He said, "Right, this is exactly what I'm saying. Don't complicate it wit' politics, don't get all righteous and stupid. Treat it like a simple business. Weapons in; money out. Business. Simple."

"Business, fine," said Salazar. "Simple, not really."

Ziggy stood there. The sun was at a difficult angle, he couldn't find a piece of shade to hide in. His head felt cottony and, after the initial glance, no one had so much as looked at him.

"Forget that politics bullshit," the short man went on, his voice staccato, his fingers busy. "Politics. Overthrow. No one's talkin' overthrow. What I'm talkin', I'm talkin' like wit' Russia. When the time comes, it overthrows itself. It just happens. Then it's fuckin' chaos. The people wit' strength, they profit. Free enterprise, bang bang. So what I'm sayin', I'm sayin' see it as an opportunity to get in good wit' the people who are gonna be profiting."

But the tall man was not content to leave it at that, he badly wanted to dress the scam in some nobility. He added, "And a chance to participate in a great—"

"Will you cut that bullshit out?" the short man interrupted.

There was a silence filled with the smell of ripening fruit. Then Salazar sucked his gums and said, "I just don't know, gentlemen. I'm flattered by your trust, of course. But the scale of what you're proposing . . . Look, what I'm running here, it's a cozy, low-risk, small-time operation. Isn't that right, Ziggy?"

Ziggy said, "Hm?"

He'd given up expecting to be addressed. Logy in the sunshine, his mind had wandered; he'd been thinking about the skin on Angelina's neck. He didn't want to think about it, but his mind kept going back to it like a dog to a buried bone. The skin on her neck was smooth and dry, so soft it felt powdery, but he could remember that, after he touched it, it turned a little pebbly and gradually grew as moist as steak.

Salazar said to him, "I was saying that, while we are fortunate enough to have associates with big-time talents, what we run here is a small-time operation. Isn't that right?"

Ziggy treaded water. "Yeah," he said, "that's right."

"And while these gentlemen," Salazar continued, "no doubt have a canny grasp of world events, these greater things might simply be beyond our scope. Wouldn't you agree?"

"Yeah, Carmen, yeah," said Ziggy, but he was feeling the unease of the hard of hearing, he understood he'd missed something and would probably now miss other things as well. Attention was a habit, a groove, and once it got away from you, it was as hard to find again as a home-run swing.

Salazar turned his attention back to his two visitors. "So you see, gentlemen, if I do choose to get involved, at least I have a savvy, top-notch workforce. Let me think it over."

The others sat in the shade. Ziggy stood in the sun. He understood that something big was being talked about and he understood that he was being mocked. But the connections eluded him. He tried to look cocky; he hoped the meeting was finished. Silently he cursed Angelina for coming to Key West and messing with his concentration. He cursed her and he thought about her neck.

✳ ✳ ✳

Angelina had slept badly, had awakened with damp and tangled sheets between her thighs, her eyes itchy behind puffy lids. Her skin felt wrong. Though unrested, she couldn't wait to get out of bed, to put the goading night behind her. She wanted coffee and daylight, and she wanted to talk to Michael.

She slipped into a modest one-piece bathing suit, and went down to the courtyard, where breakfast was laid out on a table covered with fronds from the traveler palm, and thwarted bees hovered around the fruits and juices under their pagodas of frail white netting. She took coffee and a mango muffin and a wedge of melon and sat down in a lounge chair by the pool.

She sipped and nibbled and absently absorbed the guileless intimacy, like something out of childhood, of a resort waking up. A man appeared in boxer shorts with hearts on them, took two cups of coffee and two bananas, retreated to his room. A drag queen came by in a long pink robe, his hair in curlers, drank guava juice and smoked a cigarette. The day's first sleepy-eyed nudists dropped their towels and took their wake-up dips. Angelina could estimate how long they'd been at Coral Shores by how closely the color of their buttocks matched the rest of them. For the first time ever that she knew of, she wondered how Sal would look with nothing on.

She fetched more coffee, waited for Michael to wake up.

She waited a long time. The sun got higher, shadows shrank inward like evaporating puddles. Finally the buffet was broken down like a stage set, the coffee urns rolled away on metal tables that looked surgical.

Angelina watched the little square of patio in front of Michael's room, but when Michael finally appeared, it was not by way of his own door, but through the picket gate that separated the courtyard from the heat and possibilities of the world beyond. Angelina saw him before he noticed her, and determined beyond a doubt that he was wearing last night's clothes. She knew somehow that they'd been off then on again. She waved.

He came over, said a nonchalant good morning, squinted through somewhat bloodshot eyes toward the place where the buffet had been. He said, "Coffee's gone already?"

She handed him the last half-cup of her own, and he sat down at the foot of her lounge chair.

A slightly awkward moment passed. Michael's posture was relaxed, fatigued, yet also slightly smug, puffed up. Angelina felt her forehead flushing, her mouth going dry, and she dimly realized it was because of the tweaking proximity of sex, a newly admitted awareness that desire was all around her, as various as flavor and as enveloping as air. "Nice night?" she said at last.

"Wonderful night," said Michael, sipping the lukewarm coffee, toying with his earrings. "Miraculous night." His green eyes were dreamy, a reddish stubble had sprouted on his cheeks and glinted in the sun.

Angelina gave him a moment to be coy, then said, "So tell me."

Michael said, "David. His name is David. We met at the Copa. Didn't dance. Hardly talked at first. Just, you know, locked eyes. Then walked on the beach. Saw a spectacular moonset, a perfect orange slice right down to the horizon."

Angelina smiled but also felt a pang that took her by surprise. Envy. Why hadn't she known nights like that, glorious nights with moonlight on salt water in the arms of a thrilling lover?

"Been a long time," Michael went on, "since I met someone and everything just clicked."

"I'm happy for you," Angelina said. She meant it though it took an effort.

He heard the wistfulness. He swiveled to face her, put a hand on her ankle. "Hey, we both found our princes on the very same night."

"Yeah," said Angelina, "but you knew what to do with yours."

"And praise the Lord, he knew what to do with me."

Angelina raised a hand to her face, bit the knuckle of her index finger. "I wish I knew what to do with Sal."

Michael shaded his tired eyes and pulled his sandy brows together. "Go after him, girl."

"Go after him," Angelina echoed, trying out the feel of the words. They tasted too harsh. "Jeez, you make it sound so . . . so—"

"Predatory?" Michael said. "Aggressive? Sometimes it's like

that. Look, someone has to have the nerve to lay it on the line, to make it clear, with words, with glances: I want it."

A nervous giggle started up from Angelina's tummy, didn't make it past her closed-down throat. Her legs twitched, the tanned knees rubbed together in the sunshine. "Michael," she said, "I can't throw myself—"

"Go back to that bar—" he interrupted.

"He doesn't want to see me," Angelina cut him off in turn. "You saw the way he fell back in the shadows, he looked like he wanted to be swallowed in the earth."

"The timing was all wrong," said Michael. "Your uncle was there . . . Look, go back alone. Late. Go back looking very pretty. Show a little cleavage. And make sure he feels you looking at him. Your gaze—make sure it burns right through him."

"God, Michael, I don't know—"

"You do know. You know perfectly well."

Angelina bit her lip. Searing sun rained down and naked men cavorted in the pool. The air was freighted with the promiscuity of flowers, with a lubricious perfume of chlorine and coconut and viscous oils.

"Michael," she said at last, "lemme ask you. When two people . . . I mean when, you know, it happens, I mean, like all of it, it happens—is it really as terrific as people say?"

His green eyes blinked. Was it possible? Was she really telling him what she seemed to be telling him? He tried to imagine the ripeness of her body, how the weight of that ripeness must tug at her, must pull and stretch like an over-ready fruit still captive to its vine, and he spoke to her not as a lover but as a priest of love, a guide, with a quiet holy fervor in his voice. "Yeah," he said, "it really is."

17

Uncle Louie, dressed in a turquoise cabana set and a plastic visor he'd bought that morning, sat on the seawall up by Smathers Beach, sucked at a mango smoothie, and quietly marveled at the variety of unnecessary exertions going on around him.

Along the broad but bumpy promenade, between himself and the long row of vendors' trucks that parked along the edge of A-1A, people with headphones whooshed by on Rollerblades. Bicycles went past, a few had dogs in baskets. Joggers plodded by, their skins glistening like those of basted birds. On the beach, against a background of bright green water, youths were playing volleyball, heedlessly diving on the thin layer of imported sand that imperfectly disguised the native lacerating coral.

The spectacle kept Louie entertained but could not quite cure his fretting. Since last night he'd doubted that coming to Key West was really such a hot idea; the thought was eating at him that, for all his good intentions, he'd done to himself what it seemed he'd done his whole life long—put himself in a pickle where no matter what he did was wrong. He'd found Angelina.

But what had he really accomplished? He couldn't make her go home against her will; he'd promised her he wouldn't. On the other hand, he couldn't very well abandon her down here. Whatever she was going through, love or some other crisis, she was fragile. If he left and something bad happened, it would seem an unforgivable dereliction, not just to his brothers, but to himself.

Then there was the question of contacting the family. He'd vowed to Angelina that he wouldn't give away her whereabouts. But it seemed unfair, cruel, not to let the family know she was okay. But how? Louie didn't trust himself in a position where he had to answer questions. If he spoke to someone he was afraid of, like his brother or his wife, and they pressured him, he'd spill the beans, he knew he would.

So, sitting on the seawall, his knees already getting pink, he drank his smoothie and he fretted. Then, suddenly, he knew what he should do. He walked on burning feet to a pay phone near a frozen-custard stand with a speaker that blared out, over and over again, an irritating little tune, and called the plumbing store in East Harlem.

The Dominican kid picked up on the second ring, said, "Amaro Sanitary Fixtures. You got Eddie."

"Hello, Eddie," Louie said.

"Mist' Amaro!" said the kid, and there was a happiness in it, a pleasure of reuniting that took Louie by surprise. Until that moment it had barely occurred to him that he might be missed, worried about, that it wasn't only Angelina whose absence would leave a small hole in the world. "Where ah you, mang?"

"I can't tell you that."

"Why you no can't tell?"

"I just can't, Eddie. Listen, I need you to do me a favor."

"Name it, Mist' Amaro."

"I want you to call my wife—"

"Your wife, she been calling plenny. I think maybe she been drinking."

"Call her up, tell her Angelina's okay, we're together, no one has to worry. You got that, Eddie?"

Eddie said, "Angelina? You go 'way with someone Angelina, and I'm supposed to tell your wife?"

"She's my niece," said Louie.

"Sure," said Eddie. "Your wife, she gonna ask where you're at."

"You can't tell her. You don't know."

"When you comin' back, Mist' Amaro?"

"I don't know. It isn't up to me."

There was a pause. Louie pictured Eddie leaning over the marred gray counter, shifting his crossed ankles the way he did when he was puzzling something out.

"Mist' Amaro," he said at last, "you been kidnap, something?"

"Don't be ridiculous, Eddie. We doin' any business?"

"Then why it's no up to you, when you come back?"

"It just isn't. How much money's in the till?"

"Nah much," said Eddie. "Hundred'ollars maybe."

"Take it if you need it."

"Take it?" The words scared Eddie, seemed like some crude temptation out of a fable from Sunday school, or like further evidence that something dreadful had happened to his boss. "Mist' Amaro, you tell me never touch that money."

Louie said, "And now I'm telling you take it if you need it." He ran a hand through the sparse bundles of damp hair atop his scorching head, and wished he'd bought a cap instead of a visor. Rose would have made him buy a cap. "And call my wife," he said. "Good talking with you, Eddie."

✱ ✱ ✱

Paul Amaro was pacing like a bear among the mismatched tables of the Gatto Bianco Social Club. Clumsy with fatigue, dizzy now and then, he occasionally bumped a chair back with his hip. He hadn't shaved, he gave off a faint but penetrating smell of rage and worry.

His old friend Funzie Gallo was eating a cannoli, the kind with crushed pistachios garnishing the ends. He watched the other man pace, then said at last, "For your own good, Paul, try to think about somethin' else awhile."

Angelina's father didn't stop lumbering and rocking. He fixed the other man from under tangled brows and said, "Fuck else is there to think about?"

Gallo blinked, pads of semiliquid fat shifted all around his eyes. "Business, Paul. Money. We used to make a lotta money here, remember?"

"And it's turned to shit," said Paul Amaro.

Funzie Gallo wanted to disagree. He found he couldn't. But Amaro seemed to understand that an attempt at help was being offered, he tried to meet Funzie halfway. He resumed without enthusiasm, "Okay, okay, so talk to me."

Gallo said, "These rods for Cuba—"

"Funzie," Amaro interrupted. "You're practically as old as me. Y'oughta remember. Our friends, Trafficante, Lansky, even Luciano, they lost their shirts in Cuba."

Funzie nibbled around the edges of his sweet, licked back oily crumbs of crust. "That was different, Paul. That was heavy-duty investment. This is a one-time cash transaction."

Amaro leaned against the pool table where no one ever shot pool. For a brief time he floated free of his dolorous preoc-cupation with his daughter, but what took its place was a recol-lection of the busted car-shipping scam that had sent him to the can. "International," he said, "I don't like it. Customs. Coast Guard. Fucking Navy."

"Not our problem," Funzie said. "That's the beauty part. We get the pieces far as Florida. After that, it's Tommy Lucca's problem."

Amaro tightened at the name. "Lucca's an asshole," he said.

"Did I say he's not?" said Funzie. What he left unsaid was that Lucca was active at least, doing deals while they themselves drank coffee. By cunning or good fortune, he'd left New York when the leaving was good, established himself in Miami, a wide-open town where things were happening. He'd prospered as lucky lunatics often prospered: As the world got crazier, it came his way.

Which didn't mean that Paul Amaro had to respect him. "He's a hothead and a whaddyacallit, paranoid, and he's got this bug up his ass, touchy, about how New York doesn't take him serious."

Funzie said, "But it's a sweet deal, Paul."

"Plus which," Paulie said, "I hear he's all hopped up on drugs. Rule one, ya don't do business wit' guys on drugs."

"Then I guess we're outa business," Funzie said. He went back to his pastry.

Paulie walked around the room. In spite of himself he was getting interested, he tasted in his throat the meaty joy of scamming. He said, "You telling me you trust that broke-nosed fuck?"

"Trust 'im?" Funzie said. "No. But I'm telling you I think we oughta stop sitting on our asses and do a little business. Just so, ya know, people remember we're alive."

Paulie considered. But not for long. Like a man who falls prey to dirty thoughts in church, he was suddenly furious, abashed at his own frailty, that he had allowed himself to be distracted even for a moment from his deeper meditations, the higher business of finding Angelina. He turned his face away, dropped his scratchy chin onto his chest, and very softly said, "Do what you want, Funzie. I don't give a shit."

"I do what I want, you're gonna have to get involved."

Paul said nothing.

"I do what I want," Funzie said again, "at some point you're gonna have to show your face, maybe travel, deal with Lucca."

Amaro did a kind of penance by not answering.

His old friend Funzie bit deep into the cannoli and decided, for the sake of his own sanity, that he would take the silence as a go-ahead.

✱ ✱ ✱

When the phone rang at her Bronx apartment, Rose Amaro was two knuckles deep in a tall jar of maraschino cherries, her long red nails working awkwardly to untangle the stems of the last few sugar fruits. She cursed, sucked syrup from her fingers, and took her uncompleted cocktail to the living room, where she flopped into the chair next to the telephone.

"Miz Amaro?" said a voice in response to her lugubrious hello. "This is Eddie. Eddie from the staw."

He told her of his talk with Louie, and she began, very sloppily, to sob. Big hot tears started from her eyes, got bogged in her makeup like rivers thwarted en route to the sea. Diluted lipstick stained her hand and cheek as she roughly wiped away the drool that gathered at the corners of her mouth. Her chest heaved, iced Seagram's and sweet vermouth splashed onto her blouse. "He's all right?" she managed at last. "He said he's all right? Angelina's with him?"

Eddie repeated what he knew.

His boss's wife kept crying. The kid didn't know if he should hang up or listen to her cry. He held the phone a little away from his ear. It seemed that she was stopping. Then she started again, louder than before.

"You he calls," she said. "I'm his wife, but he calls you."

Eddie leaned on the marred gray counter, reversed the cross of his ankles.

"And why?" Rose sniffled. "You think I don't know why?"

Eddie said nothing. He didn't know why.

Rose pressed herself deeper into the creased upholstery and told him. "Because I've been such a rotten wife to him all these years. The kindest, sweetest man that ever walked the earth, and I've been nothing but a selfish bitch."

The kid looked at the phone. He liked his boss, but he didn't think he was *that* terrific.

"I've been awful to him," the wife sobbed on. "I was mean. I got away with it. It got to be a game, a habit. But who was I fooling? What did it prove?"

Eddie felt bad for this unhappy woman. He searched for some way to get her to stop crying. He said, "Look, Miz Amaro, maybe he wanted to call you."

"Oh yeah?" she said, with a quick and seamless shift from remorse to complaint. "Oh yeah? Then why the hell didn't he?"

Eddie paused. He'd only been trying to give a little comfort; how had it happened that he was under attack? His splayed eyes wandered and he improvised. "Maybe he wanted to call you, but they wouldn't let him call family."

Rose Amaro sat up straighter and suddenly sounded almost sober. "They?" she said. "Who's they?"

Eddie blinked, pushed up off his elbows. He'd got ahead of himself and now he tried to backtrack. "I don't know who's they. Only, you know, he said, when he's coming home, it isn't up to him."

"So who's it up to, Eddie?"

The kid said nothing, wondered exactly when and how the conversation had gone wrong.

"You saying everything you know?" his boss's wife demanded.

"Yeah, Miz Amaro, I swear—"

She hung up on him. He looked at the receiver in his hand, replaced it in the cradle next to a dog-eared puzzle book.

In the Bronx, Louie's wife put down her drink, blew her nose, took a moment to compose herself, then called her sister-in-law Maria.

18

Having spent a damp and edgy night when she was never quite asleep, Angelina now endured a parched and vacant day when she never felt fully awake.

Hour after hour, she sat by the pool, her only activity the occasional moving of her lounge chair, chasing the slow march of a patch of shade like a refugee trailing a defeated army. Texture vanished from the sounds of the courtyard as insects rested in the cool of mounds and nests and burrows; without their buzzing and rasping, the occasional human voice or laugh seemed abrupt and harsh, a soloist without an orchestra. Beyond the picket gate, the melting streets were empty, stunned. Tourists were at the beach; locals were at home, naked under ceiling fans. Ease spilled over into a vague sorrow, sensuous languor phased toward quiet loss, as the heat of the tropics gave its gift of lassitude and claimed its price of wasted time.

She sat; she shifted her position by small increments; around five o'clock, she surprised herself by developing a vivid craving for some alcohol.

She wanted a cocktail, and a cocktail meant going out, but

she lacked the ambition to get dressed, and it was much too hot to put on makeup. At length, she shuffled into sandals, wrapped a sarong around herself and tucked it into the bosom of her bathing suit. She headed for the gate with her hair askew, her skin salty; she didn't care who saw her. She was beginning to go native, and the purest part of the process was that she didn't realize it was happening.

Her loose shoes scratched along the pavement. She found a quiet bar, took a tiny table by a shaded window, and ordered up a margarita. Sipping it, her tongue smarting from the liquor and the lime, she gave in to the pleasure of being slightly scandalized by her own behavior. Drinking alone, just for the hell of it. Drinking alone as hazy intimations of lust curled through her mind like wisps of fog. Thinking about Sal Martucci's hands and her own salty body wrapped like a present in its bright-colored cotton.

Her drink was gone. She ordered another. So this was decadence, she thought—hot days, dim rooms, notions of love growing less inchoate and more fleshly as ancient barriers melted in the sun or were vanquished by tequila, as the blank black curtains that had sequestered Angelina from passion proved only to be made of gauze.

She crossed her knees, finished her drink. From the outside she looked demure, maybe just a little sultry; on the inside she was vacillating between carnality and the giggles. She was ready for a good long nap, and the nap itself seemed an emblem of her newfound sense of the luscious. Marvelously illicit, to go to sleep in daylight and wake in all-accepting darkness, refreshed by the night and ready to go out prowling for her lover.

❋ ❋ ❋

It was almost six o'clock, there hadn't been a customer in hours, and Eddie, for the millionth time, was sounding out the flaking backward letters on the window: SERUTXIF YRATINAS ORAMA. At first he hardly noticed when the big dark car pulled up in front of the fire hydrant outside the store.

He became more interested when a thick man in a raincoat got out of the driver's seat, and held open a door for a tall man with wavy silver hair who now emerged from the back. They looked like gangsters, and Eddie watched them like he was watching television, curious, aloof, like nothing that was happening had anything to do with him.

Unease began when it became clear that the two of them were heading for his door; it ripened quickly to a paralyzing fear when the thick man reached up and grabbed the metal shutter that hid the premises from the eyes of the street. With a clatter as loud as a train and a clank as sharp as the ring of a driven spike, the steel curtain rolled down and hit the sidewalk, and Eddie realized he was doomed. Now he knew exactly what was happening: He'd been tempted, tested, and he'd failed. The consequences of his theft were coming due before he'd spent a nickel of the money he'd taken from the register.

The thick man came in first, his right wrist buried in his raincoat pocket. He said, "Okay, Jackson, put your fuckin' hands where I can see 'em."

Eddie was standing behind the counter. He raised his hands. They were shaking, his baggy shirt cuffs moved against his skinny forearms. The man with the silver hair came in. He locked the door behind him and pulled down the shade. All closed up, the store felt very small, the fluorescent lights seemed dim yet harsh.

Eddie said, "He tol' me I could take that money. I swear to God he did."

"Fuck you talkin' about?" said Paul Amaro.

"I put an IOU," said Eddie. "Exact amount, I swear."

"Where's my brother, kid?"

Eddie hadn't noticed when he started crying, but he was sniffling now, he tasted snot at the back of his throat.

"He called you. Where'd he call you from?"

Eddie was still holding up his hands, his arms were starting to get heavy. He was trying hard to understand what was wanted of him. Finally he said, "You're Mist' Amaro's brother?"

"Very good, Einstein," said the man whose hand was in his pocket.

"He called you," Paul Amaro said again. "He told you my daughter was with him. Did he say where he was calling from?"

"He didn't. I swear. I even asked him."

"What did he answer?"

"He said he couldn't tell me where he was. He said it wasn't up to him when he came home."

"What else did he say?"

"Nothing. I swear."

"What else did you hear?"

"Huh?"

"In the background, Eddie. Voices? People? Was he whispering?"

Eddie thought back. "Cars. I heard cars."

"Everywhere's cars," Amaro said. "What else?"

The kid's shoulders were starting to hurt. "Can I put my hands down?"

Amaro motioned that he could.

Eddie thought hard, said, "I heard a song that went round and round. Ya know, like a ride, maybe, at a carnival."

"Carnival," Amaro said.

"Coulda been," said Eddie. "Or maybe, like, a ice cream truck."

"This *melanzan* is fuckin' useless," said the thick man.

"An ice-cream truck," said Paul Amaro. It was April. He didn't think the ice cream trucks had started going around in April. "My brother, he sound scared?"

"He sounded 'bout like normal."

Paul Amaro rubbed a thick hand all over his face, pulled hard at the rubbery jowls. "You told his wife maybe there were people who wouldn't let him call. Why'd you say that, Eddie?"

The kid wiped his nose with his hand. " 'Cause she was crying."

Paul Amaro sighed, began to pace. For the first time, he looked past the marred gray counter to the erector-set shelves with their dusty cardboard boxes. "This place is a fuckin' dump," he said. He paced some more, then said, "It makes no sense. My schmuck brother, he's got family that can help him, and he wastes time talkin' to you."

Eddie heard himself say, "Maybe he don't want no help."

"Shut up, you cross-eyed idiot," said the man in the raincoat.

Paul Amaro looked down at the floor. Then, without another word, he walked to the door and let himself out. The man in the raincoat followed.

Eddie heard their car start, waited till they pulled away; waited an extra minute to be safe. Then he opened the cash register and reached into his pocket. He replaced the cash he'd taken as his wages, removed his IOU and tore it into little pieces. Then he locked up and walked away, and he knew that he was never going back.

19

Angelina woke up from her nap around eleven.

The air was very still, fragrant with the rueful smell of spent flowers, and she was quite confused. Gradually she remembered where she was, she recalled the mood and musings of the afternoon. But the tequila had worn off, those fantasies were now tainted by the thousand anxieties of the actual, and she was sorely tempted to slip back into sleep. To go prowling at midnight—earlier, the idea had seemed excitingly risqué, sophisticated; now it just felt bizarre. To track her lover like a hunting lioness—earlier, the notion had titillated by its boldness; now it just seemed brassy.

But that, she told herself, was fear talking, the old bafflement and reluctance that had kept her fallow for so long. She would rise; she would go. She just needed a pep talk.

She pulled on her sarong, went downstairs to Michael's. His room was dark, she tapped on the door. He wasn't there; of course he wasn't there. He'd found his lover; he'd met a possibility and seized it. Angelina pouted. Why was everyone in the world more facile and blithe than she? Why was she hemmed in by qualms and hesitations that no one else seemed bothered by?

In her frustration and in the oddness of the hour, she came dangerously close to asking the question underpinning all those questions: Why, after all this time, was she crazy in love with a man who, for every reason, she should not, could not, have?

That question loomed, Angelina dimly sensed its menace the way a person somehow knows when a speeding unseen car is just about to careen around a corner; her mind stepped back.

On reluctant feet she went upstairs to her room, resolved now, with more bravery than joy, to dress in something pretty, and to do her hair, and paint her lips, and dab perfume behind her ears, and to see what happened when she sat across the bar from Sal and told him they really had to talk.

✳ ✳ ✳

"Hi, Sal," she said, when she had climbed onto her bar stool and placed her purse on the bar and neatly squared her hands in front of her.

His eyes flicking left and right at regulars and tourists, his shirt damp and mostly open, he moved close to her, leaned across the slab of teak. Very softly, he said, "That's not my name."

"It's the only name I know you by," said Angelina.

"So I guess you don't know me very well."

"I never said I did. Can I have a drink, please?"

He didn't answer right away. Suddenly he felt caged in by the bar, squeezed between the thick wood and the pitiless mirror, oppressed by strangers' voices, choked by cigarettes and vines. He should have bolted. He'd already caught a whiff of Angelina's scent, his eyes had already tumbled into the chute between her breasts, and he realized he should have been far away by now, drunk in a hammock somewhere they didn't speak English.

Angelina went on, "One of those ones where you layer up the different colors and the cherry pulls the red down with it."

The bartender frowned. "Christ. A Virgin Heat?"

"Is that what it's called?"

"That's what it's called."

"I'll have one."

He pushed out his altered lips, grudgingly moved to make the drink.

Angelina watched him, saw his pinky delicately splay above the handle of the spoon, noted the mangled index finger that went its own way from the others, observed the round exquisite meetings between the bottles and the glass, the slow momentous pouring from one into the other. Watching, she felt powerful and a little bit nasty, like she was paying him to dance for her.

When he slid the drink across the polished wood between her hands, she watched the grenadine ooze downward and whispered, "So Sal, what is your name?"

✳ ✳ ✳

A couple hours later, as it was getting on toward three A.M., she whispered, "Now I get it. Ziggy. He zigs, he zags, you can't catch up with him."

The barkeep glanced over his shoulder at his few remaining customers, then looked at Angelina. He did not want to encourage conversation. Blandly, he said, "I never thought of that. I just liked the sound."

"Nice sound," said Angelina. "Takes some getting used to. Like your face."

He leaned closer to her, she saw dark stubble straining from his pores, a film of perspiration on his forehead. "I wish you hadn't come here," he said. "It's crazy that you came here."

"I have a long memory, Sal . . . Ziggy."

"And I have a strong wish to keep on living. If your father—"

"No one knows I'm here. Hardly anyone. Let's go walk on the beach. Hold hands. Talk."

He turned his back on her, washed glasses, emptied ashtrays, stalled for time. When he looked at her again, she had not moved and her expression had not changed. He sucked a big gulp of watery air, looked at his watch, and gave last call.

✳ ✳ ✳

"And that's my fault too?" he said as they walked side by side at the edge of the ocean.

"Fault?" said Angelina. He'd come close to hurting her feelings several times, but now he finally succeeded, and she let go of the thick strong hand she'd waited so long to feel against her skin. "Who said anything about fault? I just thought you should know."

They walked. Underfoot, sand crunched over coral, the sound was improbably loud. An orange moon was slouching toward the west. Its craters were tinged with purple and the light it threw across the water was a greenish gold. Ziggy was surprised to miss the feel of Angelina's fingers surrounded by his own, and missing it, he felt remorse. But when he knew he was wrong, his impulse was to argue.

"The way you make it sound—"

"Ziggy, let it drop. It isn't blame. It isn't flattery. It's a piece of information. I haven't wanted anybody else."

He pondered this, but couldn't really get his mind around it; against the disjunct pile of names and faces and false starts and tangled limbs that his own life had consisted of, this constancy, this continuity was unimaginable. He said, "You've been scared, I bet."

"Scared?" said Angelina. "Scared of what?"

"Scared, ya know, of men. Of sex."

At this she could not hold back a laugh. "Ziggy," she said, "I've been surrounded by naked men since I hit this town. I haven't yet seen anything to be afraid of."

That slowed him down. A flash of something like jealousy, or maybe only prudishness, slipped across his face, which was mapped into bright planes and dark hollows by the moonlight.

"Besides," she continued, "you're a funny one to tell me how scared I am. Your whole life is being scared."

She expected him to deny it. He didn't. He just said, "Yeah, but I got a pretty good reason."

They walked. There was no surf, the ocean ended in the meekest lapping against the shore and made the faintest hiss as sudsy water slipped through nubs of limestone. Angelina took his hand again, remembered again the padded bulk of the heel of it, the fibrous breadth of the wrist. "Ziggy," she said, "let's not argue. I didn't come down here to argue."

They took a few steps; for a few seconds they might almost have been ordinary lovers. Then Ziggy yanked his arm away and wheeled to face her.

His features were twisted, not in anger but in cornered desperation, the fatigued confusion of a creature whose zigs and zags have failed to carry it to safety. "You didn't come to argue," he said. "You didn't come to get me killed. I keep hearing lots of reasons why you didn't come here. I still haven't got a clue why you did."

She looked at him until his face let go, until the furrows softened in his forehead and the lines released at the corners of his mouth. Then she very softly said, "You don't? You really don't?"

He stared at her. Red moonlight spilled down on her hair, traced out her ear and gleamed on one side of her neck, then trickled into her blouse and was swallowed up in shadow. His mouth was very dry.

"We started something a long time ago," Angelina said. "I was thinking we should finish it."

He watched her. Her lips stayed parted when she'd finished speaking; her chin tilted up, her shoulders lifted. His hand began to move toward her, toward the moonlight on her skin, but then it stopped, paralyzed by guilty fear, by a sudden sickening belief that at the moment he felt her flesh, bullets would rip into him, the revenge he'd dodged for so long would surely overtake him at this new affront.

His hand fell to his side, his lungs grabbed for breath. "Angelina," he said, desire and foreboding stretching his voice very thin. "Listen, this is crazy."

"Maybe it's supposed to be," she said.

He clenched his jaw, his feet pawed at the sand. "Before . . . ," he said. "Look, you were a kid and I was a different person."

"You had the same hands," she said. "The same eyes."

He hid his hands. He looked away. "I had some feelings then," he said. "I had, ya know, a place, a future."

"And now?" she said. "You don't have feelings now?"

He stared at clumps of sand. He shook his head.

"You're lying, Ziggy. I know you are."

She looked out across the flat and softly gleaming water. The sky was clear to the horizon. There would be a moonset soon, a perfect orange slice, and she understood she would not be in a lover's arms to see it.

She crossed the small space of beach between them, put her hands on Ziggy's chest, then craned her neck to kiss him, very chastely, on the cheek.

"I've waited ten years," she said. "I've imagined a lot of things but I never imagined I'd have to beg you to make love to me. I'll wait a little longer."

She turned and walked away.

20

Uncle Louie had for decades been an early riser.

After the first years of his marriage, there hadn't been much keeping him awake at night, and besides, he had a shy person's preference for being at large when most people were not. He loved to be the guy waiting on the sidewalk as the lights were switched on in the diner, as the Venetian blinds blinked open and the fellow in the paper hat crouched down by the door to lift the deadbolt that was pegged into the flooring. He loved to be there when the grounds still swirled in the just-made coffee, before the ink was quite dry on the newspapers, when the glaze on the Danish was sticky and warm.

So now, with the sun barely up, he emerged from his motel room and headed to Duval Street for some breakfast. Shadows were long, oblique and baffling, tall children who bore no resemblance to their parents. Dogs yawned under cars; cats stretched, scratching their flanks against garbage cans. Occasionally people went past on bicycles whose fat tires hummed against the silent pavements; Louie tried to figure who was awake already and who hadn't been to bed yet.

Down on Duval, he bought a paper, sat at a café a few steps above the sidewalk. He ate a croissant, drank a cappuccino, and allowed himself to feel that watching the scene was enough to make him part of it. Transvestites still vamped, impressive in their stamina to strut all night in high-heeled shoes. Now and then a police car listlessly rolled by, cops held vials of ammonia under the noses of people passed out on the curb. The town seemed utterly peaceful in its aberrations, and, looking without judgment, Louie felt worldly and extremely calm.

He watched a hooker half a block away, could barely imagine how, for her, night phased into morning. Her dark hair was tousled and wild, her makeup, though faded, still seemed alien and guilty in the new light of day. Her bright dress was wrinkled, sexily sloppy in the way it creased across her chest. Her stride was inconsistent, less like she was drunk than like she was trying to spread around the wear on aching feet.

She moved closer, and Louie, spasmodically blinking behind his paper, saw that the hooker was his niece.

His broad-mindedness caved in like a failed soufflé and he was suddenly abashed and appalled. Panicked, he hid behind his wall of newsprint to stall for time. He thought of hiding there till she had passed, to spare them both mortification. But he remembered, even if self-mockingly, his resolve to be a hero; a hero wouldn't chicken out like that. He lowered the paper and meekly called her name.

She looked up from sidewalk level, walked slowly over, and in a voice that was not the least embarrassed but very discouraged, said, "Oh hi, Uncle Louie."

"Want some coffee?"

She came up the steps, noticed the discomfort in his face. "It's not how it looks," she said. "I wish it was, but it isn't."

Flustered to be caught in narrow, judging thoughts, he tried to splutter out a denial.

Sitting down, she said, "It's okay, Uncle Louie. You think I look like a slut. I see it. And I tried. God knows I tried."

Louie mopped his head with a paper napkin. The waitress came over and Angelina ordered coffee. Then she said, "*He* tried even harder not to want me."

"He?" said Louie. "Who?"

"Never mind," she said, and read the headlines upside down on his paper.

"Never mind?" Her uncle pushed croissant crumbs with his fingertips. "Angelina," he said, "I'm a meddling old fart and I'm only your uncle. Am I allowed at least to say I'm worried about you?"

Her coffee arrived. She blew on it and said, "Of course you're allowed."

He leaned closer, splayed his elbows wide. "You're a beautiful young woman, Angelina. A million guys would want you. Maybe something isn't right if you have to chase after—"

"Uncle Louie," she interrupted, "what was it like to want Aunt Rose?"

The query stood him up like a good crisp jab. He gestured, his mouth got ready to make words, but nothing came out.

"It's a real question," his niece went on. "I'm trying to understand. Could you just as easily have wanted someone else? Could you have *changed* what you wanted, like at a restaurant, they're out of lamb chops, you say okay, I'll have the steak? I mean, did you really *want* her, or was it just what came along?"

Louie pushed his lips out, made little circles with his hand. He was sitting there but he was traveling. He grew young, got trim, his hair returned as he remembered early kisses, the waxy taste of Rose's lipstick and the warm and thrilling breath behind it. His hand on the amazing place where waist flared into hip as they danced the cha-cha. He recalled the charged and lusty peace that happened when the clamor of loins clanged along in concert with the simple tune played by the heart, and he said, almost in a whisper, "I wanted her."

Angelina reached across the table, put her hand on his, and said, "All right, then." She took a small sip of her cooling coffee, then yawned. "Come on," she said, "you'll walk me home."

✳ ✳ ✳

The federal offices in North Miami did nothing to dress up the blah neighborhood they stood in. Squat and beige, bleakly new and cheaply functional, it seemed their sole design imperative was the ability to withstand a hurricane or a siege. Inside, furtive blinds sliced up the sun that came through narrow windows; black shoes scuffed along squares of gray linoleum; green metal desks sat in offices defined by slabs of rolling wall that didn't reach the ceiling.

In one such cubicle, a baggy-eyed but pumped-up Keith McCullough stood in city clothes while his supervisor, Manny Links, sat placidly and rocked in a chair that squeaked and scraped with every movement.

"I don't see it," the supervisor was saying. "Why continue with this guy? You got a girlfriend down there, what?"

"I am telling you," said Keith McCullough, "it's just starting to get interesting."

Links looked down at the clipboard on his desk. He had the clipboard; he had the pipe; he had the square chin and the salt-and-pepper hair: he seemed every inch the senior Fed. But in his mind he'd already moved on to the cushy private-sector security job that awaited him upon retirement. He'd practically forgotten he'd ever been an agent.

"Interesting?" he said, looking down at McCullough's latest report. "The guy's a bartender. He takes a drink on the job. I don't find that so interesting."

"It's a break in the pattern," said the undercover man. "He was very agitated."

Links took his pipe from his jacket pocket, serenely tapped it against his palm. He leaned back in his chair and didn't seem to notice that it screeched. "I get agitated sometimes. Don't you?"

"Look," McCullough said, "he changed right before my eyes. Someone came into that bar that he really didn't want to see. Who was it? Why did he flinch? I think something's going on."

"I think you like Key West," said Links. "There's nothing in this report to suggest—"

McCullough balled his fists, leaned forward so that his tie hung away from his chest. "The good stuff, Manny . . . it's not in the report."

"The good stuff?"

"I have a source."

"A source," said Links. He tapped the clipboard. "That should be in here."

"It's not ready to be in there."

"We have procedures, Keith. A source for what?"

"For what Ziggy Maxx is into."

Links slipped his pipe into his mouth, clamped down on the stem. "Keith, don't go cowboy on me. Who's the source?"

The undercover man ignored the question. "Look, suddenly Ziggy's drinking on the job. Suddenly he's late for work. I think something is breaking with this guy."

"And I think you've wasted enough time looking for it."

"Gimme one more month," McCullough said.

Links rocked forward. The chair complained. "Two weeks," he wearily pronounced.

"Two weeks is like nothing," said McCullough.

His boss's eyes had moved to other papers on his desk. "Two weeks of careful, conservative, well-documented work. You got that?"

"Conservative," McCullough said. "Well-documented. Got it." He wheeled out of the cube with two more weeks to run his show exactly as he pleased.

21

It was much too early when the phone rang at Ziggy's bungalow.

With the boundless resentment of the tired, he freed a hairy arm from underneath a sweaty sheet, grabbed at the receiver and said a gruff hello that was muffled by the pillow meant to shade his eyes.

The caller was an associate of Carmen Salazar's. Ziggy was wanted in the garden, right away.

He cursed, rolled out of bed, threw himself under a lukewarm shower. He drank a cup of yesterday's reheated coffee that tasted of aluminum and dust, then started up his rumbling old car and drove toward the bogus candy store.

The car shook his brain, the ruined springs of the driver's seat jostled his bowels, and his mood got only viler as he went. Grogginess lifted, gradually and incompletely, but what replaced it was an edgy residue of stifled lust. Angelina had offered herself to him. Lips parted. Moonlight reaching down her blouse. Why the hell had he resisted, retreating on the crunching beach instead of going forward to press against her, answering readiness with readiness? He wanted to imagine it was gallantry, and maybe it was in part—the barren chivalry of a man who keeps his pants zipped because he knows that once the sex has passed he has nothing much to offer. But if it was gallantry, didn't he deserve to feel better?

He parked, climbed the single cracked step, entered the dimness of the store. The fat guy who always sat behind the counter was sitting there again, airing out his armpits by the filthy fan.

Ziggy walked through to the back, saw Salazar perched in his lawn chair, and the first thing Salazar said to him, said it even before Ziggy had come around to face him, was, "You disappointed me the other day. You let me down."

Ziggy did not deal so well with criticism in the best of times, and this morning was anything but. Sullenly he said, "I don't need to hear that, Carmen. You fuckin' get me out of bed to tell me that?"

"Those men who were here," Salazar continued mildly, "they're important men. Men of the world. The kind of men you've led me to believe you've dealt with in the past."

Ziggy shuffled his feet. His skin itched; his loins felt irritable and heavy, the tug of them was giving him a belly ache. He said, "So Carmen, what's your fuckin' point?"

"I thought you'd pay closer attention."

Ziggy said nothing, sulked. He felt last night's sand in his shoes. It was pissing him off that he was standing up and Salazar was sitting down.

Salazar said, "Didn't it occur to you to wonder why I asked you to that meeting? I do things for reasons, Ziggy. I think you know me well enough by now to realize that."

Ziggy looked at his feet. He should have remembered, but did not in that moment recall, that last time things went sour for him, it was sometimes his attention that faltered, other times his tact. He said, "Jeez, Carmen, I thought you invited me so I could stand in the sun while you sat in the shade and played boss."

Salazar drummed neat fingers on the arm of his lawn chair.

His mouth got curvy in what was half a smirk and half a frown. He was not a nice person but he tried to be fair to his men; he tried not to place them in undue jeopardy if they could be just as useful to him doing something else. Salazar had noticed a subtly unnatural waxiness in the flesh at Ziggy's hairline. Ziggy had led him to believe he was not a stranger to mobsters from New York. If the big talker had more than the usual reasons to be wary of the Mafia, Salazar thought he should be given the chance to excuse himself. But if that chance was offered, and if all Salazar got in return was obtuseness, surliness, ingratitude . . . .

Ziggy passed the silence by plucking at his moistening shirt, and wondering how it would have been if he'd met Angelina's waiting mouth, if his fingertips had followed the moonlight down between her breasts. Much too late, he said, "S'okay Carmen, why'd y'ask me to that meeting?"

But Salazar's brief spasm of concern had passed. He was annoyed now, his reply was crisp and neutral. "We'll be doing business with those men," he said. "You'll be working with them closely. I thought it would be good if you got to know their faces."

At this Ziggy pouted, pawed the ground, bitterly mourned his interrupted sleep.

Carmen added, the mordancy unnoticed, "And if they had a chance to look at yours."

✳ ✳ ✳

"You have to go back," said Michael.

"I will not go back," said Angelina. "I have my pride."

"Pride is stupid. Go back. You're wearing him down."

"Wearing him down? What is this, a boxing match, a war?"

"Sometimes it's like that."

"Michael," she said, "I've tried. I'm done. He doesn't want me."

It was afternoon. They were sitting by the pool. Neither had been awake for very long; their schedules had gotten so bizarre that they were once again in sync.

"That's what you say," Michael challenged.

"That's what I *say*? That's what I know."

"Maybe there's another explanation."

Angelina feigned disinterest, looked off at the cool blue water staked with forms of naked men, gluteal folds jagged with refraction.

Her friend continued, "Maybe he wants you so bad that he can't let himself have you."

She tried not to let it show that she liked the sound of that. "Very flattering," she said. "Very perverse."

"Sometimes it's like that."

"Sometimes it's like a lot of things," said Angelina.

"That's true," said Michael. "You think it's always the same?"

"How the hell should I know?" She sighed. Her bathing suit squeaked as she squirmed against her lounge chair. "Let's talk about something else, okay? When do I get to meet David?"

22

Funzie Gallo, unsure if he was doing right or wrong, but certain that he'd go crazy if he had to keep on watching his old friend lumber blindly around the social club, had gone ahead and laid the groundwork for the deal down in Florida. He arranged for Paul Amaro to meet with Tommy Lucca.

The evening before the sitdown, sitting with a bourbon in his silent living room, Paul told his wife he was going to Miami on business. She didn't answer him. She hadn't answered him in days. For a long time, many years in fact, her silences had been accusations; but what had changed in the week and a half since Angelina disappeared, was that Paul now knew they were. He heard the seething questions inside the silence, they found his guilty places like dye finds tumors, and he felt compelled to respond, he seemed not to notice it was a one-way conversation.

"What else can I do up here?" he said. "You're looking at me like I shouldn't go, like there's more I should be doing. What else can I do?"

She didn't answer. A lamp was on behind her, it reduced

her to a silhouette of an old lady's hairdo and a face that was wrinkled at the edges. She turned away her eyes.

"I've talked to everyone I know. I've begged. I've threatened. I've sent messages to the Irish, to the Asians. Tell me, Maria, what more should I do?"

She said nothing. Her hands were folded in her lap, they didn't move.

"Al's here," her husband said. "Joe's here. There's any news, they can find me in a minute."

Maria was quiet.

"Life can't just stop," he said. "Life stops, ya go crazy and what the hell does it accomplish?"

There was no reply.

Paul Amaro's voice grew higher, thinner, craven. "You think I feel this less than you do, woman? You think I love her any less than you?"

Angelina's mother didn't answer. Her husband stood up heavily and left her sitting on the sofa, featureless and gray with the yellow lamplight reaching toward the corners of the room behind her.

* * *

Next day, Paul Amaro went to Florida. He was carrying no weapons, packing no contraband; there was no reason not to fly.

At Miami airport, he walked through the same corridors that his daughter had walked through, smelled the same faint salty mildew, saw the same pyramids of plastic oranges.

A driver met him, swept him past the clutter of downtown to discreet and shady Coral Gables, where rambling houses with red-tiled roofs crouched behind high walls of jagged limestone rock. At Tommy Lucca's place, a gate slid open silently, tires crunched over immaculate white gravel, and the car stopped beneath a columned porte cochere.

An Asian butler met him at the door, handed him a hot

washcloth. Another servant brought a mimosa on a silver tray. Then the butler led him down a long hallway lined with vases, paintings; and around a sunny courtyard with a fountain; and toward a separate wing whose walls were paneled in mahogany. The elegance was seamless until the servant tapped lightly on the study door, opened it, and there was Tommy Lucca's face. The nose went even more sideways than Paul remembered; twisted cartilage showed a shiny dent, the nostrils didn't match. The mouth was broad and loose and twitchy, he seemed always to be about to suck his teeth. He said a single word but clearly he was showing off. "Welcome."

Paul Amaro said, "Nice to see you doing so well, Tommy."

The compliment was insincere but still it cost him. Paul Amaro could remember being on the wrong side of the discussion about Tommy Lucca's prospects in Florida. Like most of the New York *goombahs* who didn't have the vision or the guts to make a move themselves, he thought Lucca was headed to a backwater, the minor leagues. Now they were all near the ends of their careers, and Tommy Lucca was rich, was tan, was one of the few who had never been to jail. He'd proved them all wrong, though he'd yet to prove nearly enough to be content.

He plucked imaginary lint from his shirtfront, said, "I'm getting by. Come in, come in."

Amaro stepped farther into the room, saw a sad-eyed, handsome man rising from his chair, a Panama hat in his left hand as he reached out his right to shake. Lucca made the introductions. The handsome man's name was Carlos Mendez, and his host described him as an important businessman with many friends in Cuba.

". . . where great and long overdue changes are about to happen," Mendez said.

"He wants Castro's balls," Lucca explained. "Democracy. It gives Carlos here a hard-on, he thinks it's coming any day. People are getting ready for it, buying guns. Siddown, siddown."

Amaro settled into a chair, said skeptically, "Ya read the

paper, ya'd think the Cubans had no money. Not for guns. Not for nothin'."

The handsome man tried and failed to keep a certain smugness out of his smile. "The money is no problem," he said. "America is still good to those of us who strive."

"Yeah, swell," said Paul Amaro. "So what kinda pieces ya want?"

"Two thousand handguns," said Mendez. "Preferably 9 millimeter. Five hundred assault weapons, Chinese is acceptable. You can do?"

Paul Amaro crossed his arms. He'd promised himself to be bored and distant, but the deal adrenaline was starting to flow. He said, "What about payments, transfers?"

Tommy Lucca hadn't sat. He was pacing, raking the hair on his forearms. "You get the merchandise far as Hialeah. When it gets there, I move it to Key West, where another guy—"

"Another guy?" Amaro interrupted. "Who's the other guy?"

"A Key West guy," Lucca said impatiently. "A local."

"Of Cuban heritage," Mendez added, furling and unfurling the brim of his hat.

Amaro burrowed deeper into the negotiation, knew the fugitive peace of forgetting about his life. "I don't like it there's another guy," he said. "Why's there have to be another guy?"

"Geography," said Lucca. "Right here, we're like two hundred miles from Havana, the Gulf Stream in our face. Key West, it's only ninety miles."

Paulie chewed his lip, looked out the window at spiky plants with giant leaves. "When do I get my money?"

The handsome man said, "Everyone gets paid when the merchandise reaches Havana."

"Bullshit," Paulie said. "My part's done when the goods get to Florida."

Mendez smiled. His eyes got sadder. "Guns in Hialeah don't do my friends in Cuba any good."

Amaro ground his foot against the carpet. "This is why I

don't like it there's another guy. I'm waitin' on my money while my merch is with some yokel?"

Lucca didn't like the word; his loose mouth quaked and burbled.

Mendez, diplomatic, said, "Perhaps we could pay half at Hialeah."

"And the other half before the shipment heads for Cuba," pressed Amaro.

"But if there's a problem—" Lucca said.

"A problem," said Amaro. "Exactly. This is why I don't like it there's another guy."

"Paulie," Lucca said, "the water near Cuba, the Straits, that's the hairy part. Cutters. Helicopters. The boat don't get through, someone's fucked. Who'd'ya wanna see get fucked—us, or the other guy?"

"I don't like dealin' wit' guys I don't know," insisted Paul.

Tommy Lucca's ears were getting red, lines of white were tracing out his mismatched nostrils. "I know him. That's not good enough for you?"

"No offense, Tommy, but no, it isn't."

Lucca stalled in his pacing, drummed stubby fingers on his rosewood desk. "No offense, Tommy? No offense to you, pal, but after all this time, you still got this fuckin' New York thing, like no one else knows how—"

"I didn't say that," Paulie said, though secretly he was pleased that he could sit in the enormous house of this success-ful man and so easily find a nerve where he could still be tweaked. "All I said—"

"All you said is that for you it don't mean beans that I picked this guy, that I trust him."

"Now don't get touchy, Tommy," said Amaro.

Carlos Mendez was working on his hat. His tragic eyes flicked back and forth, and he wondered if these two bullheaded gringos would scotch his deal before it started. At last he said, "Gentlemen, let's not quarrel."

"Who's quarreling?" said Angelina's father.

"I have a suggestion," Mendez went on. "Be my guests for dinner. If you like, we'll see a show, gamble, have some women. Tomorrow we'll go together to Key West, you'll meet our colleague there, I'm confident you'll be more comfortable. Is that acceptable to everyone?"

23

Angelina was feeling glum, unpretty, hopeless. She invited Michael out for a fancy dinner and, as he picked apart his lobster with great deliberation, she told him she was leaving town the next day.

He put down his tiny fork, very thoroughly wiped his mouth, looked out past the terraced tables to the ocean. "You can't do that," he said. "That's ridiculous."

"Ridiculous?" she answered. Her own plate was hardly touched, she pushed it an inch away from her, took a sip of Chardonnay. "What's ridiculous is that I came here at all."

"That's not ridiculous," Michael said. "That's romance. That's destiny."

She made a dismissive sound, fiddled with a roll.

"You can't leave now," her friend went on. "Not when you're so close."

"Close to what?"

Michael flicked his green eyes left and right, leaned low across the table, decided on a somewhat desperate stratagem. "Close to getting laid, for one thing."

Angelina was piqued. "You think I can't get laid?" she said. She said it louder than she'd meant to, heads turned here and there.

He reached for the wine bucket, poured them both some more. "So why haven't you?" he challenged.

She looked away.

"Because you're after the sublime," he answered for her. "Because you won't settle. So why settle now, when you've almost got what you've been waiting for?"

"I don't almost have it," she said. "That's exactly the problem. It feels farther away now than when I was home in my room and didn't even know if Sal Martucci was still alive."

"He's alive," said Michael. "He's here. You've *touched* him."

"And he practically dissolved," said Angelina. She sipped wine, gathered steam. "And another thing. Just in the last day or so it's finally getting through to me that it's a little pathetic to still be chasing at twenty-seven what you dreamed about at seventeen, especially when it was probably a bad idea to begin with."

"Is twenty-seven so different from seventeen?" said Michael. "Is *eighty*-seven so different from seventeen. People want what they want. They need what they need."

Angelina sighed, looked out at moonlight on the water, at misted stars that dimmed and brightened as scraps of cloud slipped past them. "It's beautiful here," she said. "And you've been a terrific friend, a godsend. But I'm leaving tomorrow."

Michael stared down at the tablecloth, fingered the base of his wineglass. He hated saying goodbye to people; no matter whose idea it was to leave, no matter what the circumstance, he always felt like he was being punished, renounced, dragged away to someplace dark and cramped and silent.

But then again, Angelina's giving up didn't mean that he had to give up too. After a long moment, he said, "What time tomorrow?"

"Hm?"

"What time tomorrow are you leaving?"

Angelina shrugged. She hadn't gotten as far as making reservations.

"Don't leave before we talk."

"Michael," she said, "there's nothing—"

"Not until we see each other," he said. "Promise?"

She pouted, pulled a deep breath in, smelled sauce and smoke and ocean. "Okay," she said. "I promise."

* * *

Maybe Louie had simply been away too long. Maybe he was tired of walking up and down Duval Street, spinning the same postcard racks evening after evening, seeing the same T-shirts, the same pierced noses, the same tattoos. Maybe he was tired of the moldy smell of his motel room, the places in the towels where the terry cloth had been rubbed away on strangers' bodies. In any case, his traveler's delight was beginning to wear that thin, he was starting to feel homesick.

Homesick for what? he asked himself. For his wife's bad cooking, grains of salt bouncing off of watery mounds of tasteless vegetables? For the not quite kitty-cornered angle of the TV set in the living room, the tangle of extension cords behind it? For the traffic, the cold, the stinking air?

Truth was, he was getting homesick for all those things.

He missed his wife; he felt that now, intensely. Missing her, he afforded her the benefit of every doubt. She wasn't sarcastic, she was witty. Not malicious, but tough-minded and savvy. She wasn't vain, she was respectful of appearances. Not pushy, but high-spirited.

Besides, what did any of that matter? He missed her. She was his wife. Quite suddenly, he wanted more than anything to hear her voice.

He was standing in a pizzeria while this was happening, waiting for his calzone to be warmed up. The air smelled of oregano and yeast, flashes of heat shot forth from the ovens. He sipped his soda through a straw. He didn't really think that he should call, but he looked around for a pay phone. He saw one in the dim alcove that led on to the rest rooms. He asked the counter guy for change.

Names and numbers were scrawled in pencil on the wall around the phone. Louie's heart was pounding. He shouldn't call because he didn't know what he would say. He picked up the receiver, heard the dial tone, put it down again. He was afraid he'd catch hell, afraid he'd be asked too many questions. He felt a desperate impulse to brag, and he knew this would only lead to trouble. *I found Angelina!* he yearned to tell his wife. Then what?

He again picked up the phone, nestled it between his shoulder and his ear as he dialed numbers, readied change. Quarters plunked, dimes tinkled. His hand shook. There were two rings, three, and then his wife said, "Hello?"

Louie heard the rasp of many decades' smoking, the thick tongue of an evening measured in cocktails. The TV was on, must've been a sitcom, he heard clustered laughing.

"Hello?" she said again, impatient now, aggressive.

Louie wanted to speak but he couldn't. Behind him, trays clattered, peels rang, a counterman sang out, "Spinach calzone!"

Rose demanded, "Who the hell is this? You there? You there?" Her own heart thumped now, she felt a burning in her tightened chest. Was this news? A ransom call? "Hello?"

Louie understood he had to talk, couldn't let things hang like this. But when he went to move his mouth, the best he could manage was a kiss, a wet and awkward smacking kiss into the phone.

There was a moment's disbelieving silence, the receiver felt like a dead fish in his hand.

Then Rose said, "Drop dead, ya fucking pervert."

The phone slammed down in Louie's ear. He blinked, then cursed himself. He knew if he called back, the line would be busy, off the hook. Why did he always make things worse when he tried to make them better?

He waited till his breathing slowed, then went up to the counter. He paid for his calzone but left it sitting there. He wasn't hungry anymore.

24

Ziggy was dreaming of lamb chops.

Or at least that's how the dream had started off. A pair of lamb chops, perfectly pink, were set before him on a clean white plate. He was ravenous. He had a big napkin tucked under his chin, and he contemplated the chops in the perfect rapture of appetite peaking, fulfillment in plain view. He admired the delicate and arcing bones, licked his lips at the prospect of the juicy resilient flesh between his teeth. But when he picked up knife and fork, the lamb chops began to change themselves into Angelina. Their curving bones became her sides, her face appeared like a medallion on the plate. The dollops of meat began to breathe; he saw them pulse, alive again, and with lascivious confusion, he pondered the dubious anatomy. These succulent pink morsels—were they her thighs? breasts? buttocks offered on a clean white plate?

The phone rang, kept ringing.

Ziggy whimpered, groaned, turned over. At last, with flustered effort he freed a hand from underneath the tangled sheet, brought the receiver to his ear beneath a sweaty pillow. "Yeah?"

"We need you here at noon," said a flunkey of Carmen Salazar.

Ziggy forced an eye to open, squinted at his watch on the bedside table. "It's not even fuckin' nine," he groused.

"It's important. Don't be late."

"Have I ever been fuckin' late?"

The flunkey hung up on him. Ziggy called him an asshole as he fumbled the phone back into its cradle.

Then he put the pillow on his head again and tried his best to dive back into sleep. He needed rest but more than that he needed sustenance; he longed to recapture the dream he now felt, bitterly, he'd been gypped out of.

His eyes closed tight, he labored at bringing back the images of nourishment and lust, projecting them like slides against his eyelids. It didn't work. The pictures were there, but without the all-acceptingness of sleep, they were ridiculous and crude, and Ziggy dimly understood he'd lost his chance to savor Angelina without the guilty weight of will, to relish the miracle of her availability without the dread of consequences.

Cursing, he gave up on rest and trundled out of bed, moving resentfully into another day of a life that, as he couldn't help noticing more and more, didn't fit him as a person's own life ought to, but pinched and drooped like someone else's borrowed clothes.

Another day, thought Angelina, another mango muffin.

Though this day, she realized, was very different from all the others that she'd spent at Coral Shores. The breakfast buffet was the same—the same thwarted bees hovering outside the tiny tents that covered the fruit. The poolside spectacle was more or less the same—the same mix of sleepy smokers and pinkened bare behinds. But everything was tinged now with the sepia of departure. Colors faded as things seen were already becoming things recalled; round objects flattened, the better to fit in the never adequate luggage of memory.

She was leaving today. She'd booked her flight. She'd tried to call her Uncle Louie, left a message for him. Thanks for everything. Sorry to be leaving so abruptly. Sometime, when she was feeling calmer, clearer, she would explain it all.

She was already mostly packed, her open suitcase sitting at the foot of the bed, piled with pastel blouses and floral shifts in hothouse colors that she doubted she would ever wear back in the austere and washed-out north. Things were very different up there, she reminded herself. Up there she wouldn't greet each sunset with a salty cocktail. Up there she wouldn't spend her evenings hopping bars, eating seafood on the ocean. What *would* she do up there, without Michael for a friend, without Ziggy for a mission, without her own awakened desires giving direction to her days? She didn't know; the question gave her the beginnings of a bellyache. She leaned back farther in her lounge chair, offered her face to the sun, and tried to think of other things, or better yet, of nothing.

She succeeded well enough in going blank that she didn't see Michael come in the front gate from the street, and it wasn't till his shadow cooled her skin that she noticed him standing above her lounge, staring down at an unsettling angle. Russet stubble bristled on his chin and underneath his nostrils. His eyes were narrow in the sun, laugh lines at the corners; his mouth was stretched in a slightly goofy smile powered by conspiracy and triumph.

"You're looking pleased with yourself this morning," Angelina told him.

By way of answer, he reached into the pocket of his jeans, produced a rumpled bit of paper which he dangled over her like a string above a cat. "Know what this is?" he said.

Without much interest, Angelina guessed, "A new boyfriend's phone number?"

Michael said, "What kind of slut do you think I am? It's for you."

"Me?"

He sat down near the foot of her lounge. With effort he tempered his grin, looked almost priestly in a pagan sort of way. "Give me your hand."

Hesitantly, Angelina reached out. Michael pressed the scrap of paper into her palm. "Ziggy's address," he whispered.

"Michael, for God's sake!"

"We followed him home this morning. Four o'clock."

"We?"

"David and me. The whole thing's so romantic, he was into it immediately."

"You tell people? I thought I was confiding—"

"It was an adventure. We tracked him to his car, grabbed a cab to follow—"

"Michael—"

"The place he lives, it's no pleasure palace, I have to tell you. Not without a certain tawdry charm, I guess . . . but you'll see what I mean."

"I won't see what you mean," said Angelina.

"Of course you will," he said. "How can you not go—?"

"Michael, I know you think you mean well. But the spasm has passed. I'm packed. I'm leaving."

"What time's your flight?"

"Five."

"That's plenty of time."

"Time for what?"

"Jesus, Angelina! Don't you see how you could put the perfect finishing touch on this vacation?"

"Finishing touch?" she said. "God, Michael, you make it sound like, I don't know—a garnish."

"Sometimes it's like that."

"Sometimes it's like a garnish?"

He leaned closer to her, put both his hands on one of hers,

closed her fingers around the precious scrap of paper. "Go there," he said. "Have a wonderful, wonderful afternoon . . . Write to me sometime, my address is on the back . . . And don't say goodbye, I can't stand to say goodbye."

*** *** ***

They took the stretch from Coral Gables so no one would get crampy, cranky on the long ride down the Keys.

Even so, Paul Amaro was feeling foul. He looked out the window as a pretext for turning a wide shoulder on his companions, but he allowed himself to take no pleasure in the sparkling greens and blues that stretched away from Seven Mile Bridge, in the effortless flight of pelicans whose wing tips hung an inch above the water.

A suspicion was gnawing at him—the suspicion that he was being duped somehow, made a fool of. But when he pondered who or what was duping him, he could come up with no villain other than himself. He was pretending he cared about this deal. He was feigning a professional's interest in the details, going through the old charade of showing he was tough and sly. He was shamming, even, the expected avidity for money, when the truth was that, once the mindless spasm of involvement had passed, he didn't give a damn about any of it, not the guns, not the risk, not the payoff. He cared about his missing daughter. When he thought about her, worry and rage brought him to the brink of madness; when he tried to distract himself with thoughts of anything except her, he felt only a cowardly dishonesty, an emptiness beyond despair.

So he stared, unseeing, out the window, his sinews stretched between the poles of grief and fakery, and at last the limo reached Key West.

The highway narrowed, lost its forward thrust as it left behind the strip malls and the billboards. One traffic light sufficed to change it into a shady avenue where people sat on porches, where matching pairs of palms stood sentinel in front of doorways.

Tommy Lucca's driver veered off toward the dusty neighborhood where Carmen Salazar had his headquarters, parked on a street of dented cars, among them a battered hulking Oldsmobile.

Paulie emerged from the air-conditioned stretch into the blistering heat of noon. Through eyes constricted by a moment's dizziness, he squinted at the candy store, with its cracked stoop and streaked and filthy windows, loose mortar crumbling in its cheap facade of bricks.

"Place is a dump," he said to Tommy Lucca.

He said it to gain the upper hand but it backfired. Lucca didn't rattle, just flashed a sour smile, and what the smile said was that the Gatto Bianco Social Club was not exactly Caesar's Palace either, and you couldn't judge an operation by its headquarters, or then again, maybe you could.

They climbed the cracked stoop. Lucca and Mendez stood aside, gesturing graciously for their guest to enter first. But by old and reasonable habit, Paul Amaro declined to lead the parade through an unknown doorway. He waited until the others were inside, then stepped into the dimness, smelled ancient chocolate and the armpits of the man who sat before the fan, and was confirmed in his determination to be unimpressed.

25

For a while Angelina truly believed she wasn't going to Ziggy's place; then she caught herself wondering if she should bring her suitcase or leave it at the guest house.

Bringing it, she reasoned, would be awkward and could be regarded as presuming; on the other hand, it would be a nuisance to come back for it before going to the airport—especially since, if she went to Ziggy's at all, it would only be to say hello and goodbye, nothing more.

But wait a second, she reminded herself. She wasn't going to Ziggy's, it was out of the question, so why was she bothering to think about the suitcase?

She was in her room. She'd had her second shower of the day, dressed a second time; her skin was already flushed again as she paced between the dresser and the bed. She realized there were lots of other things she could do between now and five P.M. There was the beach. There was sight-seeing. But her eyes kept flicking back to the torn-off piece of paper that held Ziggy's address. The paper sat in an ashtray on the night table. It was barely big enough to wrap a chewed-up piece of gum, yet the whole room seemed to pivot around it, it became the center of gravity, as if it were made of some impossibly dense stuff, a different kind of matter.

She approached the paper, or rather she was pulled in toward it. She nudged it gently with a fingernail, as if she feared it might explode. Then she picked it up, although it seemed to her that it jumped into her hand. She squeezed it hard, and ran downstairs to find a taxi.

＊ ＊ ＊

In the moment before Paul Amaro lumbered through the doorway that gave onto the garden, Ziggy Maxx was nibbling a loose thread off the short sleeve of his faded shirt. His arm was raked across his face, his mouth was buried in his shoulder. He barely listened as Carmen Salazar tried to explain to him and a man named Johnny Castro—a half-black Bahamian with smeared freckles and strange green eyes—how important this meeting was, what an opportunity it represented. Ziggy hated pep talks, always had. He shifted his weight from foot to foot and kept chewing at the thread.

He was still working it when, in a macabre reshuffling of space and time, his past in New York loomed up before him in a Key West doorway.

It seemed to Ziggy as baffling as a tumble into an alternate universe, but there, moving toward him at a stately pace, broad-shouldered and silver-haired, his expression grim and dogged, was the man he'd sent to prison, the man who'd sworn to kill him. Ziggy's breathing stalled, his arm dropped to his side, left his new face naked in the garden's dappled light. His field of vision shrank, became greasy at the edges; a taste of sour milk climbed up his throat.

But he stood his ground somehow as Paul Amaro neared, flanked by the short man with creases in his pants and the handsome man with the Panama hat; as Carmen Salazar respectfully got up from his lawn chair; as the short man led the rituals of greetings, introductions.

Through the handshakes and the small talk of the more important players, Ziggy had a moment to wonder if he'd be murdered right there in the garden, and to ponder what it would be that would give him away, since he had no doubt that he would be exposed. He mostly trusted the surgeon's knife and hammer; he didn't think Paul Amaro would know him by his face. So then—would it be the hands? The voice? A telltale phrase or inflection, the smell of his aftershave or of his skin?

Carmen Salazar was introducing the other underling. "This is Captain John Castro—no relation, I assure you." People tried to laugh, there was something uncomfortably intimate, visceral, about the gurgling sound of forced laughter. "Smuggles people, hard currency, cigars. Has a good boat, knows Havana harbor like his bathtub."

There were handshakes. Touching. Looks in the eye, and breathing of the damp and common air between close-together faces. Ziggy's nerves felt swollen with adrenaline, he imagined they were visible, sparking like snapped wires at the places where they branched.

"And this," said Salazar, "is Ziggy Maxx. Tommy, Carlos— you remember him. Utility player with big-league capabilities. Isn't that right, Ziggy?"

Ziggy didn't want to talk, didn't want to risk moving the features that, in repose, had not undone him. It would be absurd to die because of the stubborn remnants of a Brooklyn accent, to be murdered for a rasping tone that might trigger recollection. Between barely parted teeth, he muttered, "That's right, Carmen."

Eyes were turned his way; hands were lifted toward him. He shook with Tommy Lucca, Carlos Mendez, and as he did so, he thought about his mangled finger and the way it made his grip unique. His mind reeled with a dim sense of all the million details of identity, the seldom thought about codes and markers by which we know one person from the next, and in the instant before he shook hands with Paul Amaro, he tried to invent a handshake that was not his own.

His palm, now, was pressed against the palm of his sworn enemy; the two men were linked at the webbing of their thumbs. Ziggy squeezed down but only very softly; he willed his dislocated pinky to work beside his other fingers; he felt the damaged joint crackle like a broken hinge. Something told him he had to lock eyes with Paul Amaro, that shrinking from his gaze would leave his enemy's senses free to absorb signals that were harder to disguise, that did not admit of bluffing. With the moxie of the cornered, he stared straight at his former boss; what he saw in his glance almost gave him hope. Paul Amaro's shadowed eyes looked far away, indifferent, bored. Ziggy recognized the expression of a man who was only partly where he seemed to be.

He freed his hand, it felt very heavy at his side. Paul Amaro's exhausted gaze slid away to other things. A brief breeze, wet and unrefreshing, rattled the foliage, brought forth hints of fruit and flowers that mixed with the smells of sweat and cologne.

Carmen Salazar said, "So, gentlemen—to business?"

✳ ✳ ✳

The cab drove off, and Angelina walked uncertainly down a narrow lane that wasn't very nice.

Low and rusted chain-link fence separated tiny unkempt yards; the barriers were colonized by scraps of browning vine. Fronds had fallen here and there at curbside, and no one picked them up, they dried and broke in pieces on the stony ground. The sun beat down on sagging roofs and splintered porches and jalousied windows with missing slats like gaps in teeth.

Angelina, her scalp throbbing as her body worked to shed its heat and that of the midday glare, paused in front of number fourteen, Ziggy's place.

Fenceposts leaned in unmoored foundations of cracked cement. A gate hung askew before a weedy path. An ancient birdbath, chipped and dry, sat in the dirt, spotted with lichen. Two drooping stairs led up to a door whose screen was torn. She approached, breathed deep in the relative cool of the porch, and knocked.

There was no answer.

She was less relieved and more disappointed than she thought she'd be. She knocked again.

She waited. A banking plane went by, its clatter reminded her that she was leaving in a matter of hours, with nothing really changed, nothing accomplished, nothing even understood. Quite suddenly she was furious with frustration. She yanked open the screen and reached for the knob on the inside door.

She knew it wouldn't turn. Ziggy was a paranoid, saw thieves and dirtbags everywhere, was not the type to leave his door unlocked; she was mostly just performing for herself, putting on a little show of temper.

She could not know that a Federal agent named Keith Mc-Cullough had considerately picked the lock for her, then settled back in his shady car at the head of the lane, to see what would happen when Ziggy Maxx and Paul Amaro's daughter got together.

The knob turned, the door fell open, and Angelina, utterly surprised, stepped into Ziggy's empty bungalow.

26

Something was bothering Paul Amaro, he couldn't pinpoint what it was.

The garden was steamy, he was damp inside his clothes, but he didn't think it was the temperature alone that was annoying him. Pollen and fruit sap were glutting up his sinuses, he had the beginnings of a headache, but what was gnawing at him did not seem mainly physical. There was, of course, his preoccupation with his daughter, but that had become a constant droning sorrow; what he felt now struck him as outside of that.

He pondered his malaise as the meeting progressed.

Tommy Lucca was saying, "We need a safe place to move the goods from my guy's truck to your guy's boat."

"We have a place," said Carmen Salazar. "An abandoned marina, ten, twelve miles up the Keys. Extremely private. Totally secure."

Paul Amaro thought: Bad enough I can't stand Lucca. Maybe what's bothering me is that there's someone else here I don't like. Was it Salazar, this arrogant little small-timer who talked fancy and sneered at everything?

"And on the Cuba side?" said Carlos Mendez. "We have to take precautions on the Cuba side."

Salazar said, "The Cuba side is covered. Johnny, when's your next trip down there?"

"Day after tomorrow," said the captain. "Cash and Walkmans in, stogies and a couple refugees out."

"You'll have time to meet with Señor Mendez's people down there?"

"I'll make time," Johnny Castro said, and Paul Amaro wondered if it was the boat guy that was irritating him. He didn't like it when a person was doing a job for damn good pay and made it sound like he was doing you a favor. Or maybe he just didn't like the captain's hybrid looks, the yellowish skin with big oval splotches, the kinky reddish hair.

Salazar said, "He'll set the details up this trip, the goods'll be in Cuba twelve hours after they hit the Keys."

"How's that sound, Paul?" said Tommy Lucca. "Professional enough?"

Paul Amaro missed the beat. He cleared his throat to try to cover up the humiliating fact that his mind had wandered, his concentration had let down. "Sounds okay," he said without conviction. Then he vented some funk by adding, "If no one fucks it up."

"No one's going to fuck it up," said Salazar.

Paul Amaro, working to get back on top, shot him a smirk as bent and scornful as his own, then slipped once again into the morbid pleasure, seductive as a scab, of sorting through his irritations and wondering why he felt so lousy sitting there.

✳ ✳ ✳

Ziggy's place made Angelina very sad.

It was a mess and yet it looked like no one lived there. There were no pictures on the flaking walls of the living room, no keepsakes on the scratched and dusty coffee table. There was nothing that suggested an enthusiasm or a hobby, no hint of an attachment or a memory. A faded couch with wrinkled lumpy cushions. A few old magazines and newspapers lying wherever they'd been tossed. The room felt less like a home than like a place to wait for a bus or an examination.

Feeling furtive, jumpy, she stepped through a low doorway into the tiny kitchen. An old refrigerator rumbled; the floor sloped beneath crazed linoleum. The stove was stained with boiled-over drips of things. But what things? Angelina gave in and opened cupboards, saw only a few cans of soup, a bag of pretzels, a bottle of tequila. Ziggy's coffee cup was in the sink. She touched it, she hefted it. She wanted to know how his cup would feel in his hand when he had his coffee in the morning.

She moved into the narrow hallway that led on to the bathroom and the bedroom.

Above the bathroom sink she saw a single toothbrush, frazzled, dangling from a porcelain fixture whose glaze was chipped. On a shelf before the mirror was a plastic razor and a can of shaving cream, dried foam honeycombed around its nozzle. Who did he see when he shaved? she wondered. What did he think? Were his thoughts as void of the personal as his place was? Had he never learned how to care for himself, about himself, or had the caring leached away, become vestigial, obsolete, like the name he used to have?

She moved slowly toward the bedroom, raking the tips of her fingers along the wall. A breeze stirred, made palm fronds scrape against the tin shingles of the roof. Guilty, Angelina was disconcerted by the sudden sound, felt caught by it somehow, like she was being watched even as she spied on Ziggy.

The bedroom door was three quarters open, left that way, no doubt, by a random nudge of an elbow or a shoulder. She stepped inside.

The windows were covered loosely, incompletely, by louvered shutters that sliced the daylight into vivid stripes alive with silver motes of dust. In a corner of the room, a simple chair stood draped in wrinkled trousers, faded shirts. A dresser, whose veneers had parted and were riffling out like playing cards, held loose change, a spare watch, a coiled belt, but not a snapshot or a souvenir.

Angelina was standing near the bed. It was unmade, she knew that it would always be unmade. Tormented pillows lay at jarring angles, crinkled flaps of pillowcases caught beneath them. A light blanket, kicked away, was bunched into crags and valleys. The bottom sheet was not stretched tight; crests of cotton rose up parallel, like waves stopped on the water.

She reached down, touched the cloth. It was soft, old, thin, it had a feel like lanolin from the sweat and oils of Ziggy's body. She smelled him now, as if her touch had renewed his presence in the sheets. It was a yeasty smell, slightly sour but as rich as the vapors of baking bread, as beckoning and basic. She traced the wrinkles in the sheet, she breathed in deeply, and she noticed that her other hand was at the collar of her blouse.

It was a blue blouse and it buttoned to the neck. She watched the silver motes floating in the stripes of light that filtered through the shutters, and although she knew full well that she was nothing like bold enough to do what she was doing, she began unbuttoning the buttons.

She put the blouse on the chair with Ziggy's clothes, then stepped out of the skirt she'd meant to travel in. The air had become very still; the house creaked, swollen with heat; the room seemed very full of Ziggy now.

Not until the last moment did Angelina hurry. Then some old shame of nakedness, some childish fear of leering eyes and wagging fingers, made her movements angular, abrupt. She shuffled off her underthings, clingy with damp, and settled into Ziggy's bed. The room was hot but the sheets felt cool as wind-dried flesh against her skin, and she told herself she could stay there forever if she had to, her face on Ziggy's pillow, her body snug against the mattress where the man she loved, for all his attempts to zig and zag, to slide through life untouching and untouched, had stayed still long enough to leave his imprint.

27

The meeting was over.

On the glaring sidewalk, Tommy Lucca said tartly, "So Paul, this yokel, he meet with your approval?"

"I think I'd like a little time to myself."

Lucca shot a glance at Carlos Mendez. Mendez adjusted the tilt of his hat, said mildly, "Our colleague, your concerns are answered?"

Amaro said, "Later. Let's talk about it later."

"What later?" Lucca pressed. "I thought we're doin' business here?"

Paul said nothing.

Lucca twitched. He wanted to get home and he was tired of sitting on his exasperation. "Christ, Paul," he went on, "the guy's a pro, anyone can see that. Little shitass town like this, he's pullin' in—"

"Tommy," Paul Amaro interrupted, "it's nothin' against your guy, okay? He's a cocky scumbag, but that's okay by me. I have a lot on my mind, I'd like a little time to think. Ask your driver, please, to bring me to the beach."

"The beach," said Tommy Lucca. A Floridian, he did not, in the middle of a business day, see the big appeal of sand and water.

"That's right. The beach. To me, Tommy, the beach is very soothing."

✳ ✳ ✳

Carmen Salazar was all pumped up about his flirtation with the big boys. Though he tried to be blasé, he couldn't help replaying his sitdown with the mobsters, reviewing for his minions how well it had gone, how suave he had been. Ziggy, unless he wanted to reveal his panic, had no choice but to stand there in the garden, listening to his boss congratulate himself, before he could slip away and bolt.

He would bolt, there was not a shred of doubt about it now. He should have fled before, as soon as Paul Amaro's relatives had mysteriously begun appearing at his bar. He'd been stupid to stick around, and it was pointless now even to wonder why he'd done it. He felt damn lucky and stunningly surprised to have met Amaro face-to-face and not been murdered on the spot. He saw no virtue in pressing his luck still further.

He waited for Salazar to finish chattering, then said a curt goodbye and stepped briskly through the dimness of the candy store, paused on the top step of the cracked stoop, glancing left and right. Instinct was battling fatalism. If his enemy was onto him, he was dead, if not today, tomorrow; he knew that. Yet the innards counseled vigilance. He probed the glaring street for assassins, fairly tiptoed to the Oldsmobile, held his breath as the car cranked out the ignition spark that might set off a bomb.

He hadn't been shot. He didn't blow up. He put the car in gear and headed home to grab his little stash of money and a change or two of clothes, and tried to figure just where the hell he'd go to hide.

* * *

Paul Amaro left his suit jacket in the limousine as he stepped out onto the promenade flanking Smathers Beach.

It was early afternoon. The sun was white, the sky a careless blue with little clouds whose bottoms picked up green reflections from the waters of the Florida Straits. Paul rolled up his shirtsleeves, and even so he was sweating before the limo had rolled out of sight. He didn't mind. It felt good to sweat in the sunshine, salt air drawing at his open pores. It felt clean, uncalculated, simple; felt like nothing else in his baroque and convoluted life.

He walked a while, walked faster than he should have, so that his heart pounded, the pulse surged in his ears and in his feet. He looked around, and everything he saw made him feel nostalgic and remorseful. Kites bobbed on puffing thermals, they hung lazily outside of time. Vendors sold hot dogs, sausage, french fries that barefoot kids carried off in paper cones; they could have come from Rockaway or Coney Island forty, fifty years before. The beach, it never changed. People on towels, a guy red as a lobster. A couple necking, their elbows coated in sand. A little girl with a yellow pail and shovel, a naked boy with water wings, learning how to swim.

He walked, he sweated, the sweat on his face was of the selfsame stuff as tears. At length, his shirt translucent, he sat down on the seawall, mopped his forehead, felt his dreadful distance from everyone around him. They were ordinary people, the kind he usually despised. Working stiffs, taxpayers, suckers. People with mortgages, bosses, people who chewed their fingernails when it was time to pay the bills. Cowering civilians—but today he envied them. They did their jobs, they scrimped, they earned vacation and wallowed in sand and they savored it. They were decent, and their reward for being decent was that if bad things happened to them, as bad things would to some, they could at least believe that they were blameless, it was just bum luck.

He sat looking out at the ocean, life went on around him. A volleyball game on the beach. Behind him on the promenade, joggers, skaters, the small noisy commerce of people buying sodas and hamburgers and ice cream. His mind snapped back to the sitdown in the garden, the clench in his gut that told him something wasn't right. Somebody was lying; or somebody was cheating; or something was not as it appeared to be.

Or maybe, Paul Amaro dared to think, it was himself who was no longer what he seemed. Something had been shaken loose inside of him when his daughter disappeared. Settled matters of how a man should live were now called into doubt, unquestionable truths now needed to be questioned. Sitting there in the searing sun, his blood pounding and carnival sounds tinkling and clattering around him, Paul Amaro was like a man trying to pry open a long-sealed tomb, and he was also the tomb itself. Was there anything of value left inside? Would he look hard enough to change?

He knew that he would not.

He lacked the will, was too steeped in guilt and spite. Even so, the mere thought of being other than he was made him for a moment almost happy. Unburdened. His mind went empty, and in that brief emptiness he noticed something that had been there all the while but that he'd failed to focus on: A tune was going round and round. It was an irritating, catchy little tune; it finished on a warped note, caught its breath, then started in again, infernal in its cheeriness.

Paul Amaro swiveled on the seawall, looked over his left shoulder. He saw an ice-cream truck, an old-fashioned bullhorn speaker mounted on its cab.

For a moment he forgot to breathe. An ice-cream truck in April. Civilians on vacation.

His overheated brain thrashed toward sense like a swimmer in a riptide. Was it possible? His brother Louie's stupid video. His daughter's strange attention. Could it be?

He stood up too fast, blood drained from his head. When his vision returned he saw a pay phone thirty feet away. The phone that Louie used to call the plumbing store?

He stood there. With a sudden eerie calm he wondered if he was onto something or if he was going mad.

Then, wavery and insubstantial in the heat shimmer that floated off the pavement, Tommy Lucca's limousine came gliding up the road. Paul Amaro blinked toward it, bitter and confused. A deal had been set in motion; he'd gotten tangled up in business. He was supposed to go back to Coral Gables, he was supposed to play the solid and reliable capo. But there was no way he was going. Not now.

When the car had stopped in front of him, he said to Lucca, in what he hoped would pass for a calm, sane voice, "Bring me to a good hotel. I'm staying here a while."

Lucca's eyes tightened down, his lips twitched. "Staying here? For crissakes, Paul." His mouth stopped making words and chewed the air.

Carlos Mendez fretted with his hat. "But about our arrangements, Paul," he said.

"Our arrangements," echoed Paul Amaro absently, as he slid in alongside Mendez, felt cold upholstery against his sweaty skin.

The car started moving, Paul looked out the window at the beach, imagining that he might see his daughter as a little girl, playing in the sand. "Arrangements, right," he murmured. "Fine, no problem. Soon as I get settled in, I'll get in touch with Funzie."

28

Ziggy's house key was ready in his hand as, looking back across his shoulders, he strode the weedy walkway that led on to his sagging porch.

He climbed the two splintery stairs and stepped briskly to the door. He reached for the knob, which turned at his grip, before he'd touched it with the key.

He recoiled in terror, spun around, jumped down the steps, and hid behind a bush.

His bowels burned, his scalp was crawling along his altered hairline. He hadn't left the door unlocked; he never did. True, he'd been absentminded lately—left milk out on the counter in the heat, bollixed up drink orders at work. But leave his door open? No, that's not something he would do. He had to believe that somebody had broken in, that someone, maybe, was awaiting him in rubber gloves, at that very moment attaching a silencer to the muzzle of a gun.

He crouched against the foliage; sweat ran down his spine, trickled past his belt. He watched the door and riffled through his options. He could run back to the Olds, but what then?—he had no cash, no bank account, and besides, he'd be in the open, an easy target, as he ran. So he waited. He sniffed the air for smells of threat, listened for wrong sounds. There weren't any. The house seemed innocent, benign, just a funky bungalow. His fear leveled off. Maybe he *had* forgotten to lock his door.

He decided on a stratagem. Staying low, beneath the level of the windows, he started crawling through the yard to check his place out room by room. Lizards fled before his slow and cumbersome advance. He dodged the leavings of feral cats; half-buried shards of coral pocked his hands.

He came around a corner of the building and lifted his eyes to the level of the windowsill. He peered into his living room. No *goombahs* were glutting up the furniture; the place looked undisturbed.

He pressed on toward the kitchen, found it as grimy and lonely as he'd left it.

The bathroom window was frosted, he could only scan for telltale shadows.

His knees bruised, his lower back complaining, he kow-towed onward toward the bedroom. He contorted himself to avoid brittle fronds that might crack beneath his weight; he landed now and then with a hand against a thorn lurking in the camouflage of unraked ground. At length he reached the bedroom window, stretched his aching limbs before lifting up his head to peek inside.

At that moment, Angelina was lying peacefully, silently, dreamy in the doughy warmth of her longed-for lover's bed. Suddenly she saw a pair of eyeballs clicking upward through the louvers of the drooping shutter then sliding into place between two slats. She pulled the sheet up tight beneath her chin, and she screamed.

Ziggy, freshly terrified at the piercing howl, screamed right back. Then he tumbled over his heels and landed prostrate in a pile of damp and decomposing leaves.

His first impulse was to run like hell, but for a time he was paralyzed with fright, could do no more than pathetically wave his ungrounded limbs like a flipped turtle. Then his mind began to clear, to process what he'd seen. It was a woman. A woman in his bed, covered, mostly, with his sheet. He blinked, rolled over on his side.

He took a breath, then crawled back to the bungalow, slowly raised his head and took a long look in. He said, "Angelina."

She said, "Sal. I mean Ziggy."

His knees hurt pretty badly, it was a scraped-up hurt like something from boyhood. He said, "What the hell are you doing here?" His nerves were shot, it came out more unfriendly than he meant it to.

She didn't answer right away. Sorry now that she was naked, she tried to make the sheet into a tent to hide the contours of her body. Dimly, reluctantly, she admitted to herself that Ziggy's place had seemed much sexier before Ziggy had returned. Finally she said, "Do we have to talk about it through the window?"

✳ ✳ ✳

Uncle Louie had fought it for as long as he could fight it, but he couldn't fight it anymore.

He was bored, pure and simple, and, worse, he knew that he was bored. He'd come to feel he had no purpose here, and in the absence of a purpose, the touristy amusements, the mango this and Key lime that, had quickly lost their novelty. He mocked himself; his fantasies of heroism seemed wretched to him now, ridiculous. And yet he stayed on in Key West, pinned by obligation, and a fear of having to explain his actions, and a sort of timorous defiance of giving in and going home.

He'd settled into a routine. He left his dreary motel room very early every morning. He walked Duval Street, wandered the beach, and the days seemed very long. So he'd taken to drinking in the afternoons. He was more or less indifferent to the alcohol, it was mainly that he needed a pretext to sit somewhere, a way to justify his presence. He drank sweet things with rum in them. He talked to bartenders; he talked to other tourists, every bit as bored as he, every bit as determined not to let it show.

One afternoon he was sitting at an outdoor bar at the Flagler House hotel, a slushy pink drink in front of him. He was helping a couple of fellow travelers gloat about how cold it was back in Minneapolis, when, at a distance beyond the clear focus of his eyes, silhouetted against the tinted glass that enclosed the lobby wing, he saw a man who bore an odd resemblance to his brother Paul. The same mane of wavy silver hair. The same pushed-forward chest and proud aggressive jaw. But this man had his jacket off, and from the shimmer of his shirt it seemed that he was sweaty, and Louie knew his brother Paul, a formal man, a slave to dignity, would not appear that way in a fancy hotel lobby.

Still, he squinted toward the man; he had nothing better to do. People talked about April blizzards, hailstorms in May, and Louie watched the stranger leave the front desk in the company of a bellman, although he had no luggage. He watched him stride around the pool to the tiki wing where the freestanding cottages were, the most expensive rooms. The bellman opened a door, and Louie watched the guest reach into his pocket to produce a tip.

Then he almost took a header off his barstool. The man didn't come up with a wallet, like most men would. He came up with a coiled wad of bills; he put his fingers to his mouth before he peeled one off. From the bellman's scraping little two-step, Louie understood that he'd been overtipped; suddenly he knew beyond a reasonable doubt what he couldn't help suspecting from the start: his big-shot brother was in town.

He blinked, made sure he was hidden by tendrils of hanging thatch. He was utterly befuddled but at least he was no longer bored. He watched his relative slip into his room, then abruptly, his drink unfinished, he called for his tab.

"Hey, where ya goin'?" said the man from Minneapolis, who wanted to keep gloating about the frozen lakes back home.

"Things to do," said Louie. "Lotta things to do."

Once again he had a purpose. He had to warn his niece.

29

"Ziggy, look at me," said Angelina.

"I am looking at you," he replied.

"My eyes, Ziggy. Look at my eyes. Look me in the eyes and tell me you really believe I put my father onto you."

He was standing over her at the foot of the bed. His hair was awry, he had green stains on the knees of his pants, broken bits of leaf were sticking to his shirt. His stare was wild and his voice was tight and scared. "Then why the hell's he here?"

"How should I know why he's here?" said Angelina. She was propped on Ziggy's unfresh pillows. She held the sheet up snug beneath her chin, but still the soft cloth traced out the curves of her legs and hips and tummy. Her body was confusing her. One second she wished that Ziggy was naked with her in the bed and the next second she wished that she was dressed and on a plane. "Why's he *say* he's here?"

Ziggy's reply was dismissive. "Some business thing. Some thing with Cuba."

Angelina said, "All right, then. There's your answer."

The answer didn't mollify his paranoia. He paced the width of the bed, dragged his hand over the dusty dresser top. "Fuck's the difference why he's here? He's here. He's in my face."

"You said he didn't recognize you."

"Yeah, *today*. But what's it take to recognize a person? A word? A look? Christ, you recognized me by my goddam finger."

"That's different," Angelina said. "I'm in love with you."

Ziggy's hands hardened into fists, veins stood out along his neck. His face got red, his eyes narrowed down, he looked like he would scream or cry. Instead, he squeezed out, "And right there is the mystery of the fuckin' ages."

Angelina looked at him, shook her head in its nest of wrinkled pillows. "On that I have to agree."

He turned away from her and faced the wall. She watched his back heave as he battled the air to grab each breath.

After a moment she said, "I came here to make love with you. You know that, right?"

"Oh really?" he said without turning around. "I thought you just stopped by to get naked and take a nap."

She watched flecks of silver dust swim through the bright stripes near the shutters. "It was a pretty dumb idea," she said. "I admit it."

He stayed in his chosen exile at the foot of the bed, staring at the void and dirty corner of the room.

"So what'll you do now?" she asked at last.

"Go far away," he said.

She thought about that, said, "This is far away."

"Meaning?"

"Meaning," she said, "you came here because you thought no one would find you, it would be safe."

"It *was*," he interrupted.

"But everybody found you," she went right on. "*Everybody*. And that could happen anywhere. The world just isn't that big."

Finally he turned to face her. "Ange," he said, "you have no idea how big the world is. You think—what?—the world is Pelham Manor, New York, and Florida?"

"It makes you feel better to insult me, Ziggy?" Then her voice changed and she added, "It's been ten years since you called me Ange."

He stood with his hands on his hips, sucking wretched, labored breaths.

After a moment she went on, "Besides, you have a life here."

This was news to Ziggy. A life? He had a so-so job and some second-rate action that was never going to make him rich. He had a nothing place to live and occasionally he got laid. Was this a life? Was this what other people had in mind when they talked about a life? Fact was, Ziggy was pretty clueless about what a life consisted of, still less how to get one.

This lack flooded over him now, enraged him, made his movements violent, jerky. He tore open a dresser drawer, reached in deep for his passport and his stash of funds beneath a heap of socks. Stuffing money in his pants, he wheeled back toward the naked woman in his bed, said, "Sorry things didn't go better, Angelina. I'm outa here."

At once he was moving toward the bedroom door. It wasn't far and he was moving fast. Yet the time it took for him to reach the doorway was time enough for Angelina to do a hundred oscillations. She wanted him to vanish. She wanted him to stay. She cursed herself for being here; she should have been the one to catch a plane, to turn her back on him, not the one walked out on, undressed and absurd. But loss was loss, what did it matter who left who? . . . She heard herself say, "But you don't know where you're going."

He had one foot in the hallway. As torn as she, he couldn't

drag the other leg across the threshold and have this madness over with. He stopped to argue, his momentum stalled. He said, "At Miami airport there's this screen, it lists the whole world—"

Angelina said, "I have an idea."

Ziggy went on, "Jamaica, Paris, Bogota—"

"Coral Shores."

"—Puerto Rico, Italy—"

"Coral Shores," she said again. "No one would think to look for you at Coral Shores."

"—Antigua, Hawaii—"

"Ziggy, think about it. You have an edge—you know him, he doesn't know you. You stay in town, you see what happens, maybe there's a chance to work things out."

His voice turned shrill and raspy, the simple fear cut through. "Work things *out*? This isn't something you work out, Angelina. This isn't something you talk over. He wants me dead."

"And he wants me to be happy."

He looked at her, her violet eyes, the earnest and neglected body wriggling in his bed. "Your father, Angelina, happiness is bullshit to him. What he cares about is honor, and the balls of honor is revenge. You know that."

"Ziggy, you'll be safe a while, you'll see how things play out."

He knew he shouldn't even think about it, but he thought about it. He couldn't pull his eyes off Angelina. Her neck, her breasts, they'd kill him yet. "Coral Shores," he said, "it's fulla queers."

"It would be more pleasant," Angelina said, "if you called them gays."

The sun was moving, there were patches of light across the sheet where Angelina lay; he imagined that they made the cloth translucent, revealing swaths of flesh. "I don't see me hangin' out around a buncha queers."

Cautiously, she rolled onto an elbow, a browned shoulder with a pale chaste tan line came into view. "Think about your situation, Ziggy. Who's it make more sense for you to hang around with? A bunch of queers or a bunch of mafiosi?"

PART THREE

30

"It's very important," Uncle Louie said. "Family emergency."

"I understand," said the desk clerk at the Coral Shores Guest House. He had a shaved head above bleached blond eyebrows, and an expression so concerned that it put creases all across his scalp. "But there's no one registered by that name. Are you sure that's the name?"

"She's my niece," said Uncle Louie. "Of course I'm sure."

"And you're sure this is the place?"

"I've walked her home. In broad daylight."

The clerk leaned on an elbow, as intent as his visitor to puzzle this thing out. "We don't get that many lesbians. What's she look like?"

Uncle Louie said, "My niece is not a lesbian."

The clerk's expression darkened for a moment, the east-west furrows moved north-south. "You have a problem with lesbians?"

"Me? I don't have a problem with lesbians. I have a problem with relatives. But my niece, I never said she's a lesbian."

"Why else would she be here?"

"She's a single woman, on her own."

"Oh, *her!*" said the clerk, and in his relief he gave Uncle Louie a light slap on the arm. "Why didn't you say so? There's only one of those. Dark hair, a little chesty, right? That's Jane Starr."

"Excuse me?"

The clerk leaned closer across the orchids on the counter. "Alias, I guess. We get a lot of *noms de sex* down here—people closeted back home mostly, nervous. They pay in cash, it's all the same to us. Live and let live, right?"

"Uh, right," said Uncle Louie.

"You're welcome to wait out by the pool. Want a cup of tea?"

✳ ✳ ✳

Half a dozen blocks away, Paul Amaro stood in his shower and entertained dark thoughts.

He wondered if his life was finally, irretrievably unraveling. He marveled at how little he cared. He noted with an odd detachment, almost a chastened ecstasy, how brittle his strength must always have been, if it could be undone so easily.

Hot water hit him in the face; he let it scour him, hoping vaguely that it would carry off dead skin, chip away old sins along with rotten flesh, leaving something better underneath. His mind raced. An ice-cream truck and a pay phone. Did those things mean his daughter was in Key West? Or did they only mean he'd taken too much sun, that the searing heat had put his sorrow over the edge into outright delusion?

He soaped himself, sought refuge in the practical. If Angelina was here, how would he find her? Who did he know that knew the town, who did he know that would help? Only Carmen Salazar. An arrogant pissant, but ambitious and not without intelligence, a man who understood the value of favors owed—as long as they were owed by people more important and more powerful than himself. Which meant that Paul Amaro would, as usual, have to hide his grief and his confusion, have to bend on the stiff mask of the formidable boss.

He rinsed, watched dirty suds go down the drain. For a long time he stood beneath the water, coaxing his mind to rest. He forgot about guns for Cuba. He forgot about calling Funzie Gallo. Or maybe he didn't forget. Maybe it was some dim defiance, some penitential courting of trouble that led him not to call. Maybe he just didn't dare distract himself. Like a weary actor mustering conviction to go out and reprise an ancient role, he needed to be empty of everything except the craft that might allow him to keep persuading others of what he himself had an ever harder time believing—that he was still a big shot, and that any of it mattered half a damn.

✳ ✳ ✳

Less happened in the summer, but what happened was more strange. Ziggy had noticed it for years, but it had never been like this.

He stood now in the courtyard at Coral Shores, Angelina at his side, and he saw things that, in his staunch blue-collar prudishness, he was simply not prepared to see. At one end of the pool, two pairs of men, young, frisky, and innocent of bathing suits, were sitting on each other's shoulders, staging chicken fights. On the lip of the hot tub, a white man and a black man, bare-assed both, were sipping wine and exchanging enraptured stares. Buttocks gazed up from lounges, scrotums half-floated in clear water, diffuse as poaching eggs. Ziggy said, "Christ, Angelina, this is naked city."

"Don't say I never take you anywhere."

"I mean, I can't believe you sit around and look at dicks all day."

"Don't be crude, Ziggy. You feeling insecure? Listen, you get used to it. You practically stop noticing."

"I'm not getting used to it," he said. "I'm leaving."

Angelina surprised herself. Out of Ziggy's bed, she felt less sentimental. Back on her own turf, clothed, she felt more in control. She said, "Okay. So leave."

The baldness of it, the lack of protest, caught Ziggy off guard. He had nothing to add but his feet were planted in hot gravel, they weren't in a position to carry him away.

Then they both heard Angelina's name.

It came from a patch of shade at the far side of the pool, where a dressed man and a naked man were playing backgammon. Angelina looked toward the voice, said, "Jeez, it's Uncle Louie."

"Uncle Louie?" Ziggy said. "Zis a family fuckin' reunion?"

But in the next heartbeat his thoughts curdled and he realized he was trapped. Angelina, after all, had set him up, brought him to this sealed-off courtyard, this place of no escape. This was Paulie's brother. If Paulie's brother knew, that meant Paulie knew. That meant there were killers lurking. He wished he had his gun, which was taped beneath the dashboard of his car. All he was carrying was a good-sized pocketknife. Should he grab a hostage? His head swam. The hostage should be Angelina. Could he do it, could he point a knife at her, wrap his arm around her throat?

All this transited his mind in a second. He didn't move. Uncle Louie was walking quickly toward them, agitated, jerky. The knife was in Ziggy's right pants pocket and for now he left it there. The sun was on the back of his neck and there was splashing in the pool.

Angelina said, "Uncle Louie, what are you—"

"We have to talk," he whispered breathlessly. He barely glanced at Ziggy; in that moment he seemed too full of his own momentous news to recognize the bartender from Raul's.

"Okay," she said, "let's talk."

Her uncle's eyes flicked nervously toward the stranger,

whose hand was in his pocket. Angelina's gaze told him he should go ahead. "Your father's here," he told her.

Wearily, Angelina said, "I know."

"You know?" said Louie, deflated as usual. He blinked down at the damp apron of the pool. "How d'you know?"

"How do *you* know?" she asked right back.

"I just saw him," Louie said. "At Flagler House. He took a room."

"Shit," said Ziggy.

"How do *you* know?" Louie asked.

"It's a long story," Angelina said.

Louie stood there. He had time.

His niece said, "I don't really know where to start."

A team of naked chicken-fighters went down with a plunk like a depth charge, water lapped over the edges of the pool. Uncle Louie said, "The beginning might be good."

Angelina bit her lip. She sighed, and said at last, "Uncle Louie, you remember Sal Martucci?"

"Ya mean the skunk sonofabitch that—"

He broke off suddenly. He fell back half a step, squeezed his chin between a thumb and index finger, and for the first time he looked hard at Ziggy Maxx, tilting his head and narrowing his eyes. He said, "Angelina, no."

She nodded yes.

"*Marrone*, Angelina," said her uncle. "Of all the people."

"What can I say? You see now why I couldn't tell you?"

He nodded vaguely.

Her tone went thin and young. "You still on my side, Uncle Louie?"

Ziggy's hand was on the knife deep in his pocket. He liked the feel of it though he knew it wouldn't do him any good.

Louie stood there in the sun. He thought about his family, its cockeyed way of giving everyone a favorite. He thought about his brothers, about their strength that had made him weak, their wadded bankrolls that had made him poor, their crooked confidence that had made him a quailing little man. He looked at the ground, said, "I'm still on your side. Of course I'm still on your side." Then he added, "But who's gonna break it to your father?"

"No one's gonna break it to her father," Ziggy said.

"But if he's here—" said Uncle Louie, and then he fell silent.

All three of them were silent amid the splashing and the laughing and the scratching of the fronds, and in the silence it was gradually dawning on each of them that they were captives there at Coral Shores. It didn't take a gun and it didn't take a knife to hold them hostage. The town was too small, the streets too narrow; the airport was a fishbowl. For as long as Paul Amaro was around, they didn't dare go out. They were marooned together in the naked city, their best hope the camouflage of undressed men and drag queens all done up in heels and rouge.

Uncle Louie pursed his nervous lips, shot his niece a resigned and sheepish smile. "Guess I'll see about a room."

31

"I see," said Carmen Salazar, when Paul Amaro, sitting in the stretched and loopy shadows of the garden in late afternoon, had told him as much of the story as he felt like telling. "I'm glad, of course, to help in whatever way I can. But perhaps it would be easier if I better understood a couple things."

Paul Amaro gave the smallest of nods. The nod told Salazar he was free to ask questions; the smallness of it told him he'd better be careful how he phrased them.

"Your daughter, Mr. Amaro—"

"Paul. People I do business with, they call me Paul."

Salazar smiled inwardly. He hadn't been invited earlier to use first names. "Paul," he said. It felt good in his mouth, seemed to promise income growth, prestige. "Do you believe that she was kidnapped or do you think she ran away?"

Amaro took a deep breath, slowly blew the air into his fist. "At the start, I thought that someone grabbed her. But I don't know who, I don't know why." He faltered, shrugged, stared off into knotted shrubbery that swallowed up the light. "Now I don't know what to think."

"Forgive me, but was she involved with drugs? I ask because there are certain neighborhoods—"

"My daughter isn't into drugs."

"A love affair?"

"She didn't run around."

Salazar saw that a change of tack was called for. "And your brother, you think your brother's down here too."

"He's the one who called New York," Amaro said. "Vanished a couple days after she did."

Salazar drummed fingers on the arm of his lawn chair; it made a dull cheap sound. "Your daughter and your brother. Excuse me, Paul, but the connection, I'm not sure I see—"

"I don't fucking see it either," admitted the capo. "That's why my first thought was vendetta . . . Look, my brother comes here on vacation. Gets back all excited. Comes to my house, shows his asshole video. Next thing I know, my family's torn apart."

When Carmen Salazar was thinking hard, he didn't scowl; instead, his top lip rode up on his teeth and quivered, rabbit-like. After a moment, he said, "That video—who has it?"

Paul Amaro shrugged, said, "His wife, I guess."

"Maybe there's some hint, some landmark. Might be interesting to watch it together."

Paul Amaro sucked at wet thick air, smelled musky fruits and overripe flowers. He looked down at his hands, grudgingly admitted that this Salazar was bright, already he was bringing some reason, some promising dispassion, to all this infuriating muddle. "Yeah," he said, "it might."

✻ ✻ ✻

"Lucky me," said Uncle Louie, though he didn't really sound like he meant it. "Got the last room."

"The last room?" said Angelina. "What about Ziggy?"

They'd moved back from the pool to a shady little grouping of chairs around a stone table, and now there was an embarrassed silence. Louie was of the school that preferred to consign to genteel oblivion any discussion of the sex lives of unmarried female relatives. As for Ziggy, though he hadn't had much leisure to think about it, he'd been quietly assuming that he and Angelina would shack up. Behind his terror and his plotting, he'd retained an image of her lying in his bed; burned on the backs of his eyeballs was a picture of the roundness of her breasts beneath the sheet, the canyon where the cloth banked down between her thighs. His scruples about deflowering her had been eroding, as scruples do. His testicles had framed a new logic: if he was a dead man anyway, why deprive them both of a little joy? And if there was the remotest chance of making things right with Paul Amaro, being his daughter's lover might help his case as easily as hurt it.

The only problem was that Angelina no longer felt like making love with him.

Not then. Not there. Not holed up like fugitives, with Uncle Louie practically next door. Her nerves had fired to exhaustion; she felt both spent and spared. Unkissed, untouched, she yet felt that she had gone to the very brink, and now she was pulling back again, moving away from the dizzying edge of the diving board.

The silent stalemate carried on, and she caught a fast and ill-hid glimpse of something in Ziggy's face. She'd never seen it quite so bare before but she recognized it instantly. Desire. Desire quickened by frustration. She almost smiled at the wicked pleasure of being, at long last, the one withholding union rather than the one from whom it was withheld. Sweetly, she said, "I guess you two are roommates."

"Not a chance," said Ziggy.

A pause. Then he frowned as Angelina glanced briefly toward the picket gate that led on to the wider world with all its many perils, its blithe murderers in trench coats, its ice picks and piano wires. He shot a sour look at Louie. "How many beds in that goddam room?"

Uncle Louie raised an index finger.

"Jesus Christ. King, at least?"

"Queen."

"Figures."

Angelina smiled, said, "I'll leave you two to settle in." She looked full on at Ziggy. "I feel a little soiled. Think I'll have a warm bath and a nap."

✱ ✱ ✱

Tommy Lucca, eager to finalize the details of the smuggling operation, tried to reach Funzie Gallo as soon as he and Carlos Mendez had returned to Coral Gables.

It took four phone calls and several go-betweens, and by the time he spoke to his New York colleague, Lucca was more irritable than usual. This should have been a simple business, and it was turning out to be nothing but delays and aggravation. "You New York guys," he groused to Funzie. "Still so fucking paranoid about the phone."

Funzie, who in fact was paranoid enough that he only took calls on a pay phone in a bakery across the street from the Gatto Bianco Social Club, was too cautious to respond to that.

"Ya heard from Paul?" asked Tommy.

"Was I s'posed to?" Funzie said, noncommittal.

"Yeah, you were supposed to," Lucca said. He jerked back in his study chair and plucked at the crease of his trousers. "Ya should've heard from him hours ago."

They were baking cookies in a huge black oven near the phone that Funzie used. A batch was taken out on an enormous wooden peel and a smell of anisette and almond filled the air. "Well, I haven't."

Lucca choked back exasperation, said, "Our arrangement, it's a go."

Funzie motioned to the baker. He wanted some cookies

while they were good and hot, the pignolias soft and chewy. He said into the phone, "I gotta hear that from Paul. You know that, Tommy."

Lucca knew it but he didn't like it. He snarled. He smacked his thigh. Carlos Mendez gestured to him, be nice, go easy. Lucca said, "But fucking Paul isn't exactly on the fucking case."

On that Funzie offered no opinion. His mouth was watering at the thought of the warm cookies.

A moment passed, and the Florida mobster said, "You call me soon's you hear from Paul. Soon. You got that, Funzie?" Then he slammed the phone down, the futile momentum of his arm seemed to propel him from his chair and start him pacing.

Carlos Mendez tracked him with his eyes, rolled his hat brim in his lap, said mildly, "It's only been four, five hours, Tommy."

"How long's it take to make a fuckin' phone call?" Lucca said.

"Maybe he had other things to do."

"Like what?" said Lucca, and threw himself back into his unhappy twitching march.

He paced and scowled until an ugly thought assailed him. Then he said, "Like stay in Key West and find a way to cut me out of this?"

"Tommy," said Mendez, "the money comes from me, remember?"

But suspicion had grabbed on to Tommy Lucca, and on a man like him suspicion was a ratchet, it only went tighter once it grabbed. "Salazar's boat guy, that fuck with the freckles, he's in Havana like every other week—ya don't think he knows other people who want guns?"

"There's no reason to imagine—"

"Fuckin' Paul was acting weird. *Take me ta the beach. Lemme see the water.* Weird."

"The man's a northerner," said Mendez. "He comes to Florida, he wants to see the beach."

"And all of a sudden, just like that, check into a hotel?"

For that, Carlos Mendez had no answer.

"The fucking guy is jealous of me," Tommy Lucca said. "Always has been. My house. My tan. Now he's looking for a way to screw me."

"Tommy, you're getting way ahead—"

"Either that or he's losing his marbles."

"It could be a million other things," said Mendez.

But Lucca couldn't see a million things, he could only figure two. "He's fucking me or he's crazy. And either way, I don't like what I smell."

✳ ✳ ✳

"Ziggy's *here?*" said Michael. "*Stuck* here?"

"Looks that way," said Angelina. It was early evening, and she was sitting on the end of her friend's bed, kicking her bare feet against the sisal rug. "In a room with Uncle Louie."

Michael said, "God, it's so romantic."

"For Ziggy or my uncle?"

"For *you*," said Michael. He was standing near the mirror, lifting his lip to check for specks between his teeth. "It's this perfect little dance. First you chase him, then he chases you—"

"And my family chases both of us."

"Sometimes family's involved," said Michael. "Sometimes it's like that. Like, look at *West Side Story.*"

"I seem to remember that ended badly."

"Now don't get pessimistic. We'll order in Chinese." He went to the bedside table, found a phone book, looked up Chinese restaurants.

Angelina sighed. "Spare ribs," she said. "Uncle Louie likes spare ribs."

"And Ziggy?" Michael asked, the phone tucked between his shoulder and his ear. "What does Ziggy like?"

It was a question to which Angelina could only shrug and shake her head.

32

The instructions that Rose received from Paul Amaro by way of her sister-in-law Maria were simple and specific. She was to take the Key West video to Federal Express and have it shipped to the Flagler House hotel for hand-delivery to a Mr. Paul Martin, the name under which her brother-in-law was registered.

That's all she was supposed to do. It was easy; it was clear; but Louie's wife had chosen not to do it. She'd sat in her steam-heated Bronx apartment, looked out the sooty windows, and she got to thinking. Why would Paul be staying in Key West, why would he want to see her husband's film, unless he had reason to believe that her Louie was down there? And what had always been the problem in her marriage, why had her husband finally abandoned her after all these years, except that she had taken him for granted, she had never gone out of her way to show him that she cared? She resolved that she would show him now.

She'd brewed a pot of coffee, got as close to being sober as she had been in several weeks, and booked an early morning flight to Florida. Something like hope, like tenderness, awakened in her as she packed badly folded clothes into a suitcase.

She arrived in Key West just before midday, the video in its black box in her purse, and took a taxi to the Flagler House. At the front desk she inquired as to the number of Paul Martin's room, had the savvy to slip the clerk a twenty when he said he couldn't give it out.

Tired, nervous, and with a cumulative hangover like a lingering flu, she walked around the pool, among the palms and past the thatched roof outdoor bar. She reached the tiki wing and knocked on her relative's door.

Paul Amaro coughed out a gruff, "Yeah?"

Rose groped for poise against the wet and draining heat. She made her voice husky and official, choked off the New York accent. "Delivery for Mr. Martin."

A moment passed, a bolt slid free. The door opened. Paul Amaro stood there in a hotel bathrobe, blinked into the daylight. Then he said, "Rose, you look like hell."

It was true. Her eyes were yellowish and soupy, her skin had the stretched and bluish sheen of rising dough. Her lipstick missed the outline of her lips, got grainy at the edges like something badly printed. She said, "You always knew how to make a girl feel good."

"What the hell are you doing here?"

"You don't look so hot yourself."

He didn't. His eyes were caving in like sinkholes, the flesh around them was pebbled and gray. Blood pressure was tormenting capillaries, his face and neck were tending toward the color of beef. Wearily, he said, "Why didn't you do like I told you, Rose?"

The sun was at its zenith. It beat down on her head and made it pound, seemed to call forth vaporous memories of every Manhattan she'd ever drunk. She tried to sound strong; it didn't work, it came out petulant and whiny. "I wanna help."

Paul Amaro briefly closed his eyes. The woman was a lush

and a hysteric and a general pain in the ass. "Ya wanna help, gimme the video and go the hell home."

He held out a meaty hand. It stayed empty. His sister-in-law said, "I'm getting a room."

"Rose, you got no fucking business here. Now gimme the tape, and go."

Just for a moment, she wondered if he would dare to grab her purse or hit her. She was braced, her shoulders tilted bravely forward. She said, "Not without my Louie." Then she pivoted to walk away, spoke across her shoulder, "Lemme know when you wanna watch the movie."

* * *

A phalanx of rolled-up towels separated Ziggy's side of the bed from Louie's, and Louie had been told that if he crossed the line he would die.

So he really hadn't slept that well. Aside from the fear of rolling over, there was the fact that Ziggy's feet were very near his face, his own feet in danger of tickling Ziggy's chin. Through the night he'd done no more than doze. He'd smelled the fleeting perfume of things that bloomed in moonlight, watched the thin curtain sway like a skirt on puffs of breeze that whispered through the open window.

As was his custom anyway, he rose from bed before the sun was up. He pulled on plaid Bermudas and went down to the quiet courtyard, where he used a rumpled cloth to wipe the heavy dew from a lounge. He sat back like he was at a show and watched the same old miracles that launched the day. Stars dimmed in the sky and in the pool. Hunks of purple cloud bulged out of the blackness in the east; the purple went pink, the first yellow rays spoked through. An unseen hand hurled the morning papers over the picket fence; they landed on the walkway with an authoritative slap. Streetlamps switched off, and only then did one notice they'd been humming all along.

The breakfast cart was rolled out, Louie savored coffee. People appeared, rubbing their eyes. The sun topped the metal roofs and, sudden as a toaster, it was hot.

Around nine, Angelina came down, kissed him good morning. A little while after, Ziggy showed up, grumpy, restless, not yet shaved. There didn't seem to be much to say this morning. They sat around uncomfortably, acquaintances on a group vacation that wasn't working out.

Sometime after ten, Michael and his lover, dressed in jeans and T-shirts that fit like glaze on doughnuts, walked through the picket gate; and, quite suddenly and with no warning whatsoever, what had been merely awkward became insane.

Michael spotted Angelina, waved and moved toward her around the pool. But he'd barely murmured a hello when his partner, having decided to seize the advantage of surprise, looked square at Ziggy and said, "You and I should talk."

Ziggy blinked toward the sun, rubbed his scratchy chin. Caffeine had not yet washed away his grouchiness, and he wasn't that fond of gay people to begin with. He said, "Yeah? And who the hell are you?"

Protectively, Michael said, "His name is David."

"My name is Keith McCullough." He said this while somehow getting a hand in his taut pocket and producing a wallet with a badge.

"You're a cop?" said Michael, dazedly. "You told me you—"

"We'll talk about this later," said McCullough. To Ziggy, he added, "Witness Protection Program."

Ziggy looked away, said, "I got nothin' ta say ta you, dickhead."

McCullough said, "I think maybe you do."

Michael was staring at his feet, trying to get the earth to firm up beneath them. He said, "A cop. A *cop*?! You were just using me all this time?"

"I hear that Paul Amaro's camped at a very comfortable

hotel a quarter mile from where you sit," McCullough said to Ziggy. "I don't think you can afford to kiss me off."

"Paul Amaro?" Ziggy said. "I don't believe I know a Paul Amaro."

Michael was shaking his head. "A queer Fed! God Almighty, how'd I end up with a queer Fed?"

Ziggy went on, "I used to know a guy named Sal Martucci. *He* knew Paul Amaro. But this Amaro guy and Ziggy Maxx, nuh-uh, they don't know each other."

"This time around you're brave," McCullough said. "This time you're playing by the code. Last time around you didn't, remember? Paul Amaro, you can bet that he remembers."

"Just using me," said Michael. "Pumping me for all the romantic details. Who's this one, where's that one? You faggot bitch."

McCullough said, "Shut up, Michael. I'm not gay, I've got a wife and kids."

"Ha!" said Michael, loud enough to catch the ears and sympathies of people having breakfast all around the pool. "I don't care if you've got a harem and a flock of sheep. Homo is as homo does, sweetheart, and you're as gay as Liberace."

McCullough turned his back on his former boyfriend. "Paul Amaro isn't down here for the weather," he said to Ziggy. "You're gonna tell me what he's doing here."

"Kiss my ass."

"And I might help you stay alive."

"I've been doing fine without you assholes," Ziggy said.

"Fine as a guy who's fallen thirty stories off a forty-story building," said McCullough. "Paul Amaro, what's he up to?"

"Lemme ask *you* a question," Ziggy said. "You got a wife and kids, what're you doing fucking guys?"

"And hurting people's feelings," Uncle Louie could not help putting in.

McCullough said, "Ziggy, you're trapped here. Pinned. My guess, you're not a person who likes to feel trapped. Feeling trapped makes your skin crawl. You don't have to like me. I don't have to like you. I'm your ticket out of here. Remember that."

He turned, his tight jeans creaked. He said to Michael, "Sorry I couldn't let you know some other way." And he left.

An unnatural hush followed his leaving, time flattened out like the water behind a big boat that has passed. Uncle Louie absently sipped at tepid coffee. Michael very slowly sat himself down at the foot of Angelina's lounge. "God," he said, "I feel so stupid. How's it possible to be so wrong about a person?"

Angelina slid forward, put her arm around her friend, kissed him on the cheek. "Sometimes it's like that," she said. "It'll be okay."

33

The TV and the VCR were set up on a plastic milk crate in the garden. A long extension cord, orange, snaked away through the gravel and the shrubbery, climbed the cracked step up into the candy store. One of Carmen Salazar's goons pushed some buttons and turned some dials, and Uncle Louie's video began to play.

Pictures of Key West filled the screen, which in turn was framed by a shady background of Key West, and there was something unsettling in the doubling of the place, a little spooky, like those sets of dolls that are gobbled up inside of other dolls. The ocean appeared, as flat and green as the real ocean that was simmering a mere five hundred yards away. Tourist attractions flickered by—Hemingway House, Curry Mansion, Southernmost Point; the machinery suggested they were distant, exotic, touched by some unearthly magic, when, to locals, they were ordinary buildings practically around the corner, shabby monuments in need of paint, obstacles you had to go around to get to a gas station or a liquor store.

The images rocked and bounced and quivered. There was

no rhyme or reason to their sequence. Now and then the screen went black or blazed with a painful glare.

Rose, formerly too critical, now felt she had to make excuses for her absent husband. "He hadn't had the camera very long," she said.

Carmen Salazar had promised himself to be nothing but gracious to this relative of Paul Amaro's. "Actually," he lied, "it's very good. He's really capturing the high points."

"But what the hell's it telling us?" Amaro said.

So far it was telling them nothing. Here was a glimpse of the harbor, a sailboat full of people going snorkeling. There went the laundromats with the names that Louie found so droll. Foliage rustled, it was hard to tell if it was in the garden or the soundtrack.

Then, with no transition, the scene jumped to a bar, an open-air place, at twilight. Matches rasped; glasses tinkled. A smoky mirror, partly blocked by ranks of stately bottles, was edged with tangles of grabbing vine. Just for an instant, the wobbly camera skated over the barkeep's turning face, revealed dark hair, olive skin already stubbly, a feisty guarded mouth.

Salazar said, "Whaddya know, there's Bigtime."

"Bigtime?" Paul Amaro said, with no particular interest. By the time he said it, the bartender's face was gone, the screen was filled with his hands instead as they layered liquors in a pony glass.

"Guy who works for me," Salazar casually explained. "You met him yesterday. Ziggy."

"Ah," said Paul Amaro, watching the barkeep's tics and swoopings as he built the drink. "Why ya call him Bigtime?"

Salazar gave a little laugh. "Ya know, I can't even remember how it started."

But by now Paul Amaro found he couldn't move his eyes from the television. A vague unease, like yesterday's, a feeling of inchoate wrongness, had started churning in his gut. "Try," he said.

Salazar felt a little scolded, rubbed his chin. "When he first came to me for work, he dropped these hints, you know, of bigger things he'd done, important people that he knew."

Amaro leaned far forward in his lawn chair, squeezed one hand tight inside the other. "Like what?" he said. "Like who?" On the screen, the stripes of booze were mounting to the top of the pony glass.

"Never got specific. You know how people are. They're dying to have you know something, and they know they shouldn't tell you."

"He's a northerner," said Paul Amaro.

It was not a question and Salazar just nodded.

"Go back," Amaro said. "Go back to where the camera's on his face."

The goon stepped forward from the shadows, rewound the tape. Again appeared a sour, harried Ziggy, shying from the lens.

"Stop it," Paul Amaro said. "Stop it right there."

The frame froze in the instant before the camera abandoned the bartender's face, caught him in a look of scowling sorrow. Stopped, the image was grainy and distorted, swaths of it moved out of register like strata on a hillside. Paul Amaro studied it less with his eyes than his belly, took the measure of this stranger's face by the way it tugged his innards, mocking and insistent as a half-remembered dream.

There was a long silence.

Rose broke it, her voice as sharp and sudden as a tooted horn from the back of a resting orchestra. "Angelina," she said. "The way she hugged Louie when she said good night. I just remembered how she hugged him. The way she thanked him, like he'd done something so terrific for her."

Paul Amaro sat there, hunched forward in his chair, fists clamping down on nothing. Foul stuff was rising in his throat and he was not sure he could speak. He stalled a moment, pointed a thick finger at the tortured image on the screen. "I wanna find that guy," he said.

Salazar, for the moment blind to the direness of the request, said lightly, "That's easy as a phone call."

"No phone call," Paul Amaro said. "I wanna go to his house. And you're lending me a gun."

✳ ✳ ✳

"Now do you believe that something's going on?" said Keith McCullough, not even trying to keep the note of gloating triumph out of his voice.

His boss's answer was circumspect and bland. Manny Links cradled the phone against his ear, tapped his unlit pipe against his palm, said, "Might be something. Might be nothing much."

"Nothing much?" said the undercover man. He was back in his motel room, looking out the window at the parking lot where spaces were marked off by opposite diagonals, like the skeletons of fishes. "Manny, Ziggy Maxx, okay, Ziggy Maxx is nothing much. But Paul Amaro's here on business. That's not nothing much."

"So what's the business?" asked the supervisor.

Exasperated, McCullough said, "I don't know what the business is."

"Exactly."

"That's what Ziggy Maxx is gonna tell us."

In Manny Links's cubicle in North Miami, there was a thoughtful pause. "You know," he said, "I've been in this business nineteen years. I'm trying to think, in all that time, has there ever been a case where an informant ratted out the same guy twice?"

"Manny, he's desperate. He's terrified. He's holed up in a gay guest house and he can't come out."

"He's gay?" said Manny Links.

"He isn't gay. That's part of why he's desperate."

Links put his pipe in his mouth, yearned briefly for the halcyon days when he used to burn tobacco in it. "Keith," he said, "if this guy turns again, that means he has to change identities again. How many times can we cut and paste this one poor bastard's face?"

"I'd say that's his problem," said McCullough.

"And I'd say that's why he isn't gonna turn. The pain, the craziness—I don't see a person going through all of that a second time."

"He'd rather get rubbed out?"

"I would," said Links.

"Manny, this guy, I don't think he's as deep a thinker as you. I think he wants to live no matter what name we give him or how many times we relocate his nose."

The supervisor sighed. "So you're saying you want more time."

"I want time and I want backup."

"Backup?"

"Manny, this guy's gonna give us the goods to get Paul Amaro right back off the street. I want two agents for a week."

Links leaned back in his office chair, the squeak came through the phone. "I don't have two agents. I'll send you Sykes."

"Sykes? Oh Christ, not Sykes."

"Only guy available," said Links.

"I wonder why," McCullough said.

"And Keith, about your source, all this terrific information—you still haven't told me who you got it from or what you gave away to get it."

"It's none of your business, Manny. Terry Sykes. Jesus, some backup."

34

"And the worst of it," Michael was saying—"well, maybe not the worst, but part of it that's bad—is how I told him all this stuff about you and Ziggy, and your family—"

"It's okay," said Angelina. "I know you meant no harm."

"One of these years," he said, "I'll learn to keep my mouth shut."

"Honestly, I doubt that," Angelina said.

"And I won't be such a slut for romance."

"I doubt that even more."

It was late afternoon, the time when the sun loses its knockout punch and throws instead a sluggish heavy hook that is almost an embrace. Uncle Louie had found his naked backgammon partner, was rolling dice in dappled shade, had lost a dollar and a half so far. Ziggy was upstairs napping or maybe only sulking. Angelina and Michael reclined on poolside lounges, among men taking siesta in the open, confident as cats, their less-tanned places swathed protectively in towels.

Answering a thought of his own, Michael said suddenly,

"But jeez, I hate a closet case. The harm they do, those chicken-shits."

Angelina caught herself picking at a cuticle, forced herself to stop. Cautiously, she said, "Michael, I wonder if somewhere, somehow, you knew . . . Not that he was a cop, I mean, but that he wasn't really there for you, you couldn't really have him."

"The allure of the unavailable?" said Michael. "Lust with an escape hatch?"

Angelina changed the cross of her ankles, rocked her knees from side to side. "Something like that. But more like . . . like you had enough of an involvement so that you could believe you were involved, but what the involvement really did was keep you *un*involved."

He fingered his earrings, took a moment to sort that out. Then he said, "We talking about me, old girl, or you?"

"Both," admitted Angelina. She didn't hesitate, just half-turned on a hip and rearranged her arms.

Michael blinked, his sandy eyelashes became a blur. He'd had a measly week or so invested in David/Keith; Angelina had bet a decade on Ziggy/Sal. He didn't think it was his place to question the wisdom of such a huge investment.

She did it for him. "It's just, you know, now that Ziggy's here, now that we're this close to getting together, I think back on what kept me going all those years, what kept me lonely and not minding it, and it just seems, I don't know, so *thin*."

"Thick enough to bring you down here," Michael said.

"I know, I know. But now—" She couldn't find the words, just gestured in the air, let her legs flop flat against her lounge.

"You know what I think?" said her friend. "I think you have postcoital depression."

"Michael, we didn't—"

"Without the coital part," he said. "You think you need coitus to have postcoital depression? You think life's that fair?"

"But what I'm feeling—"

"You're feeling let down, right? You're feeling you were with your lover, the whole universe should have been transformed, and here it is, the same old world, a mess. Am I right?"

Angelina didn't say he was and didn't say he wasn't, just lifted her behind a second and fretted with the elastic on her bathing suit.

"So now you feel regret," Michael went on. "It happens. You try for sex without remorse, sometimes you get remorse without the sex."

"I don't feel regret," protested Angelina. "What I feel . . . I feel uninterested."

"Uninterested?! There you're kidding yourself, old chum. Look at you." He sketched the air along the length of her body. "You can't sit still a second. If ever a woman needed either a man or a hula hoop—"

"Michael!"

But Michael was launched upon the gospel of passion and he wasn't stopping now. "Uninterested? Then why'd you bring him back here? Just a good deed? A pure unselfish rescue mission?"

"It was the only thing I could think of," she maintained.

"And how convenient that it was!" said Michael. "You bring him here, excuse me, like a half-dead moth back to the nest, so you can watch him flit and flutter and then enjoy a tasty morsel at your leisure."

"That's a terrible thing to say!"

"Is it?" Michael parried, and did not unsay it, just crossed his arms on top of his stomach from the gym and gave a pagan little smile. Angelina pouted, untwisted a shoulder strap, shifted her disgruntled hips. A scrap of breeze put shivers on the pool and raised a smell of chlorine and damp towels.

After a moment Michael said, "Sweetheart, can you look me squarely in the eye and say it isn't so?"

* * *

In New York it was one of those heartbreaking April days when spring, like a drowning swimmer, gets sucked back into the cold gray eddies of winter.

Looking out the bakery window at a chilly slanting rain, Funzie Gallo hunkered closer to the warmth of the big black oven, nibbled sesame *biscotti,* and held the phone a little distance from his ear as Tommy Lucca raved. When the Florida mobster paused for breath, Funzie softly said, "What could I tell ya, Tommy? He hasn't called."

"Why?" insisted Lucca.

"Why what?" said Funzie mildly.

"Why the fuck hasn't he?"

"Tommy, if he called, I could tell you why he called. If he doesn't call, I really got no waya knowing why he doesn't call."

"He looking for a fucking beef or what?"

"He's not looking for a beef. He has a lot on his mind."

"Well he's finding one. He's finding one but good."

Funzie took another bite of biscuit, brushed crumbs from the corner of his mouth. "Am I hearing a threat here, Tommy?"

Only then did Lucca realize he'd been moving to the brink of war. He pulled back half an inch. "Time is money and rat shit isn't raisins. Y'unnerstand me, Funzie?"

Gallo looked out the window, wondered if the rain would harden into sleet in time for rush hour. "Not really," he admitted.

Lucca, pacing in his study, looking out the window at Haitian gardeners on their skinny knees, tending to his flowers, had a brainstorm. "Hey, why the fuck don't you call *him?* He's staying at the Flagler House hotel."

"Under what name?" Funzie said.

"How the fuck should I know?" Lucca said.

"Well, how the fuck should *I* know?" Funzie asked in turn. "I didn't even know he wasn't coming home."

Air hissed through Lucca's teeth and whistled through his mismatched nostrils. "So you're telling me I gotta drag myself down there and find him?"

"You don't gotta do anything," said Funzie. "What I think you *oughtta* do is find some tweezers, pluck the hair outa your ass, and sit tight for a day or two."

"A day or two," said Lucca. "While he finds a way to screw me."

"If he was screwing you," said Funzie, "I'd know about it."

"I sit tight a day or two and he does what he wants."

"Yeah," said Funzie. "He does what he wants. I don't see what the problem is with that."

Lucca put on the squeezed face and singsong voice of a man who knows damn well he's being lied to. "Innocent," he said. "So fucking innocent . . . Tomorrow, Funzie. I don't hear something by tomorrow, I'm going down there."

"Suit yourself," said Paul Amaro's number two.

"Don't say I didn't give you notice."

35

Finding Ziggy proved, of course, to be far more complicated than Carmen Salazar had thought.

He lent Paul Amaro a thug and a pistol that had never been fired and could not be traced, but he was not without misgivings. He was a crook, a con man, a small operator with medium-sized ambitions; a murderer he was not. He had no special affection for Ziggy, but even so, he knew the man, had nothing personally against him, was unhappy being party to his demise. Maybe what he felt was nothing nobler than squeamishness; that, and a fear of being implicated in someone else's grudge—a grudge of which he neither knew nor cared to know the details. Still, a mocking little voice was telling him that maybe he'd been better off before getting into bed with these big-time hoods, his heroes; maybe peace of mind lay in remaining a pissant little second-rater hunkered in a shady garden in a pissant little town.

But that was idle thinking. He'd come this far, had Paul Amaro asking favors of him now—money in the bank. Saying no was not an option. He watched the two assassins head off to do their business.

Graciously, he put a second car and a second sweaty driver at the disposal of Paul Amaro's relative. Rose made her chauffeur drive the melting streets of town for an hour and a half, hoping that, among the tourists with their peeling noses and the locals with their worn-down sandals, she might spot her Louie. When she didn't, she had the flunkey drive her to the office of the local paper, the Key West *Sentinel*. She went inside a while, then was driven back to Flagler House where, over the weak objection of a mumbled promise she'd made to herself, she ordered a cocktail, and then another.

In the meantime all that had been found of Ziggy was a fresh and damning absence.

Paul Amaro and his new accomplice had climbed the softly rotting steps of his bungalow, their damp hands wrapped around the butts of guns held in their pockets. Salazar's thug, choosing the theatric, kicked in the front door, which had not been locked, and which sent forth wet and darkened splinters from the decayed wood at its edge. The living room was empty. Paul Amaro shook his head in some strange vindication at the stained furniture, the mildew on the ceiling; it pleased him that his enemy lived in squalor. Guns ready, they moved to the un-peopled kitchen, the abandoned bath. In the bedroom they saw the signs of a fast disorderly retreat. Dresser drawers stood open, dripping underwear and shirtsleeves. Shutters hung undecided, not open, not closed tightly, prepared for neither day nor night. The bed was unmade, the pillows crushed, the sheet whipped into pointy crests and troughs. Paul Amaro stared a moment at the guilty mattress but no scent or imprint told him that the bed's most recent tenant, naked and hopeful, had been his beloved daughter Angelina.

Frustrated, spiteful, Amaro smashed the dresser mirror with his gun butt. Then the would-be killers left.

At Raul's they learned from a jumpy manager that Ziggy had not showed up the past two days, no phone call, nothing, their entire schedule was all screwed up, and he'd better have a pretty damned original excuse if he ever planned on coming back to work.

Out on the glaring sidewalk once again, Paul Amaro tried to think, but found that he had nothing of substance to think about, and so his mind burned and rumbled like an empty stomach looking for something to digest.

Just around then, in Carmen Salazar's garden, the telephone rang. It was Tommy Lucca, and he was pissed.

"Carmen," said the man from Coral Gables, "just one question: Paul Amaro been back to talk to you?"

Innocently, maybe even with the slightest hint of bragging, Salazar said, "Yeah. A couple times."

"That's all I fuckin' need to know," said Lucca, slamming down the phone.

Slowly but uneasily, Salazar hung up, stared off at the tangled shade of natal plum and passionflower and philodendron and aralia. His garden, his operation, his life—in that instant they all seemed incredibly puny and totally precious, because Salazar was realizing he had somehow got himself in the middle of things he didn't really understand and that could easily undo him. He tried to think of the juncture when he'd begun to lose control. He couldn't pinpoint a moment when it happened or a decision that brought it on. No matter. Even if he had it to do all over again, he would have done the exact same thing, because he had always wanted big-time friends. Now he had them. Big-time friends, and big-time headaches.

36

That evening the hostages of naked city had Cuban food.

Michael brought in rice and beans and *picadillo*, and a double order of fried plantains whose ample grease soaked through the bottom of the bag. He brought in six-packs of beer and a liter of tequila, and for dessert he found a mango torte—the only thing with mango in it that wouldn't melt in the stubborn warmth of early evening.

But for all the food and alcohol, dinner was anything but festive. Ziggy and Angelina had reached a new and mutually grumpy stage in the long slow dance that they were doing. Thwarted desire had put a dull but unremitting ache in Ziggy's loins; the distant pain made him mostly silent, and sarcastic on the rare occasions when he spoke. As for Angelina, some mix of pride and tactic and confusion was making it difficult for her even to meet the eye of the man she'd wanted for so long. They hated each other that evening, and yet it was the merest membrane of restraint and doubt that kept them from falling berserkly into each other's hot and gripping arms. Their standoff, with its musky smell of strangled lust, made Uncle Louie thoroughly uneasy, and flung Michael back into the throes of his own recent heartbreak and humiliation.

So they ate with meager appetite, their faces toward their plates. Ziggy, from the start, was drinking heavily. He'd rub a wedge of lime on the meaty place between his thumb and index finger, then salt the spot, then lick it, then toss back a swallow of tequila, followed by a good long suck of beer. Uncle Louie, to his later sorrow, became intrigued by this technique and tried it on his own. He liked it.

The sky dimmed, a half-moon brightened near the zenith. Michael and Angelina finished eating, threw away their Styrofoam plates. Ziggy and Louie surrendered their plastic forks and knives but not their glasses. Locusts buzzed. Michael got up to leave, and rest, and then go out to look again for romance, reassurance.

"Thanks for dinner," Louie said, eyeing the sweet glaze on the mango cake still perched on a snack table.

Michael smiled and withdrew. Angelina followed him, saying only the tersest of good nights. Ziggy bitterly watched her hips as she walked around the pool.

He kept drinking. Louie tagged along. For a while there was not a word of conversation. Ziggy was in a sulk, and he was one of those men who had a gift for it, a boundless stamina, so that, for him, a funky mood could dig itself broader and deeper until it became something bleakly spiritual, a morbidly ecstatic meditation on the subject of gloom and festering resentments. Uncle Louie, however, had no such talent for silent, self-glorifying woe; drinking made him chatty, curious, emboldened him to inquire into things that, sober, he would only meekly wonder about.

After a time he heard himself saying, "Ziggy, no offense, it's none a my business, but I gotta tell ya, the way you're being so cold t'Angelina, I just don't get it, I think you're acting like a putz."

Ziggy blinked, turned his head very slowly, and said in a brooding monotone, "Fuck asked you how I'm acting?"

Uncle Louie said, "She loves you. Don't you see how much she loves you?"

By way of answer, Ziggy salted his hand and licked it.

"How many men are ever loved like that?" said Louie. "Ten years she waited for you! You should throw yourself at her feet, you should drink the water she bathes in."

Ziggy drank beer instead. Tree frogs croaked out answers to other tree frogs croaking from across the courtyard. Louie raised his glass for emphasis, took a bigger pull of liquor than he'd meant to.

"Ya know what drives me nuts?" he said, against the sour burn that was raging in his throat. "What drives me nuts is a guy who doesn't know how lucky he is."

Ziggy lifted an eyebrow, looked away. The attempt to seem uninterested was the first crack in his lack of interest.

"Ya think about it," Louie rambled, "why should anyone love any of us? We're funny-looking, hairy in ridiculous places. We snore, we're moody, we smell bad—"

"Speak for yourself, old man—"

"We make terrible mistakes, we promise things we can't deliver, we disappoint in bed, in life . . . Ziggy, ya think about all that, and ya don't see how lucky you are, how amazing it is, to have this woman love you?"

Ziggy turned toward Louie then, but it was hard to read his face, a face whose flesh and hinges had been rearranged long after the emotions had been formed, a disconnected face whose tragedy was that its expressions, made of reused parts, could not be trusted to match its owner's feelings. He leaned in close to Angelina's uncle, beer and cactus on his breath. His eyes gleamed dully in the blue light that spread upward from the pool. His voice was a clenched and gravelly whisper. "You think I don't know that it's amazing? I'm fuckin' ashamed, it's so amazing. That doesn't mean it makes me happy."

"It should," said Uncle Louie, softly and simply, sure beyond all argument that he was right.

✳ ✳ ✳

The mango torte was not a good idea.

Louie had eaten a big hunk of it after Ziggy went to bed, licking glaze and runny custard off his fingers, and when the sugar hit the alcohol already coursing through his veins, it sent up fumes that made him dizzy. Still sitting in his lounge chair, he'd closed his eyes and shallowly dozed, nauseously dreaming that he was an astronaut under whose humid capsule a wobbly earth was rocking. He woke to a wheeling sky and blundered off to his room, where he fell heavily on his own side of the barricaded mattress. Ziggy grunted, then went back to snoring.

Louie slept, peed, drank water, slept again. By five-thirty he was no longer drunk and not yet hung over, arrived at a sort of delicate oasis. His mind seemed improbably clear, though his nerves felt scraped and raw, his emotions as fresh and full as fruits just peeled. He rose silently and went downstairs to watch another day begin.

He smelled chlorine, saw stars erased by the approach of dawn. Vaguely, he recalled the conversation of the evening before, wondered if he'd said anything to regret or be embarrassed by; to his surprise, he didn't think he had. Somewhere a cat mewed; far away, a motorcycle revved. He briefly dozed again, woke up when the streetlamps stopped buzzing.

Out of the corner of his eye he saw a sheaf of newspapers come pinwheeling over the fence, heard their slap against the ground. With effort he rose from his lounge, went over and picked one up, carried it back to his seat. There was just enough light to read by, if he squinted.

The paper was wonderfully skinny, a slender testament to how little really happened; the headlines were refreshingly trivial, evidence of how little really mattered. Louie scanned the front page in a minute: The mayor was awaiting trial again; a barracuda had flown into a boat and bit an angler on the leg; a giant crane had fallen into a hole that it was digging. He was about to turn to editorials, had, in fact, already spread the paper and snapped the crease, when his mind belatedly registered a tiny item at the base of a page one column. He refolded the paper, braced it on his knees. He took a breath before he read the ad. The item said:

> Louie,
> I love you.
> Please come back.
> > Rose
> > Flagler House,
> > room 216

There are times in life when a person does not, should not, trust his eyes, when something wished for takes on such a weight and substance that it seems to caper across one's field of vision though it isn't really there. Louie second-guessed his eyeballs. He rested them a moment. He rubbed them, coaxed sleep out of their corners. He rustled the newspaper and brought it a little closer to his face, in light that every moment was growing brighter. He read the ad again, a third time, a fourth. It was not until he realized he was crying that he really believed he'd read it right, that it actually said what it said.

He put the paper down, sat there in his lounge chair in the exploding yellow dawn, and wept. His wife loved him. This was staggering. It rewrote history. Decades of shame and disappointment, of feeling like a failure and a fool, were washed away by a few smudged lines printed at the bottom of a page. His whole life became more dignified in retrospect. He was, after all, a man worth loving, a man a woman could care for.

Astonishment spread all through his scoured nerves, the glad news was passed along from one transfigured fiber to the next, and for a long time he lay very still, as if his newfound peace was a fine silk blanket that could easily slide off. Tears dried on his cheeks as the morning warmed. He pulled the scents of just-opening flowers into his expanded chest.

Then, as the breakfast table and the coffee urn were being trundled into place, his joy took pause to look at itself, and the first cruel jabs of doubt assailed him.

This ad—it said what it said, but what if it was for some other Louie, put there by some other Rose? The chances of there being a mirror-couple, he realized, were remote; but lives were shattered every day by odds that long, or longer.

Uneasy now, he shifted in his chair, but qualms pursued him no matter how he turned and twisted. His brother Paul was at the Flagler House. Was it conceivable that Rose was in cahoots with him, that this love message was nothing but a horrid strategem to flush him out?

For that matter, couldn't it be imagined that his wife was not at Flagler House at all, had not cared enough to track him down, was back home in the Bronx, and the whole heartless ploy had been set in motion by his brother?

Having known contentment for half an hour, Louie was already wracked by a dread of losing it again—of learning that he'd never really had it. Dread ushered in the looming hangover. A headache started clamoring in both his temples. His mouth went dry, his tongue suddenly felt thick. He went to the buffet, brought back juice and coffee.

He fretted as Coral Shores woke up around him, bit his lip as yawning men emerged in boxer shorts or towels. He couldn't stand not knowing if his fragile joy was real or fake. If the ad from Rose was on the level, he longed to hold her in his arms at once; if, God forbid, it was a sham, he needed to find out before the habit of believing he was loved became any more entrenched, making its loss even more of a calamity.

But he feared to go to Flagler House. Paul was there. If the whole thing was a trap, his brother could corner him, threaten him, beat him even, squeezing out the whereabouts of his daughter and his betrayer.

His brow furrowed, his scalp pinched, he went to the buffet for another cup of coffee. Ahead of him in line was a tall slim man in a green kimono, with eyebrows that were plucked and arched, a memory of rouge across his cheeks, a hint of shadow beneath the powder on his upper lip. An idea slipped like a fish through Louie's mind, was dismissed almost before it could be tracked. He got his coffee and went back to his lounge.

He sat there. Heightening sun scorched his eyes; inside his skull, hope and apprehension were colliding like a hammer and a gong. Finally he thought: Why not?

He walked over to the man in the kimono, stood before him as he sipped his coffee and smoked a thin brown cigarette, and said, "Good morning."

"Morning, hon. How are you?"

"I . . ." said Louie. "I was wondering . . . I mean, I wanted t'ask you . . ."

The man blew smoke out both his nostrils. "Life's short, sugar, say what's on your mind."

Louie leaned in closer, couldn't keep his eyes from flicking left and right. "I was wondering," he whispered, "if you have some woman's clothing you could loan me."

37

"Key West!" said agent Terry Sykes, as he filtered Flagler House coffee through his brushy blond moustache and looked out at the flat green water of the Florida Straits. He was wearing a loud floral bathing suit, a Miami Dolphins T-shirt, and the kind of chunky sunglasses cops wear when they want to look relaxed. "McCullough, you really get the postings."

"It's not vacation," said the undercover man.

Sykes fingered his way through a basket of warm rolls, touching every one. With the grin of the chronic shirker, he said, "It isn't hardship duty, either."

McCullough swallowed his annoyance, glanced off through the sweetly muted sunshine of their umbrellaed table to the tiki wing where, as far as anyone could tell, Paul Amaro was still asleep. "Hardship's not the point," he said. "Results is the point."

Sykes pulled his Marlins cap lower over his forehead as his light eyes tracked a woman in a thong bikini. "Supe thinks results'll be zilch."

That's why he sent you, thought McCullough. He said instead, "Supe always thinks that. Comes from sitting on his ass too long."

Sykes fished out another roll, thickly smeared it with strawberry jam. "This Ziggy guy, how long's the hit been out on him?"

"Coming up on his ten-year anniversary," McCullough said.

"We kept someone alive ten years?" said Sykes. "Whaddya know—sometimes the system works."

"Does it?" said McCullough. "Amaro only went away for nine."

"And you think Amaro's here to do the dirty deed himself?"

McCullough searched for patience. "Amaro came here for something else. What, we still don't know. That Ziggy's involved, that's a lucky break."

Sykes swabbed his moustache on the back of his hand, gave a goofy laugh. "Not too damn lucky for Ziggy."

McCullough kept an eye on the hotel's long and arcing row of cottages. Sykes watched a woman with her top undone, taking sun across her back.

"Not lucky for Ziggy at all," McCullough said. "Which is why, when the screws get just a little tighter, Ziggy's gonna crawl to us and beg to be allowed to spill his guts."

Sykes said nothing, hoping for a glimpse of breast.

"And when that happens, Terry, I hope you'll be paying attention."

"Sure thing, Keith," he said. "No problem."

✳ ✳ ✳

"Where's Uncle Louie?" Angelina asked, shading her eyes and looking up from her lounge at Ziggy.

Ziggy swigged coffee before he answered. "Guy's my roommate, not my wife. How the hell should I know where he is?"

"I see you're gonna be all charm again today," said Angelina.

Ziggy's eye sockets felt too small for his eyes. He wasn't quite awake yet, and mid-morning sun was already scorching the back of his neck. He surprised himself by going on the offensive, and realized only afterward that the attack was a sure sign he was caving in. "Don't talk to me about charm," he said. "The way *you're* acting—that's charming?"

Angelina looked away, gave her thick black hair a shake, successfully tweaked him by her silence.

"First you're all over me," he went on. "Flirting. Kissing. In my bed, for Chrissake. Then it's like, I don't know, I became a frog, a leper. When a woman acts like that, there's a name for it, Angelina."

"And I'm sure it's a quaint and lovely name," she said.

He turned his back, looked out across the pool. Men in tiny bathing suits stood thigh to thigh and talked. Another man rubbed suntan lotion on the bare shoulders of a friend. Did it make him queer, Ziggy vaguely wondered, that he realized this whole place pulsed with sex, that the atmosphere seeped into him, that it was a lousy setting in which to have satisfaction dangled then withheld?

Facing her again, he said, "I just don't get it, Angelina," and he felt the vibration of his clenched voice in his gonads. "I just don't understand."

She looked up at him, rearranged her edgy knees, and made a considerable concession. "Maybe I don't understand either, okay?"

He'd stopped expecting her to yield an inch; the frank perplexity in her eyes now disarmed him and gave him hope. He sat on the edge of a lounge next to hers, tried to rid his own voice of its mordant rasp. Almost gently, he said, "If you don't understand, and I don't understand, maybe we're making it more complicated than it's s'posed to be. Desire, Angelina, it's really pretty simple."

"I know about desire," she said, the hardness, unbidden, back in her voice. "I know more about it than you do. Desire's all I've had."

Ziggy's frustrated hands squeezed the flesh above his knees, his freshly discouraged head hung down between his sagging shoulders. "Should we argue who knows more?" he said. "Would that get us anywhere?"

She didn't answer. She looked off at a frangipani tree, at the creamy yellow tucked deep within the bright white petals of the flowers.

After a time, Ziggy said in a tone of seething calm, "This place is driving me crazy. You're driving me crazy. You and me, Angelina, I got no idea how it's gonna end up with us, but I'm telling you, I gotta bust out of here, and soon."

She'd heard the bravado before. Her eyes stayed on the flowers, she scratched an ankle with the bottom of the other foot.

"Angelina, look at me," he said. There was no bombast in his voice, just a quiet urgency. Grudgingly she turned to face him. "Your father," he went on, "he's involved in something down here. Something that's not kosher. You know that, right?"

She hesitated, bit her lip, and nodded. That her father was a criminal, that threats and fixes and plunder had always provided the family livelihood—she'd absorbed that dirty knowledge; but when had she first known it, first *really* known it? Vaguely, she remembered being a regular kid with what she thought was a regular daddy; then she'd become a strange young woman with a lot of things she couldn't talk about to anyone. But the transition eluded her. Was it gradual or was there one grim buried day when it happened?

Ziggy said, "I'd really like to find a way out of this without sending him away again."

Angelina stared at him, felt her pupils squeezing shut then spiraling open. Her face flushed, strands stood out in her neck.

What was he saying to her? Was it a threat? Blackmail? An ugly proposition, silence in exchange for sex?

He saw the affront in her face, said, "I'm not asking you for anything, Angelina. I'm telling you as an old family friend— I'd really like to find some other way."

Embarrassed now, blood trapped in her face, she said, "I wasn't accusing you—"

"Yes you were," he interrupted, a surprising lack of resentment in his voice. "It doesn't matter. I'd like to find another way, and I don't see how I can. No hard feelings if I can't. Okay?"

38

The stockings were hot, but a lot less trouble than shaving his legs.

As for the lacy bra with its built-in boobs and exaggerated nipples, he practically stopped noticing it as soon as his chest hair had been untangled from the cups. The feel of a rayon skirt softly lapping between his thighs took some getting used to, though he'd insisted on wearing his jockey shorts, and there was great comfort in that scrap of the familiar. The only things that really bothered him were the pumps with their pinching toes and mid-height heels that made his butt stick out for balance; and the auburn wig, whose starchy backing made his bald spot itch like crazy, and whose stability on his sweaty head he didn't really trust.

Big sunglasses with winged frames avoided the need to do his eyes; a few sweeps of Cover Girl, tinged apricot, did a passable job of masking the stubble on his cheeks. Lipstick, a pale coral shade for morning wear, softened the crinkled corners of his mouth. His new ally the drag queen had said, "You're no Joan Crawford, sweetie, but you'll do."

He took a taxi to the Flagler House, forgot to keep his knees together as he exited. He caught the doorman's eyes flicking rudely toward his crotch, trying to chalk up a flash of panties. Men were beasts, he realized.

Now he was skulking through the lobby, his heart thumping so that his left falsie chafed against his chest. Half-deafened by his own clicking footsteps, he moved slowly, his eyes panning without respite. He peeked furtively around potted palms, looking for his brother or his henchmen, wondering if he'd be recognized, waiting for the trap to close.

When he was not immediately grabbed, he sidled to the front desk and asked the whereabouts of room 216. In his nervousness he neglected to disguise his voice, but the clerk, unflappable, barely blinked at the unlikely baritone; he directed the visitor to a bank of elevators.

The doors slid open on the second floor, and the first part of Louie to emerge was the winged sunglasses beneath the auburn wig, big silver frames turning left and right along the corridor. Finding it vacant, he stepped out, took a breath, dragged his heels along the carpet until he found room 216.

Standing before the door, he took a final trembling glance around him, then raised his hand to knock. But his nerve deserted him, he couldn't move his arm. This was it. Either Rose was there behind that door, and he was loved, his life fulfilled, or she was not, and he'd been duped, he might as well be laughed at, used, because his whole life was a travesty. He licked his lips, tasted wax and fragrance. He reached up to mop his forehead, his wrist bumped the wig a little bit askew. He knocked.

His answer was a silence, a pause beyond all measure.

His squashed feet fretted against the carpet, his heart fell in his chest, quivered like a dying mouse against his ribs.

Then he heard the tiny click and slide of a peephole being opened. As sure as a person feels a clammy hand, he felt an eye on him, though he didn't know whose eye it was.

Inside room 216, Rose Amaro, just now waking up from an unsober sleep, was thoroughly confused. Who was this dumpy brunette with the geeky sunglasses, and why was she knocking on her door? Softly but not warmly, she said, "Yes?"

Her husband's voice somehow issued forth from the painted mouth of this unattractive woman. "Rose," it said, "it's me!"

The voice, its incongruity, only deepened Rose's confusion. She struggled to wake up. For a moment no thought whatsoever would resolve, then what streaked across her mind was the befuddling notion that, after all these years, it turned out that her husband was a fruit. Had it happened in Key West or had he always been, down deep? Was it something he was born with or had she failed him even more miserably than she thought?

Out in the hallway, exposed to gangsters and relatives, Louie was extremely nervous. "Rose," he said. "Open up. Please."

After an interminable moment, a night chain rattled, a bolt scraped free, the door of 216 fell open.

Rose Amaro stood there in a cotton nightie, her silhouette revealed by silver shafts of daylight streaming in through the partly open blinds behind her. But Louie didn't see the loosening flesh, the contours surrendering, didn't see tired eyes or a jawline going slack; he saw his wife, the woman he had courted and won and loved forever, whose occasional affection was the greatest compliment he'd ever known. He scuffed his pumps across the threshold, closed the door behind him, and moved to take her in his arms.

Rattled, she fell back half a step, said, "Louie, you could have told me, we would have worked it out."

He swept off the itchy wig, tossed it on the bed. "Told you what?"

"This dress-up thing," she said. "I hear it isn't really that abnormal."

The acceptance with which she said it, the compassion, made Louie for an instant almost wish he was a real drag queen.

His wife said, "I would've tried to understand. I would've loved you anyway."

"You would have?" Louie said, his voice soft but taut with wonder. He took a bold step in his mid-heel shoes, closed the space between them, and held her hard against him.

✳ ✳ ✳

It was sad, how easily Tommy Lucca's enforcers got the drop on Carmen Salazar's bodyguards, how puny the local tough guys seemed when the outside world invaded.

Next to the practiced bone breakers from Miami, the homegrown goons were slow, flabby, indecisive, almost humane. They'd hardly reacted when the out-of-towners bulled through the narrow passage of the candy store and stormed through the doorway at the rear, their hard hands readying their guns. The defenders had fallen back, spontaneously surrendered; there was no fight but only a weirdly dancelike ritual of dominance and obeisance, as Salazar's two guards stood dwarfed by Lucca's men like pawns immobilized by rooks.

A third Miami hood strapped a dazed and silent Carmen Salazar into his lawn chair, swaddling him in a dozen ravels of shiny silver tape. With each wrap, Salazar's usually languorous posture grew more rigid, until finally he sat there squeezed and snug as a sausage. He didn't have time to be afraid, exactly. His thoughts were bleak but resigned: I've made a dumb mistake; I should have realized sooner; I'm dealing with a madman.

Tommy Lucca, twitchy and snarling, paced through the dappled light of the garden so that broken sunshine painted him one moment in stripes, the next in leopard spots. He pointed a finger at his taped-in host, said, "You're fuckin' me. You and Amaro, you're cuttin' me out."

Salazar groped for composure, said, "Tommy, I don't know what you're talking about."

"Tommy? . . . To you, fuckeye, it's Mr. Lucca."

Salazar never sweated. He sweated now, his shirt grew wet beneath the coils of the tape.

Lucca paced. "Amaro's been to talk to you. Yes or no?"

"Yes. I told you that."

"What the fuck about?"

Salazar tried to breathe in deep but the tape was like a second set of cramping ribs. Paul Amaro might kill him if he spilled his secrets. Tommy Lucca might kill him if he didn't. This was what happened when you got ambitious, moved beyond the small safe confines of your garden. "Personal stuff," he said. "Family stuff."

Lucca said, "Do better, asshole."

Foliage scraped. Salazar swallowed, reluctantly told Lucca about Paul Amaro's daughter and his brother, and the video brought down from New York, and the search for Ziggy Maxx.

Lucca paced, stalled, paced again, unsatisfied. "The two of you watch videos. He's looking for his relatives, for a man that everybody knows has not been seen in a dog's age. A bigger crock of bullshit I have never heard."

"Mr. Lucca, why would I lie to you?"

"Cocksucker Amaro offered you a bigger cut."

"We haven't even talked about that deal."

"How's he routing the guns?" the mafioso chipped away. "Through Tampa? Through New Orleans and down the Gulf?"

Salazar tried to move against the tape; the effort made the bonds seem tighter. "I told you, Mr. Lucca, there aren't any guns."

Lucca mugged toward his underlings, showed them he was not fooled for a moment. Then he moved very close to Salazar's chair. Fear sent a sharp pain through the seated man's bowels; he braced himself to be smacked or pummeled but Lucca reached out very slowly, with a mocking gentleness intended to humiliate, and grabbed him by the chin. "Carmen," he said, "I used to think you were bright, that I could work with you. Now I see you're one more second-rate scuzzball, I gotta watch you every second."

He released the other man's face, took half a step away, swiveled toward him once again.

"Carmen, we're gonna do this deal. I want it and we're gonna do it. But I have to tell you, I'm disappointed in you. That it turns out you're the kinda scumbag that would rather take money from a has-been from New York than do right by your people here in Florida."

"I haven't taken any money," said Carmen Salazar.

"Your *neighbors* in Florida," Tommy Lucca said. "Don'tcha have no fuckin' sense a neighborhood?"

39

Love gives a man courage, or at least makes him feel that he should act courageous.

Uncle Louie, having lain with his wife, having been reminded that she'd missed him, now remembered what feeling strong was like; he resolved to confront his brother Paul. He'd come to Florida to try and make things right for Angelina, to show his family that he had some brains and nerve, that he could be of use. Here, finally, was his chance. Feeling loved himself, he'd make Paul understand Angelina's love for Ziggy, make him see that love was more important than revenge. He'd be the hero by being the peacemaker.

He kissed Rose one last time, gave her the address of his guest house, asked her to take a taxi there and wait for him. Then he got back into the only clothes he had, the bra and stockings, the skirt and the wig, and went out through the lobby, past the pool, and onward toward the tiki wing.

Agent Terry Sykes, alone on stakeout now, Keith McCullough having gone to watch the picket gate of Coral Shores, looked out from underneath his beach umbrella and saw a frumpy aging hooker knock on Paul Amaro's door. Sykes pursed his lips, shook his head, and t'sked. A man of Amaro's power and prestige should certainly have rated a less weatherbeaten chippy.

Inside the room, Angelina's father heard the knock, leaned away from the rolling table at which he was just finishing late breakfast. He wiped his mouth on a napkin, said, "Yeah?"

Louie spoke into the crack between the door frame and the door. "Paulie," he said in a rasping whisper, "it's your brother Louie."

There were quick footsteps. With a reckless and forgetful lack of caution, the door was yanked open, sunlight bleached the walls. Paul Amaro squinted at the man in drag, chewed his lip a second, then said, "Louie, what the fuck?"

"I was afraid," the younger brother said by way of explanation. "That was before." He ducked beneath Paul's arm and scraped into the room.

"Before what?"

Louie didn't answer. The door closed behind him, shutting out the naturalness of day. He swept off his winged sunglasses in the dimness.

"Where's Angelina?" Paul demanded.

"No hello?" said Louie. "No how am I?"

"Louie, where's my daughter?"

"Your daughter's fine."

"I'm asking where she is."

Louie glanced around the room, noted the small sad luxuries of the guest who dines alone—the single curling rose in the bud vase, the paper cap atop the streaming glass of water. He said, "Maybe we'll get to that. First we talk."

Paul Amaro was wearing a hotel bathrobe. His barrel chest stretched open the lapels. His breathing came with effort and his skin was splotchy red. "Don't fuck with me, Louie. My patience is used up."

"I'm not gonna let you spoil things for her."

Paul stared at his brother, surprise and contempt swirling through the look. This runty man in a skirt and a wig, this meddling nobody with tits and wrinkled stockings, was telling him what he would and wouldn't let him do? "If you're gonna be an asshole—"

Louie interrupted him. "Paul, your daughter's in love with Sal Martucci. She came down here to find him. Haven't you figured that out by now?"

Paul Amaro turned his back and clenched his fists. The room, a big room, was feeling very small. Two beds left only narrow open lanes. The mirror didn't double space, it halved it, throwing back hard edges, jutting corners that blocked ways of escape. Angelina's father didn't turn around. He said, "She doesn't even know Sal Martucci, not really, what a piece a shit he is. What she felt for him, that was long ago, childhood, a crush."

"That may be," said Louie, "but she isn't gonna stop feeling it just because you want her to."

Paul half-turned, glanced briefly down at his breakfast table with its cooling coffee, its plate striped with streaks of drying egg. "What that fucker did to me," he said, "that's death. Even you know that, Louie. That cunt put me in jail."

Louie remembered all at once that the wig was on his head, he yanked it off and tossed it away. He ran a hand over his sweaty bald spot but before he could think of what to say he was saying it. "Paul," he told his brother, "for once in your life be honest. He didn't put you in jail. *You* put you in jail. You're a criminal, Paul. A bully and a crook and a criminal."

For a moment Paul Amaro just glared at him, his eyeballs throbbing and his body churning and heaving in his robe like something being born. At last he said, "You little twat, you have the fucking balls—?"

"Yeah," said Louie, more surprised than anyone, "I do. I do, Paul. Finally I do."

At a loss for logic, Paul Amaro spluttered, "Your asshole video, Louie. This whole mess started with your video."

The younger brother refused to be deflected. He put his hands on the hips of his skirt, leaned forward on his tippy shoes. "Okay, Paul, so say you kill 'im. Big man, you rub 'im out. What then? Your friends respect you more? Your enemies know to be afraid?"

Paul said nothing, stared vaguely at softening butter, hardening toast.

Louie hammered on. "One thing that happens, Paul? I'll tell ya one thing that happens. Kill 'im and your daughter hates ya."

There was a long pause filled with the hum of the a/c and a faint rustling of foliage from the world outside. Then some words leaked out of Paul Amaro. They were words he didn't know he had inside him, and could never in a hundred lifetimes have imagined he would say. He met his brother's eyes in the instant before he said them but then he looked at nothing. "She hates me anyway."

Louie sat down at the foot of a bed. He didn't remember moving, but there he was. He was not a father and he had no answer for what had just been said. He couldn't lift his eyes up off his lap.

After a moment Paul went on like he was talking to himself. "She didn't hate me, why would she be doing this?"

Louie's chest and arms were damp, he rearranged his blouse. Not sure if he was chiding or trying to give comfort, he said, "You think all of this, it has to do with you?"

"You think none of it does?" said Paul Amaro. Moving slowly, heavy, he slipped between the breakfast table and a bed, sat down, shoulders slumped, across the narrow space from his brother. "Of all the guys inna fuckin' world, Louie. Coincidence she's stuck onna guy I hate the most?"

Louie brought his knuckles to his mouth, chewed on them

a moment before he answered. "With love," he said, "I don't think you can look at it like that, like there's rhyme or reason."

"And what about wit' family? You think there's rhyme or reason wit' family?"

Louie had no answer, his eyes strayed toward his cast-off wig, which shone with an unwholesome luster like the pelt of something poisoned.

"I tried to make her a nice life," Angelina's father muttered. "Big house. No worries. All I did, I made her ashamed of her old man."

Louie said nothing. He thought of reaching for his brother but couldn't lift his arms to give an embrace that might have been welcomed, might have been pushed aside.

"That's why I gotta kill 'im," Paul resumed, his voice weary, trancelike. "That's the real reason. Businessman, Louie. To my daughter I was a businessman. Not a criminal, not a thug. Went ta work in nice clothes, brought home lotsa presents. Executive, like. Wit'out that fuck I mighta got away with it. To my daughter. Maybe she never woulda known."

"But Paul—" said Louie.

He got no farther. Outside the room there was the scratch of footsteps, a low rumble of knotted voices. Then a knocking on the door, loud, rude, insistent. Someone tried the knob; it turned, Paul Amaro had neglected to relock it.

Sunlight flooded in, Tommy Lucca and his three gorillas rode it like a wave. Nobody was smiling.

" 'Lo, Paul," said the man from Coral Gables. "Nice ta find you in."

Paul Amaro didn't answer.

Lucca took his shades off, his eyes flicked with mockery to the man in drag. "And who the fuck is this?"

Paul said, "That's my brother Louie."

The goons snickered.

Lucca said to Paul, "You poor bastard, you're even worse off than I thought." To the fellow in the skirt he said, "Take a hike, Sis. Us men, we gotta talk."

40

Keith McCullough, hidden in deep shade across the street from
Coral Shores, did not immediately recognize Uncle Louie; but he
could tell a real transvestite from someone merely improvising,
and the clumsy walk and crooked wig led him to look a whole
lot closer. The stubby build and bowed out knees persuaded
him that this was Paul Amaro's brother, and while he had no
idea why he was out on the street in woman's clothing, he was
encouraged. There was movement, maneuvering; the stalemate
was easing.

Once inside the courtyard, Louie drew a couple of facetious whistles from men in the hot tub. But he had too much on
his mind, he didn't stop to kid around. He walked around the
pool, high sun scorching his wig, heels sliding over damp tiles,
until he found his family. Rose and Angelina, in wet bathing
suits, were lying side by side on lounges; Michael, in a towel, sat
upright in a nearby chair. Ziggy lazed a little distance away, in a
sulk as usual.

Rose lit up at her husband's approach, fluffed her hair

where the bathing cap had squashed it down. "Louie," she said, "you must be broiling. Sit by me, I'll help you get undressed."

He perched on the edge of her lounge. She took off the wig, unbuttoned his blouse, couldn't help giggling as, for the second time that day, she unclasped the deceiving bra.

Angelina said, "So Uncle Louie, how'd it go?"

For a time he didn't answer. He was sweating, his head itched. His thoughts were going round and round. Too much had happened for one morning, he felt an exhaustion such as an animal must feel when it sheds a skin and wills a layer of wet flesh into a new one. Finally he said, "You hate your father, Angelina?"

He regretted it the instant the words had passed his lips. It wasn't fair to put her on the spot like that. He thought she flushed, but he couldn't be sure, she was very tan by now. In any case, she didn't answer, and Louie tried to erase the question by talking over it. "Try not to hate him," he said. "He loves you very much."

She looked away. At the far side of the pool, somebody splashed. From the street came the buzzing whine of rented mopeds. Rose said, "Swivel a little, I'll unzip the skirt."

She pushed the rayon down over his hips, he shimmied out of the garment like he'd been doing it all his life. He kicked the stockings off. He was so numb, so raw and new, that it seemed almost normal to be sitting on a lounge chair in the tropics in his underwear, discarded women's clothing at his feet.

He looked over his shoulder at Ziggy, said, "I tried to talk 'im out of killing you."

"Thanks," said Ziggy, without conviction.

"I don't think it worked."

Ziggy tried to sound blasé. "You don't *think* it worked?"

"We didn't really get to finish talking. A guy came in, seemed pretty mad."

"He have a name this guy?"

Louie said, "I think my brother called him Tommy."

"Short guy? Sideways nose?"

Louie nodded. "Had three, like bodyguards. Big. I'm very tired, I think I gotta go lay down."

He hitched up his briefs, began to rise. His wife said, "I'm going too then, Louie. I wanna be by you."

Angelina watched them walk away together, honeymooners after thirty years of waiting for the honeymoon. She shifted her knees, then said to Michael, "I'm really sorry, hon, but I think you just got Ziggy for a roommate."

Ziggy glared at the woman he still desired, though his desire was turning each hour more rancid and spiteful and surreal. Then he looked at Michael with an expression that was both nervous and aggressive, a look that the gay guy had seen from certain kinds of straight guys many times before.

Michael met his gaze, said, "Don't worry and don't flatter yourself. I don't like hairy men."

✳ ✳ ✳

"Right in my own backyard," said Tommy Lucca. "I can't believe you're tryin'a fuck me right in my own backyard."

Paul Amaro was still sitting on the bed, his bare toes squeezing the carpet underneath his breakfast table. "Tommy," he said, "you're crazy."

Lucca mugged over at his thugs. "*I'm* crazy? Me? You got a brother wears a dress, a daughter runs and hides, and I'm crazy?"

Quite evenly Paul Amaro said, "Don't say another fuckin' word about my family 'less you wanna have to kill me here and now."

"Who said anything 'bout killing?"

The goons shifted foot to foot, arms twitched at the prospect of some exercise.

"You're touchy 'bout your family," Lucca went on. "Okay. Everybody's touchy 'bout something. Me, I'm touchy 'bout being screwed in business."

"For the last time, Tommy, I'm not screwing you."

"Then fuck didn't you call Funzie like you said? One phone call, Paul. That's all you had to do."

Amaro pursed his lips, crossed his arms against his stomach. "The truth?" he said at last. "I didn't call Funzie 'cause I don't give a fuck about your guns and I don't give a fuck about your deal and I don't give a fuck about you."

Tommy Lucca took that in, didn't seem offended in the least. He said simply, "But you said you'd do it."

This was hard to argue with. Amaro had given his word to a colleague and he hadn't followed through. Inaction on a promise was not so different from betrayal.

"The Paul Amaro I know from years ago," said Tommy Lucca, "he wouldn't let a deal sit there and get cold. That he'd fuck the other guy, take the profit for himself—tha'd be more easy t'believe."

Amaro sat before his plate with its streaks of egg and edges of toast and said nothing.

Slowly, Tommy Lucca reached a hand out toward one of his underlings. Almost tenderly, the thug put a gun in his palm.

Lucca pointed it at the forehead of his sometime ally, close enough that the muzzle would scorch skin before the bullet shattered bone. "So tell ya what, Paul," he said. "While we're sittin' here, all together like, why don't you call Funzie right this fuckin' second, before it slips your mind again?"

41

Later on, when the sun had slid far enough down the sky so that the pool was in the shade and fringed shadows had crept along the gravel walks to climb the clapboard walls on the east side of the courtyard, Ziggy retrieved his extra socks and underwear and pocketknife from what was now Louie and Rose's room.

Like the homeless person he'd become, he brought them in a tattered plastic bag to Michael's cottage, and found his new host doing sit-ups on the floor next to the queen-size bed.

Michael ignored him altogether, just kept bringing his elbows to his knees, a hundred times, two hundred. Secretly, Ziggy admired the striations and pebblings of the gay guy's stomach.

After sit-ups came a string of yoga poses—stretching, folding, standing on one leg. Ziggy sat down in a wicker chair and sort of watched. A master of the sulk, his funks had many aspects, and he was now at the stage where he was feeling very sorry for himself. Michael's vigor mocked him. He felt forever cut off from the kind of self-affection that gave rise to the discipline to work out, to take care of oneself. Also, he was newly oppressed by the realization that he'd become the pariah of the little group of hostages at Coral Shores. Everybody else got along. Everyone else made a show, at least, of keeping up their spirits. Not him. He'd gone into a sulk to push them all away, and now that he'd succeeded, he moped because he felt isolated.

Gloomily, he watched as Michael breathed deep, focussed, and brought a foot against the inside of the other thigh. At some point he surprised himself by saying, "I guess you think I'm a real shithead."

Maybe it was the yoga, the calm it induced, but Michael was not the least bit ruffled by the comment. He said softly, "I don't for the life of me get what she sees in you."

In some unconscious parody of Michael's exercise, Ziggy folded up his thick unlimber legs.

"I mean," said Michael, his green eyes straight ahead, just the slightest waver in the limb that held his weight, "Angelina has a spark. Life. Warmth. She's romantic."

"I useta be romantic," Ziggy said.

His only answer was a skeptical silence, which, now that he'd taken the leap and started talking, he found extremely frustrating.

"I *was*," he went on. "Flowers. Candy. Little presents, the whole nine yards. Then . . . Michael, can I ask you something? Y'ever like girls?"

The gay guy was switching poses, kicking a leg behind him, keeping it parallel to his flattened back. "In high school, sure. That's what people did back then. Boys liked girls, girls liked boys. It was cute."

"You had dates? Caught some sex maybe?"

"Dates, sure. Sex, enough to know my heart wasn't in it."

"Exactly!" Ziggy said. "Exactly. 'Cause you were going through the motions, it wasn't who you were."

Michael dropped to his knees, spread his elbows on the

floor, and lifted himself into a headstand, feet arched, toes pointed at the ceiling. Upside down, he said, "That's fair."

"Well that's what it's like for me," said Ziggy. "Since they changed my name, my face, since I can't go back to where I'm from. Before . . . look, I'm not saying I was a good person, but I knew who I was, I knew—"

Ziggy really thought that he was being honest, even bravely open. So he was surprised when Michael, still standing on his head, his inverted eyes oblique and haunting like something out of Egypt, cut him off. "Ziggy," he said, "I think that's all a load of bullshit, just a big excuse."

Ziggy spluttered, found no words. Over the course of several seconds, a feeling of affront grudgingly gave way to the secret thrill, the relief, of being caught.

"I mean," continued Michael, his mouth moving disconcertingly above his nose, "what I understand, you used to be a little cheese hoping to become a big cheese. You had to be afraid of stronger guys and you had to be afraid of cops. Tell me what's so different now?"

"What's different—" Ziggy started, but then could only rearrange his cramping legs and gesture in the air.

"You know what's different?" Michael said. "What's different is that now it's just you and Angelina, period. She's not the boss's daughter. She's not the girl from the neighborhood whose family is in your business. There is no neighborhood. There's you and there's her, and the only question that matters is, come what may, do you want to be with her."

"It's not that simple," Ziggy said, squirming in his chair.

"It *is* that simple," said Michael, his face flushed with conviction or from standing on his head so long. "The rest is crap."

"Her father wants to kill me. That's crap?"

Michael dropped his legs, assumed a graceful jacknife. "Fathers always wanna kill the boyfriend. It's, you know, a dick thing, universal. Okay, maybe not as much as this . . . Look, run away. Elope. Wait it out, pick your moment, and run."

The idea pressed Ziggy back against his chair. "Run where? Mexico? Cuba? Live under a tree till we fuckin' starve to death?"

"Imagination, Ziggy. You'll figure something out."

Ziggy pursed his altered lips, shook his tight-skinned head. "Wouldn't be fair t'Angelina."

"More crap," said Michael. "More excuses. No one knows what's good for someone else. No one knows what's fair."

Ziggy said, "It's fair I bring her into this fuckin' mess I've made outa my life?"

"She seems to think it can be fixed."

"She's stubborner than I am."

Michael pancaked down, then rolled over and sat back against his heels. Blood was draining from his head but his face was still a ruddy pink, sparse freckles showing through the tan. He said, "You're pretty fucking stubborn yourself. You've made up your mind it's hopeless."

Ziggy looked off at a corner of the room, saw wisps of cobweb swaying slowly in the small breeze from the ceiling fan. "No," he said softly. "That's where you're wrong. I don't believe it's hopeless."

Michael sat there and said nothing.

"I act like it's hopeless," Ziggy went on. "Force a habit. Maybe I wish it was hopeless, it'd make things easier."

Michael kept very still.

Ziggy said, "But in my heart I don't believe it's hopeless. And that's the sadass truth."

Michael studied him a moment, said, "You sent flowers? You really used to do that?"

Ziggy leaned far forward, propped his elbows on his knees. "Look, there's no reason you should help me but I could really use your help."

Michael said, "Would it be good for Angelina?"

"Ya just got done telling me that no one knows what's good for someone else."

"Don't ask me to do anything that would hurt her."

"Ya think she really hates her father?"

"Partly, yes," said Michael. "And partly loves him too."

"I been thinking about a couple things," said Ziggy. "I'm asking you to trust me."

Michael considered, then glanced over at the only bed and felt the peace of knowing and of being unafraid. "Looks like you have to trust me too."

Ziggy swallowed, said, "I can do that, Michael."

"Then so can I," said Angelina's friend.

✳ ✳ ✳

Angelina lay back in a tepid bath and steered a jagged course among all the things she didn't want to think about.

She didn't want to think about Ziggy, about her battered half-dead love for him, about his brooding simmering manner that put her off and still somehow seduced her.

She didn't want to think about her father, about the taboo suggestion of her rage against him; didn't want to call up recollections of childhood happiness and safety, grotesque now against a backdrop of newspaper headlines, prison records.

She didn't want to think about her own body, half floating, half sunk in the tub, water immersed in other water, her skin wrapping a befuddling amalgam of nerves and secrets, sadnesses and appetites, recklessness and qualms, a mass of tangled circuits sucking juice out of an overloaded brain.

So she stared at the horizon line of water in the tub and tried to think of nothing. It didn't work and she grew annoyed. Other people, she imagined, managed to go blank; the tropics, as advertised, nurtured the process. But the draining temperatures, the restful whoosh of fronds—for her they weren't working.

Sitting there, she was assailed by unremitting images of men's hands and big dark cars and sharkskin suits and more toys than a little girl could ever get around to playing with, bought with pilfered funds. From decades before she remembered "uncles" bringing gifts—coming to the house, she more lately understood, to talk of crime. And Sal Martucci, visiting on business, stealing gutsy moments in the hallway to kiss her ear, stroke her neck. Crime, sex; father, boyfriend; shame, virginity; innocence, freedom. The warring pairs clapped together in her mind, seemed to set the bathtub water roiling like tremors underground.

Angelina, giving up on blankness, embraced the promise of riot instead, felt both hope and terror as she realized that some grand collision was on its way, had been set in motion weeks before; and that if the tumult didn't drive her totally insane, there was the chance, at least, that, in its noise and heat, rage might be resolved and overripe childhood finally finished, that she would walk away a grown-up woman and calm would come at last.

42

Up north, webby trees just coming into leaf were silhouetted against a red-reflecting sky.

At a warehouse on the Hudson, an hour or so above the city, the guns for Cuba were being loaded onto a truck that usually serviced the Hunts Point produce market. It had a picture of a cauliflower painted on the side, and its trailer smelled of tangerines, bananas; between its soft wooden floorboards was a residue of flattened grapes.

Funzie Gallo, eating a cheese Danish that would see him through till dinner, supervised the operation. "The nine millimeters," he said, "put 'em underneat' the broccoli. T'ree fifty-sevens, mix in wit' the cantaloupes. Uzis, make sure ya keep 'em separate, bury 'em good in escarole. Got it?"

The two guys loading just grunted under the weight of crates of firearms.

"Ya drive the speed limit," Funzie said, "don't fuck around. Hialeah. Ya got the address in Hialeah?"

One of the guys loading, a little testy at Funzie feeding his face while other people might have slipped a disk, said, "We got it, Funzie, we got it."

"Carlos Mendez. He hands ya a hunnert twenty-five. Right?"

"Right, Funzie. Right."

"Make sure ya coun' it. Guy's a spick."

The other guy loading slapped his crate down on the lip of the truck, said, "Funzie, watch it, huh. I'm a spick. Remember?"

"Jesus, sorry," Funzie said, and for solace he bit deep into his Danish, sweet cheese glued his teeth together. What had happened to the fucking world, he wondered, when you couldn't even recruit Sicilians anymore?

* * *

Agent Terry Sykes did not know much, but he knew who Tommy Lucca was, and he was awfully pleased with the results of his day's surveillance—so pleased that, when Keith McCullough joined him for a poolside dinner at Flagler House, he wanted to go over every detail of his day.

Cramming a french fry in his mouth, he said, "First this old bag hooker comes in—"

McCullough took pleasure in correcting him. "That was not a hooker, that was Amaro's brother."

Sykes pulled on his beer, wiped foam from his moustache. "His brother? In drag? I don't see—"

"You don't have to see," McCullough said. "Tell me about Lucca."

Sykes looked down at his plate: half-eaten cheeseburger, the bun scalloped with bite-marks; fries cooling in a pool of ketchup. He took a deep breath, as though he had a long tale to tell, but then realized he hadn't in fact seen much. Tommy Lucca had marched around the pool, looking purposeful and hell-bent—but then, he always looked like that. He had three paloo-kas with him—but that, as well, was pretty standard. It seemed they'd gone right in—no key, no argument. The geek in woman's clothing came out a couple minutes after. In all, Lucca was in Paul Amaro's room twenty-two minutes, and when he emerged he looked perhaps a half-shade less pissed-off than when he'd gone in. Paul Amaro had not left with him.

"Maybe Lucca killed him," Keith McCullough said.

"If he did," said Terry Sykes, "room service didn't notice. Guy went in a little while after, rolled his table out."

"So they're doing business," McCullough said. "Lucca and Amaro. Fairly interesting."

Sykes's blond hair was slightly lavender in the blue light from the pool. He reached up and scratched his head. "But I thought this Ziggy guy—"

"The connection," said McCullough, absently pushing his plate away, "it's starting to make sense."

Sykes went back to eating, fried onions squeezed out the edges of his burger. "What connection?"

"Why Ziggy's involved," McCullough said. "What I couldn't figure out, is how Ziggy would get hooked into a deal with Paul Amaro. I mean, he's not that stupid. But if it started off as someone *else's* deal—"

"Someone else's deal?"

"Lucca's deal. See, it's Lucca's. Amaro comes in later, and boom, there's Ziggy, suddenly in the sack with the guy that wants to kill him. That make sense to you?"

Sykes's tongue chased scraps of dangling food. "Not really."

"Not really," McCullough intoned, impressed anew at his partner's obtuseness. "Okay, it doesn't have to. But Terry, try to figure it out by the time you have to testify, 'cause it looks like we're bringing down two big guys and not just one."

✳ ✳ ✳

The Feds were still at dinner when Michael stepped through the picket gate of Coral Shores to carry out, with great misgivings, the first of two errands he'd agreed to run for his roommate Ziggy.

As quickly as possible, he slipped away from the bustle and glare of Duval Street, its carnival vapors of candy and grease, and disappeared into quiet residential precincts where cats slunk through the lattice under porches, and household shadows sent mysterious patterns through the slats of louvered windows. He skirted the cemetery, saw the whitewashed multi-level crypts where unburied bones waited for the trumpet blast that would rehinge them and send them dancing in the sun; crossed White Street, that slacking locals' boulevard, with its hand-scrawled shop signs, its beer bottles poking out the tops of paper bags next to old men playing dominos.

He passed into a neighborhood where the houses were cinder block and the dogs unfriendly, till at length he came to the candy store in whose garden Carmen Salazar held court.

He stood before it a long moment, licked his lips, smoothed his hair, approached with tremulous resolve the cracked stone step. He went inside.

Dim in daylight, by evening the store was rudely bright with a bluish grainy glare. Behind the counter sat the fat man in the undershirt, torpid and expressionless as ever. The greasy fan turned side to side, strings of matted dust fluttered on its grille. As instructed, Michael didn't speak, just moved steadily toward the open doorway at the rear.

He was halfway through it, one foot searching for the ground on the far side of the threshold, when he was suddenly grabbed by a man who sprang from the shadows, with garlic on his breath and a tire iron in the hand that wasn't clawing into Michael's shirt. His snaggled teeth yawned open before the emissary's eyes and he said, "Fuck you want, my friend?"

Michael's foot still dangled in midair; it made spasmodic stabs at terra firma. Ziggy hadn't mentioned a welcoming committee. But then, Ziggy didn't know that Carmen's bodyguards had been recently outmuscled and embarrassed, that Michael would be their means of saving face. "I want . . ." he managed, "I want to speak with Carmen."

The goon increased the torque on the front of Michael's shirt, squeezed like he was wringing out a sock. "For why?"

"Ziggy sent me," said the messenger.

There was a pause, Michael's suspended leg still groping for the earth. Then a voice came from the dimness of the garden. "Pat him down, Pablo."

The big man gave a last squeeze, then let Michael come to ground. He felt the visitor's sides, his legs, his crotch. "He's hokay," he said back to his boss.

Michael mustered his nerve. "You don't know the half of it."

"Bring him here," said the voice from the garden.

Pinching his arm, the goon led him under vines and through the foliage to where a pensive and deflated Salazar was sitting in his lawn chair, a sticky residue of duct tape making linty coils around the frame.

Glancing up at his guest from under sullen brows, he said, "Ziggy sent you. I guess that means Ziggy's still alive." He tried to say it with his usual lilting cynicism, but the mordancy fell flat, his blitheness had deserted him.

"Very much alive," said Michael.

Salazar strove once again for bravado. "Hiding like a worm, I take it."

"Trying to work things out."

The seated man crossed his knees, came forth with a bitter and percussive little laugh. "Work things out? He still thinks there's a way to work things out with these crazy big shot lunatics?"

"Not exactly *with* them," Michael said.

Carmen Salazar uncrossed his legs, propped an elbow on his sticky chair arm, put his chin on his palm. "Let's not talk in riddles, friend."

"Okay," Michael said, and he tried to sound insolent yet

chummy, just like he'd rehearsed. "Ziggy wanted me to tell you that you can take your chances with the big shots or you can maybe come away on top by helping him to plan a little party. It's up to you."

A breeze moved through the garden at a walking pace, delivering aromas like a mailman drops off letters. Carmen Salazar pulled on his chin and mocked himself. He was a small-time guy, but a small-time guy with brains; he knew, he'd always known, that when a little life collided with big ones, only trouble could result. Why did people go against what they knew? Why did they scorn even the few small scraps of wisdom that they had? Sitting there, he understood quite clearly that the illicit but congenial life he'd built around his garden was over. He'd overreached; he'd placed himself between two strong men and probably made enemies of both; he'd wrecked himself. Ruthlessly lucid in his depression, he saw that no matter what course he chose now, either he would be destroyed or everything would have to change.

He said, "Pablo, bring the man a chair."

＊ ＊ ＊

On the balcony of the room that had been Louie's, then Louie and Ziggy's, and now Louie and Rose's, a single candle was burning. It was not an elegant taper; it was bug-flecked citronella in a galvanized bucket. Still, it cast a flickering flattering light on the man and the woman who sat at their small table eating Chinese food that had been delivered on a moped.

Comfortable together, they ate mostly in silence. Dinner companions for ten thousand dinners, they knew not only each other's favorite dishes, but each other's favorite bites within the dishes. Rose knew that Louie loved the baby corns, the tickle of the tiny kernels against his gums. Louie knew that Rose enjoyed the crunch of water chestnuts, he picked them out for her and lay them, tiny offerings, on the edge of her plastic plate.

He put his fork down, watched her eat an egg roll, the way her full lips locked securely on the crumbly wrapper before she bit. She watched him gnaw a spare rib, his unswerving method of nibbling one side of the bone, then flipping to the other, saving the knuckly knob of meat for last.

She poured him tea and beamed. He took a sip and glowed.

She blotted her lips on a paper napkin, reached across to put a hand on his. "Louie," she said, "isn't it amazing? We were happy all those years and didn't even know it."

43

"Hungry?" Ziggy said.

It was night and he'd realized he was lonely. His sulk had fallen away at last, and it seemed to leave him skinless, undefended, needy. He'd ordered in a pizza and two bottles of Chianti. Then he'd wandered the grounds of Coral Shores, hoping to find someone to eat and drink with him.

His heart did the leap of the friendless when he spotted Angelina sitting at poolside in a blue sarong, looking up at misted stars. But she said, "I don't feel like eating."

"Sit with me?" he asked.

She didn't say no, and he dragged a little table and a chair up next to her lounge. He opened the pizza box; an insinuating smell of cheese and garlic and oily cardboard wafted up. "Tempted?"

She shook her head.

"Glassa wine?"

"Okay," she said. "A glassa wine."

He poured, his mangled pinky arched away from his other fingers. They clinked. Ziggy smiled. Angelina didn't.

"Hey," he said, "I'm the mopey one, remember?"

Angelina shrugged so that her flipped hair rested briefly on her shoulder, then looked off at the sky. Ziggy started eating pizza, a long string of topping stretched between his fingers and his face. After a moment Angelina said, "I never should've come down here."

Ziggy chewed, sipped some wine. Then he said, "Jeez, and I've just finally decided I'm glad you did."

Angelina didn't look full at him, kept his face on the edge of her vision. "My reasons," she said, "I thought they were pretty simple. Find you. Make love. See what happened."

Ziggy said, "Sounds good to me."

Angelina kept on going. "But it was much more complicated than that. The whole family thing. I see it now. If I'd seen it then, the complications, I never would have come."

Through pizza, Ziggy said, "People, I don't think they ever see how complicated something's gonna be. If they did, nobody'd do nothing."

Angelina finished off her wine, held out her glass for more. "My father," she said. "My poor, loving crook of a father. You gonna make trouble for him again?"

Ziggy stalled, refilled glasses, didn't answer till he'd tossed down some Chianti. "I'm not mad at anyone, Angelina. I want for you to know that. But I'm gonna do what I gotta do."

The rim of her glass was resting on her teeth, it rattled when she spoke. "It's gonna be my fault."

"Nothing's your fault."

She looked off at the stars. The brightest ones throbbed through wisps of cloud, the dimmer ones struggled not to be smothered by warm vapor. "Something weird?" she said at last. "I really thought I had a happy childhood. The greatest parents, all of that. Now I look back . . . Ziggy, d'you think it's possible for a person to be unhappy a lot of years and never even know it?"

Ziggy cocked his head. But before he could frame an answer, she went on.

"Or get everything exactly wrong? Like love. Like imagine something is love when it isn't really love, it's part of that same thing of pretending things are peachy when they aren't, wanting to believe that something's impossibly romantic when maybe it's just impossible?"

That made Ziggy nervous. He said, "Ya turn these things over and over and round and round, I don't see where it gets ya."

Angelina looked away again, was gone what seemed a long, long time, and when she turned back she was smiling. The smile made Ziggy more nervous than before, it seemed to him there was something in it that was moving on, that was leaving him behind. "Ziggy," she said, "I wonder what would happen if we didn't know each other from before, if we just met now, as strangers?"

He looked at her, the ears he knew were ticklish, the neck that would grow pebbly and as moist as steak, and he was tweaked once more by a lust that swam so deep it had scars for eyes. "What would happen," he said, "is that I'd try to get you into bed with me, and you'd say yes or no."

She looked at him, the thick strong hands, the lips she barely recognized. "I'd probably say yes. 'Cause then it would be simple."

"Yeah," said Ziggy. "Then it would be simple."

Muffled by escarole and melons, the guns for Cuba barely rattled as the produce truck proceeded at a legal crawl down I-95.

In south Jersey, the guy who wasn't Italian said, "Burns my ass, the way Funzie talks about spicks."

"You getting paid?" the other guy said.

"That ain't the point."

"That is the point. Shut up."

Two hours later, just outside of Baltimore, the Italian guy said, "I hate the fucking speed limit. Fucking government. Everything they do, I hate it."

The Hispanic guy agreed, but for spite he didn't say so.

At Richmond, three hours farther down the road, there were tolls. The Italian guy picked up his line of thought. "See what I mean? Middle'a fucking nowhere, the fucking government puts in tolls."

The Hispanic guy stayed silent, but some time later, near the Carolina border, he brightened, saw his chance to be the star. "This Mendez," he said, "I speak to him in Spanish. You'll see, he'll treat us good."

* * *

After leaving the garden of Carmen Salazar, Michael took a long walk on nubbly Smathers Beach, then went downtown and stopped off at a dance club, then had a couple beers at a leather bar and watched some guys shoot pool.

Around two A.M. he realized he could stall no longer, he should head off on the second of the errands he'd said he'd do for Ziggy. His stomach milky with nervousness, he hailed a pedicab and went to the motel where Keith McCullough stayed.

As he'd done before, he climbed the outside stairs, their cantilevered steps showing dizzy slices of the parking lot below. He walked along the outside corridor, under dim fixtures splotched with flies and moths, past drawn curtains backlit with the sickly glow of televisions. At length he came to his old lover's door. He knocked before his agitation could catch up with him.

Keith McCullough, on stakeout since breakfast, was fast asleep. But he woke up quickly at the knock. "Who's there?"

"It's Michael. We have to talk."

There was a pause, a clear reluctance, and Michael knew precisely what it was about; it was about the dumper not wanting to be bothered with the heartache and recriminations of the dumped. But after a moment a bedside lamp came on, it glowed weakly through the window. Footsteps padded to the door, and Keith McCullough, his hair mussed and his eyelids heavy, undid the locks and stood there in a towel.

Michael could not help saying, "Hello, David."

McCullough, put upon, slumped his shoulders, said, "Michael, listen, I'm sorry for what happened, but this isn't a good—"

"I'm over it," Michael cut him off. "I'm here on business. Invite me in?"

The agent hesitated, then stood aside. Michael entered. He saw the little .25 revolver on the night table, gleaming softly in the light of the lamp. Shaking his head, he said, "A cop. A cop is really what you are."

McCullough closed the door, sat down heavily in a vinyl chair, snugged the towel across his thighs. "What's the business, Michael? Ziggy?"

Michael sat on the edge of the bed, said, "He wanted me to tell you he hates your guts but he might be ready to deal."

"What's he got on Paul Amaro?"

"The same thing he has on Tommy Lucca."

"Which is what?"

The ambassador looked around the dimly lighted room, the jerky paintings, the crummy carpet. "This is one tacky place you have. How did I ever get excited here?"

"Michael, don't be coy with me."

He toyed with his earrings, looked daggers at McCullough. "Nah, no matter what, let's not be coy."

"What's he got on Paul Amaro?" the agent said again.

Michael was staring at the bedside table. "Can I touch your gun?" he said. "Such a small gun for a cop."

McCullough, wide awake now, said, "Leave the gun alone. This information Ziggy's peddling—"

"You paying in trade this time?"

McCullough squirmed, rearranged his towel. He said, "Michael, don't flirt." But having said it, he wasn't quite sure he meant it. Things were breaking fast now; come what may, his posting to Key West was nearly over. He thought with guilty abashedness about his little house on a discreet cul-de-sac in Fort Lauderdale. The PTA meetings. The toys with plastic wheels in the driveway. His wife in bed with face cream on.

Michael said briskly, "You should get some people here tomorrow. Half a dozen, Ziggy says. Ready for outdoor work. Exact time and place, we'll have to let you know."

McCullough shook his head. "I need details, assurance. What if he's jerking me around?"

"Terrible thing," said Michael. "To jerk someone around."

The agent frowned, fiddled with his towel, felt in his loins the shortness of time and the opportuneness of the hour. "Michael," he said. "Michael. I have my job to do. That doesn't mean I'm not genuinely fond of you."

Angelina's friend smiled at that, seemed to relax, leaned back on his elbows so that his shirt stretched taut across his ripply stomach and his jeans pulled snug along his thighs. Turning green eyes on McCullough, he sweetly said, "Do you even *know* when you're being a conniving scumbag?"

The agent wanted to believe the banter was part of the seduction; he managed an uneasy laugh.

His mouth was still twisted from it as Michael rose and headed for the door. "About tomorrow," he said as he left. "Someone'll be in touch."

44

At Coral Shores, the next day went as slowly as a boat becalmed. Time flattened out like water stained with oil, the sun labored across the sky as if pulling an enormous train behind it.

The rituals of the guest house moved with a deliberateness almost Japanese. Carefully, the breakfast buffet was trundled into place; unhurriedly it was removed again. Men who'd been out very late settled, yawning, onto lounges, finishing up their short night's sleep in sunshine. A few people swam languorous laps; their arms rose and fell in a mesmerizing pattern like a dream of cresting dolphins.

But beneath the uneventful calm, everything was changing for the hostages. For good and for ill, old patterns were crumbling, old habits of the body and the heart seemed quite suddenly archaic.

Uncle Louie no longer got up before the sun. His eyes sprang open early, but now he lingered near his sleeping wife, savored the familiar smells of hair spray and old cigarettes. When he finally arose, it was to bring juice and coffee back to the room. Wife and husband plumped each other's pillows, then talked with the earnestness of newlyweds about what their life together should be like.

For Angelina, too, sitting on her lounge, nibbling mango off its skin, the contours of the universe seemed altered. Ziggy and her family—those were the two fixed points her life had long revolved around. Now she was moving, inch by inch, away from them; the process was as draining as a climb against some multiple of gravity. But did she dare, did she *want*, to break loose into something altogether new, or was she only testing the outermost limits of her orbit, waiting with hope as well as resignation for the moment when the only life she'd ever known would reach the end of its elastic and pull her back?

Through that hot slow day, Ziggy fell again into the outward semblance of a sulk—but what seemed to be old grouchiness was in fact a new kind of concentration. He was painfully aware that he'd never gotten anything exactly right in his life—in either of his lives. He'd done okay on certain things, he'd gotten by. But at every crucial juncture, every moment when he was truly tested, he'd fallen short. He'd blamed it on distraction; or on fatigue; or on lust for Angelina's neck. But it was something else as well: He'd screwed up because he knew that he'd screw up. That knowledge had always been the trigger of his failure, and he spent the day trying to sweat it out, to lose it and the other self-made poisons that went with it.

For Michael, the afternoon was a befuddled meditation on the dangers of the vicarious. He felt like he'd been watching someone else's movie and a giant hand had come out of the screen and grabbed his throat and pulled him in. Cops and robbers. Smuggling and vendettas. Murderous fathers and bisexual Feds. Somewhere along the line, watching had been transfigured into doing, and he couldn't shake the feeling that if he was in this far, he'd be called upon to get in farther still.

He was right. Around four o'clock, Ziggy, speaking for nearly the first time all day, said to him, "Michael, couple more things. Can I ask you to help with a couple more things?"

Michael nodded. He'd been yanked into the screen, he couldn't help but nod.

Ziggy said, "My car, it's on the side street. Underneath the dashboard, taped up, like, there's a gun. Can you bring it here?"

Michael's eyes got wide, he swallowed and his Adam's apple shuttled in his ropy neck. His voice congested, he said, "God Almighty, you're gonna need a gun?"

"No," said Ziggy. "You are."

✳ ✳ ✳

Manny Links had been dubious as ever when Keith McCullough called that morning to ask for reinforcements.

"Lemme make sure I have this straight," the supervisor had said into the phone. "You have Amaro there. You have Lucca. You have Lucca and Amaro together. You have an informant right smack in the middle of Lucca and Amaro. And yet you have no idea what it is that Lucca and Amaro are up to."

Somewhat sheepishly, the undercover man had said, "That's right."

Links's chair squeaked, through the wires came the faint sound of fingers drumming on the desk. "And I'm supposed to send you six men, heavy weapons, infrared, to intercept this activity that you don't know what it is."

"Right again," McCullough said.

"And this course of action," Links went on, his teeth now grinding against his unlit pipe, "was suggested by a source who you acknowledge hates your guts and presumably would take great pleasure in making you look like a horse's ass."

"Probably so," the agent said.

There was a silence. McCullough could picture his boss's eyes flicking here and there around his office, the way they did when he was feeling most beset, like he was scouring the universe for some shred of sense or solace. "Sykes have a hand in this?" the supervisor had asked at last.

"This one," McCullough said, "you can't blame Sykes for this one."

"Oh, I'll know who to blame, Keith. Depend on that . . . Six men you want?"

"A.S.A.P.," McCullough said.

✳ ✳ ✳

It was almost six P.M. when the produce truck arrived at the address in Hialeah.

The place turned out to be an auto shop, up near Opa-Locka airport, that specialized in the dismantling of stolen Lexuses and Jaguars. The Italian guy and the Spanish guy pulled into a vacant bay then watched through road-bleary eyes as a giant red sun went down beneath the muffler and transmission of a half-stripped car that was raised up on a lift.

Carlos Mendez was gracious as he paid the northerners. But he was so excited to get his guns, and so accustomed to hearing Spanish, that he noticed nothing remarkable about the New York mob guy speaking in his native tongue; he didn't even acknowledge it. Crestfallen, the Spanish guy decided he wouldn't say a word the whole way home.

While the weapons were removed from underneath the vegetables and fruits, and repacked in a different truck under iced crates of pompano and conch, Mendez retreated to the chop shop's small office and called Tommy Lucca at his hotel suite in Key West.

"Now that's more fucking like it," Lucca said. He was even more excited about the guns than Mendez was, because to him it wasn't just a piece of business but a victory, a triumph over all the sneaky bastards that were always trying to do him out of what was his. "How long till they roll?"

Mendez parted dusty slats of a Venetian blind and checked on the progress of the loading. "Fifteen, twenty minutes."

"I'm calling that pissant Salazar right now," said Lucca. "He'll get to you with location, timing."

"Fine," said Mendez. He started to hang up, then added, "One thing bothers me. His captain."

"That mongrel with the freckles?" said Lucca.

"Johnny Castro," Carlos Mendez said. "It's just not a lucky name."

✳ ✳ ✳

Lucca called Salazar, and Salazar set the details of the rendez-vous.

Ten-thirty, at a place that had once been called Sand Key Marina. You took an unmarked right just past mile-marker twelve; drove five or seven minutes down an unpaved road half closed in by mangroves. Where the road ended there was a cement block building overgrown with vines, some rusted gas tanks on the water side. The boat would be there, tied up at the end of a dock half-fallen in the ocean.

Lucca said he understood, he had it. He told Salazar to contact Mendez. He himself called Paul Amaro, still holed up at the Flagler House.

It was a terse unfriendly call. "You tried your best to fuck it up, Paul, but you couldn't," Lucca said. "Be there at ten-thirty. You've done dick t'earn it, but you'll get your other hundred and a quarter."

Salazar, meanwhile, gave directions to Mendez, assured him that the unpaved pitted road looked like it couldn't possibly be the right road, but it was.

Then he hung up the phone, stared off at his violated garden, and absently rubbed duct-tape scum from the metal tubing of his chair. He wondered what it would be like to change careers, to segue out of crime, with its uncertainties, its maniacal colleagues, its double crosses. He took a deep breath, called up Coral Shores, got Ziggy on the line.

"Good luck, Bigtime," he said to his old errand boy after he'd conveyed the forbidden information. "Just leave me fuckin' out of it."

"Word of honor," Ziggy said.

Carmen said, "Fuck you, word of honor."

Then Ziggy called up Keith McCullough and the circuit was complete.

45

At nine P.M. the moon was going from egg yolk yellow to egg-shell white as it topped Key West's metal roofs and put a silver sheen on the limp fronds of the palms at Coral Shores. It was bright enough so that the gingerbread on balconies threw shadows, and pool water glinted blue and viscous with every random ripple.

But the hostages were hiding from the light. They huddled in the dimness of the overhang next to the room that Michael shared with Ziggy. They sat on low chairs that made them hunch; their backs defined a snug circle that blocked outsiders' eyes. They spoke in soft and furtive voices.

Ziggy was saying, "Okay people, here's the night it either works out or it doesn't."

Louie was sitting hip to hip with Rose. He ran a hand over his head, raked a few bundles of sparse and stringy hair. He said, "I'd feel better, I knew more what you had in mind."

Ziggy said, "The details, they wouldn't do you any good to know." Saying it, he felt odd, like he was faking, just mouthing things he'd heard other leaders say. He'd never been in

charge before. There was an excitement in it that he could not
deny, but also a burden, a dull weight between his shoulder
blades; he didn't think the one was worth the other.

After a pause he said, "A little while from now, there's
somewhere that I gotta be. If I'm there, that means Paulie can't
be there. That's all you really have to know."

He glanced left and right behind himself, then reached beneath his shirt flaps, into the waistband of his pants, and came
out with the gun that Michael had brought him. The weapon
somehow drew a moonbeam that made it glow obscenely, made
it stand out from everything around it and seem to leave a phos-
phorescent track as it moved in Ziggy's palm.

It moved inexorably toward Michael, and when it was in
front of him Ziggy said, "What you gotta do for me, Michael, you
gotta keep him in his room."

Michael didn't answer, he was staring at the gun. His green
eyes had gotten very big and it seemed they could neither blink
nor move away.

"Can you do that for me?" Ziggy coaxed.

Michael licked his lips, gave a very small nod, but at that
moment Uncle Louie said, "Now wait a second, that's not fair."

Ziggy said nothing, just lifted up an eyebrow.

"It's not his problem," Louie said, "It's not his family."

Across the courtyard, the Jacuzzi switched on. There was
the sudden whine of the compressor, the faint hiss of exploding
bubbles. Ziggy considered, then moved the gun in the flat of his
hand like he was passing hors d'oeuvres around the table. He
said to Louie, "So *you* wanna go?"

Louie stammered, but only for an instant. Then he said,
"The poor guy just got outa jail. We're supposed to help you
send him back again?"

"Did I say I'm sending him back again?" asked Ziggy.

"You didn't say you weren't," Angelina said.

"All you said," Rose added, "you said you didn't want him

where you were. And let's face it, that's 'cause you're scared of him."

With his free hand Ziggy pulled down hard on his synthetic face. "I'm scared of 'im. Sure I am. We're *all* scared of 'im. Why the hell else are we sitting here like goddam refugees?"

No one answered that and after a moment he went on. "Look, I've known this family a lotta years—"

"An' ya wanna be honest," Uncle Louie interrupted, "it hasn't been the happiest association."

"Ya wanna be honest," added Rose, "you've been a fink."

The word stung; Ziggy felt a futile impulse to argue it away. Instead he said, "You don't trust me. Fine. You think I'm trying to save my own sorry ass. You're right. But one thing's for sure. Paulie shows up where I'm goin', he's headed right back to the slammer."

Louie said, "And if he doesn't show up, you could whaddyacallit, implicate him anyway."

Ziggy said, "That's absolutely true. I could. Nothing would be easier . . . Now, is someone gonna take the goddam gun and keep him in his room or do I carry it along for self-defense when he tries to murder me in front of half the cops in Florida?"

There was a pause. Streetlamps hummed. Toads answered one another's rumblings from shrub to shrub.

Uncle Louie looked down at his shoes, saw instead the road signs that had hovered over him on the morning that his steering wheel had turned itself and sent him careening toward Key West to be a hero. "Okay," he said at last. "Me, I'll go."

His hand started moving toward the offered weapon, but his wife's forearm came down like a board and clamped him at the wrist. "Like hell you will."

"Rose, someone's gotta—"

"Your brother's a violent lunatic."

"What's to be violent? I'm saving him from—"

Rose said, "He won't know that. Why should he believe it?"

"Excellent point," conceded Ziggy. "Maybe he won't."

"You see?" said Rose. "You see? He'll get crazy, Louie."

"I'll explain to him, I'll make him see—"

"Understand," said Ziggy, "you'll be standing between him and a payday. And one other thing—his paranoid nutcase of a partner is gonna be extremely pissed if he doesn't show."

"You see?" said Rose. "You see? No matter what, he's gonna wanna go."

Louie felt his courage leaking away, he clamped his throat to hold some in; his voice got very pinched. "Alla more reason—"

"Louie, I didn't track you down just so you could—"

She was silenced not by a word but a gesture.

Angelina had been sitting very still, seeming to fold within herself, her expression blank, her gaze turned downward. Now her hand came up slowly, resolutely. It came up before she raised her eyes and before she spoke. At last she said, "I'll go. It's my place to go."

Ziggy chewed his lip before he answered. "Angelina, I don't think—"

"He's my father," she said. "I'm the one should face him."

"But—"

"Ziggy," she said, "if you trust your plan, if you trust yourself, give me the gun."

He looked at the ground, sucked hard at an elusive breath, then very gently placed the pistol in Angelina's outstretched palm. As he did so, his fingertips raked lightly over hers. It was the first time that they'd touched in days.

Six Federal agents, dispatched amid misgivings from North Miami, had driven down the Keys in two bland cars. They'd passed the afternoon at the cheap motel where Keith McCullough stayed, and at dusk they dressed in camouflage fatigues.

They blackened their faces with shoe polish and headed for the ambush site near mile-marker twelve.

Off the highway, they drove along an unpaved and slowly disappearing road that wound among encroaching mangroves. Panicked lizards scuttled across the headlight beams that rocked crazily as the vehicles bounced through potholes filled with fetid water. Twigs poked out from both sides of the path, wasps' and hornets' nests hung on them like Chinese lanterns.

Where the road was finally smothered, just before a ruined building blanketed in vines, the agents got out of the cars. They unloaded floodlights and rifles with infrared scopes. Then two men drove the vehicles back to the highway, and the others took some time to orient themselves.

The clearing had been a going business once. It featured corroded gas tanks caked in guano, some shreds of awning still stuck on random sections of rusted frame, a dock warped and crumpled like a mangled xylophone. The whole sad enterprise was subsiding now, being patiently reclaimed by shifting waters and the obstinate progress of the mangroves.

Looking for good sight lines, for nests where they could hide and shoot, the agents plodded over coral rocks and tented roots, splashed through puddles and dragged their feet through traps of muck along that uncanny edge of Florida that was neither land nor sea. They took up positions in a spacious ring around the old marina's pier. The moon got higher, rained milk down on the unmoving water of the inlet.

They waited. It was still but not quiet. Mosquitoes found them, buzzed in greedy swarms around their eyes and ears. Spiders dropped from waxy leaves, then rode their own threads home again. Frogs croaked, confused by human legs pegged in the ground like pilings where no pilings were before. The air smelled of anchovies and rotted seaweed and iodine.

After a time a boat was heard. Its engine noise was at first a low and steady groan, barely distinct from the seldom-noticed murmur of the surfless ocean. But then the sound resolved into the steady beat of pistons, cylinders popping one by one as the craft crawled, unseen, through the winding, unmarked channel.

When it hove into view around the last barrier islet, Terry Sykes whispered to Keith McCullough, "Hot damn, first guest at the party."

McCullough kept his eyes on the water as Captain Johnny Castro expertly idled toward the dock. He said softly, "Lucca and Amaro, Terry. You're gonna get a citation, you know that? Frame and everything, hang it right up in your den."

Sykes said nothing, but McCullough felt him smiling, felt the moonlit whiteness of his goofy teeth between his blackened moustache and his painted chin.

46

Paul Amaro was getting ready—standing in front of the mirror, brushing back his silver hair and trying to summon up the old square and cocksure set of his jaw—when the knock came at the door.

It was a soft knock, not quite timid, but polite. It was probably the housekeeper; it was nothing to worry about. But Paul Amaro worried. He had reached that state of gloom and disillusion where dread bypassed the brain and burrowed directly into the pit of the stomach. It had become impossible for him to imagine that anything that happened could be good, and if nothing happened, that was bleak as well.

He put down his hairbrush, made one last try at firming his expression. He took a half-step toward the door, wondered if he should speak before looking through the peephole, decided what the hell. In a weary growl he said, "Who is it?"

"It's Angelina."

He heard it clearly but he didn't quite believe he had. His footsteps stalled a moment; a readiness to cry sprang up behind his eyes. Somewhere in his gut, hope was crawling like a crushed bug that would not stay dead, that roused itself for one more wingless and pathetic stab at getting off the floor. His daughter was okay. She was coming back to him. They would be reconciled.

He lunged toward the door, he was winded by the time he got there; blood was singing in his ears. He undid the locks, pulled the portal open. He saw her, his daughter. She was unharmed; unchanged. Her forehead, in spite of everything, was still unfurrowed, placid, blameless. Her violet eyes were clear and deep, the eyes he loved coming home to see.

He said her name. Some bashfulness or guilt took hold of him, he found he couldn't step toward her, but only leaned across the threshold to embrace her. She let herself be leaned toward, although her father seemed suddenly a stranger. She felt his cheek against her hair.

Then she fell back half a step. Paul Amaro grew very confused. He saw her hand in her purse, he saw it come out with a gun.

"Pop," she said, "I'm really sorry. You have to step back now. You have to step way back into the room."

✳ ✳ ✳

Feeling for the moment safe, feeling unaccountably on top of things and confident, Ziggy didn't notice the pink taxi that followed his hulking Oldsmobile as it slowly plied the streets of Old Town. He didn't see it stop half a block away when he parked in front of the candy store on Bertha Street.

He climbed the cracked step, strode past the filthy fan, the torn seats leaking sisal, the fat silent man behind the counter.

He was halfway through the door frame at the back when his progress was arrested by a turnstile of an arm that slammed across his chest then clawed into his shoulder. In the next instant the muzzle of a gun was pressed against the hollow just behind

his ear. He didn't go limp, exactly; he went extremely coopera-
tive.

He was walked through the vines to where Carmen Salazar
was sitting in his lawn chair, rubbing his chin so feverishly that
the sound of beard mingled with the crickets and the rasping
leaves. Standing before his sometime boss, Ziggy managed to
say, "Carmen, what the fuck?"

Carmen didn't answer right away. The thug who held the
gun on Ziggy pressed it in a little harder; the muzzle found a
nest among the sinews. "Ziggy," said Salazar at last. "I have a
question for you. You ever been afraid of me?"

Ziggy wondered if there was a right and a wrong answer to
this. Being unsure, he told the truth. "No," he said. "Not really."

"I thought this might be a good time for you to start."

"But, Carmen, hey, we're onna same side—"

"This is where you're wrong," said Salazar. "This is why
we're having this discussion, to impress upon you that we're not
on the same side."

"But we talked all this—"

"I don't wanna be on your side, Ziggy. Your side's always
afraid. Always hiding."

"Carmen, look, I said I'd leave you out of it, I gave my
word."

"Your word means shit," said Salazar. "And leaving me out
of it isn't nearly good enough. This is why my colleague here is
poised to blow your head off."

A shaft of moonlight filtered through the foliage, seemed
to pour from leaf to leaf. Ziggy said, "But—"

"Listen, Bigtime. Listen hard. You're gonna rat me out with
the others. Got that?"

Ziggy tried to lean away from the pressure of the muzzle;
the pressure followed him. "I'm not sure I do," he admitted.

"We'll go through it nice and slow," said Salazar. "I'm telling you to rat me out. Turn me in. Sing. Make sure everybody

knows it. But only on the gun deal. Nothing else. You understand?"

Ziggy blinked. It was a confusing world. Some guys would kill you if you squealed on them, some guys would kill you if you didn't. "Okay, Carmen, sure, " he said. "Any way you want it."

"I want it that I don't end up like you," said Salazar. "I want it that I keep the face I have. I want it that I can stay in my town and not wet my pants whenever a stranger walks into the room. You see? Now let's go get this over with."

They left the garden together, climbed into Ziggy's car. Uncle Louie, now the shepherd of his sundered family's interests and its tremulous defender against betrayal, told the driver of the pink cab to follow, not too close behind.

✳ ✳ ✳

Carlos Mendez didn't like the smell of fish, and even with the windows open wide he was queasy in the seafood truck.

On the long ride down the Keys, he hadn't watched the moonlit pelicans that swooped from bridge to bridge, hadn't noticed channel buoys leaning in the current like palms bent back by heavy wind. He'd only watched the mile markers tick past, and it had seemed a long time between one marker and the next.

He was relieved to see Tommy Lucca's limo parked at the appointed place, the little semicircle before the mock-important gate that closed off Shark Key from the highway.

But as soon as he'd stepped down from the truck and slid into the backseat next to the Miami mobster, he could see that Lucca wasn't right. His pupils were opening and closing, his hand kept plucking at his collar, his tongue was too busy in his mouth, looking for a place to rest. He started saying something emphatic but impossible to follow about swamps and bugs and real estate swindles, and Mendez thought, What a stupid time to get hopped up.

The car and the truck eased back onto the highway to drive the last few miles. There had been vehicles parked all up and down the Keys—people fishing, drinking, groping under steering wheels; no one paid particular attention to the two dark sedans stopped on a bridge a few hundred yards north of mile-marker twelve.

Just past the agents, Lucca's driver slowed, threw his high beams at oncoming traffic, until at length he found the break in the low canopy of mangroves that gave onto the unpaved road. He turned hard, skidded briefly on the gravel shoulder. The truck with its payload of fish and weapons clattered behind, its boxy trailer leaning.

The car bounced and squeaked through puddles and ooze and a sulfurous stink, and Carlos Mendez wasn't feeling well at all. He held the strap above his window and tried to keep his gorge down. Lucca seemed not at all bothered by the battering, the jerks; in fact he seemed to like them. He gave forth little yips, like he was at a carnival or imagining that he was riding on a horse.

Mendez ignored the giddy and demented sounds; with his free hand he calmly rolled and unrolled the Panama hat that was cradled on his lap. But when Lucca actually spoke, Mendez turned to face him, saw that he had pulled a pistol from his jacket and was slapping it lightly against his leg. "That has-been fuck," he said. "He's done nothing on this deal. Nothing but stall and fuck things up and try to screw me. Am I right?"

The car was pitching like a storm-tossed ship. Lucca's finger was toying with the trigger, he was a mass of tics and twitches, his synapses were firing at random. Carlos Mendez thought it politic to offer no opinion.

It made no difference to Lucca, he paused an instant then rolled along. "And I'm supposed to share the payday with this fuck? Balls to that. I'll show 'im."

The car bounced, Lucca's neck swayed like that of a spaniel on a spring, his spastic finger was wrapped around the trigger. "The guns get loaded," he said, "I'm gonna kill that has-been fuck. Leave 'im right there in the slime. You give a shit?"

The deliberate Mendez tried to frame a tactful answer.

Lucca saved him the trouble. "I don't care you give a shit or not. I just thought you oughta know."

He raised the pistol, aimed for practice at the back of his driver's head, narrowed down his eyes and made a popping sound with his dry and twitching lips.

47

"Sal Martucci," said Paul Amaro.

He was sitting on the bed, maybe twelve feet from the door. His knees were wide apart, his elbows rested on them. His head hung down between his shoulders, and he was shaking it, but he did not seem angry at that moment, more bemused, bewildered, like a beaten fighter who's the last person in the stadium to realize that he's lost. "The bitch of it?" he resumed. "I think, deep down, I knew it all along."

"Deep down," said Angelina. She'd pulled a chair over, right next to the door. The gun was in her lap, her right hand absently rested over it. "Where no one ever looks if they can possibly avoid it."

Her father said, "But what he did to me, Angelina. My world, that's the absolute worst thing a person can do."

Angelina said, "There's other worlds, Pop. I guess there's a worst thing you can do in each of them."

"And still you trust him," Paul Amaro said. "More than you trust me."

She didn't answer that. She didn't know how to. How did you compare smithereens with smithereens?

There was a silence. A near silence, marred by the buzz a building makes, air sliding through ducts, wires humming in conduits.

Then Paul Amaro said, "Whatever I did, Angelina, I tried to do the best for you."

Even to himself it sounded lame, and no less because it happened to be true. But it was what every parent felt when looking at his child and seeing the wounds, the disappointment; when looking at the world and knowing that one had done nothing to make it any less unkind, any less fickle or grudging in its comforts. Paul Amaro looked at his daughter and understood that for every pain he thought he'd spared her, another had been heedlessly inflicted; for every opportunity he'd yearned to give her, some other path had been closed off. Suddenly he felt very very sorry. Not for her, exactly. Not for himself. Not even for anything he'd done. Just sorry, like regret was taking him over the way spores and lichen take over the fibers of a tree that's dying from the inside out.

He tried to smile. It came out wrong—tormented, cloying. He said, "I have this stupid daydream. I had it every day in prison. That I'd come home and things'd be like they used to. You'd meet me at the door, we'd hug. We'd go for rides, remember? Restaurants, parties, everybody'd make a fuss over you, blue dress, you were so pretty."

Angelina said, "Like I'd be ten years old forever . . . And never know my father was a criminal."

He said, "You hate me that much?"

She said, "I don't want to. I don't know."

He said, "Sal Martucci, he's not a criminal?"

"He's trying not to be. Besides, where I come from—who else understands?"

Her father said, "So now you found 'im, now you're gonna be with 'im?"

Instead of answering, she said, "He hasn't asked me."

Paul Amaro nodded, almost calmly. But with every labored heartbeat, calm regret was losing ground to sorrowful fury, to reckless desperation. If he'd truly lost his daughter, if he'd repulsed forever the one person who really mattered to him, then he had to cling to something else, to business, or danger, or oblivion, or revenge. In a moment his expression hardened, the jaw clenched, there was a tightness at the corners of his eyes. He said, "I'm going to that meeting now."

Angelina wasn't ready for the sudden change of subject, didn't answer.

Blood was roaring in Paul Amaro's ears, there was a searing glare at the edges of his vision. He said, "A bust. That's crap. You don't understand nothing, Angelina."

She'd almost forgotten the gun was in her lap. She remembered now, her fingers clenched around it.

Her father went on with a defiant rage he half-knew was aimed at self-destruction. "Sal Martucci's with Lucca now. I see it. They're tryin' to cut me out, put me inna wrong."

"That's not what it's—"

"Enough! I'm late already."

"We're staying here."

"Don't try to stop me, Angelina."

He stood up very fast, an invisible but heavy wake of air spread out around him.

The gun was in Angelina's lap and the door was at her back and she barely had time to swallow as she watched him rise. She measured the distance between them with her eyes, and wondered exactly how much time she had, and exactly how much nerve.

✷ ✷ ✷

Lucca's limo and the seafood truck arrived first.

Mendez and Lucca stepped out into the clearing, next to the abandoned marina building that was being swallowed up in vines. Lucca took a leak in a shallow puddle ringed by mangrove roots.

His hand was still on his zipper when Ziggy's rusted Oldsmobile came hulking down the road, its pitted paint and faulty muffler at one with the general decay. He parked. With the engines all turned off, the place seemed very quiet for a moment but then grew loud with the noises of frogs and locusts, the burble of doves and the peeps of warblers.

On the edges of the clearing, the Feds in camouflage hunkered lower in the muck, pulled in cautious breaths, steadied weapons at their sides.

Ziggy and Carmen Salazar got out of the car. Tommy Lucca stared at them, counted them, and the first thing he said was, "Fuck's Amaro?"

Eyes flicked around the clearing, like maybe the New York mobster was lurking in the shadows. People looked back up the road but there was no other vehicle approaching. Mendez glanced at his watch, then at Salazar. Salazar looked at Ziggy. Ziggy blinked and shrugged.

Lucca's eyes were pulsing. He said, "The cunt don't even show? We're supposed to pay 'im and the cunt don't even show?"

Ziggy said, "He mighta missed the turnoff. Pretty easy turn to miss."

"Didn't stop nobody else from finding it," said Lucca.

Johnny Castro had strolled over from his boat, his odd freckles big dark ovals in the moonlight. He didn't care about the differences among the men on land. He cared about conditions for the crossing to Havana. He said, "Come on, we gotta load. We fuck around, it's daylight before I make the harbor."

Pacing among the mangrove roots, Lucca spluttered, "But the fucker said he'd be here."

As soothingly as he could manage, Carlos Mendez said, "We don't need him here, Tommy."

Lucca paced until he found a victory in this. "Fuckin' A, we don't," he said. "Isn't 'iss what I been sayin' all along?"

They started transferring the crates of guns.

The driver of the seafood truck dragged them to the edge of the trailer. He shook off watery ice that had slipped down from the pompano and conch, and handed the boxes to Ziggy, who carried them as far as he dared along the rotting pier, then hefted them over the gunwale to Castro, who stashed them in the hold.

On U.S. 1, the agents in charge of the dark sedans counted off ten minutes, then started driving very slowly down the unpaved road, blocking off escape.

Keith McCullough watched as the crates of guns moved steadily past in the moonlight. He, too, was wondering where Paul Amaro was, why the group was incomplete. But he was running low on time. Boards creaked on the dock. The truck emptied and the boat filled; it rocked just slightly with Johnny Castro's movements, water lapped against its sides. McCullough understood that if he wanted the full symmetry of the smuggling—guns moving, guns in smugglers' arms, the bosses gazing on—he had to grab it now.

He hesitated. He wanted Paul Amaro. Amaro was target number one. But finally he filled his lungs, screamed out above the frogs and the birds and the bugs, "Freeze, assholes!"

In the next instant the floodlights came on, called forth from the night a crisply etched tableau of guilt and shock. Johnny Castro ducked by reflex into the cockpit of his craft. Carlos Mendez wheeled, cringed, sought anonymity behind the halo of his hat. Ziggy made a point of dropping a crate of guns, they bounced off the dock's edge and spanked through the skin of the water.

McCullough's voice rang out again. "Hands way up in the air."

Everybody's hands went up but Tommy Lucca's.

Lucca, heroically paranoid, obsessed more with betrayal than with life itself, lashed out at the darkness. "Amaro!" he screamed. He made it sound obscene, a curse that coated the night like oil stains water. "Where the fuck's Amaro? Cocksucker ratted us out."

"Hands up in the air," McCullough yelled again.

"Fuck you," said Tommy Lucca, and though he was blinded by the floodlights, had no chance of seeing his tormentors, he pulled his pistol from his pocket, insanely confident that in a world filled with enemies, a bullet anywhere would find one.

Terry Sykes, not a bright fellow but a fine marksman, was sighting on the mobster's chest.

Maybe Lucca meant to fire, maybe his hopped-up finger twitched around the trigger. His bullet whined and scratched through mangrove leaves and lodged somewhere in mud.

Sykes, with the unhurry of the practiced, squinted down, held his breath, and shot the mobster through the heart. The frogs fell briefly silent as the dead man stumbled back a step, then paused, as though to reconsider, to call for time, a replay. At last he pitched forward, facedown in the marl at that undramatic edge of Florida that was not quite land and not quite sea.

48

The others sleepwalked into custody, bleakly stoic at the demise of Lucca, unsurprised in the face of getting caught.

When they'd been patted down and handcuffed and herded into a small tight group against the ruined building with its grasping vines, Keith McCullough took Ziggy aside into a shadowy knot of mangrove and said, "So where the hell's Amaro?"

Ziggy said, "Who?"

"Don't be cute with me. I don't find it cute."

Ziggy stared at the agent's blackened face, his eyes that seemed yellow and bulging in the moonlight. "I don't find your makeup cute."

McCullough swatted at bugs, said, "Where the hell is he, Ziggy? We have a deal, remember?"

"Fuck you, G.I. Joe. You got Tommy Lucca dead. Be content with that."

Air whistled through Keith McCullough's teeth, he kicked at a coral rock with the toe of a boot that fine, gray mud was drying on. He said, "Don't be an asshole, Ziggy. With you or without you, I'm pulling Paul Amaro into this."

"Lotsa luck."

"Salazar'll turn."

"Wrong."

"We'll trace the guns."

"Fat chance you'll trace the guns."

"We have the truck."

"The truck's from Hialeah. Face it, Jolson, you got nothing on Amaro. Nothing."

McCullough turned away, watched moonlight gobbled up by foliage, nibbled leaf by leaf till there was nothing left but shadow. Hands on hips, he wheeled slowly back around, said, "Ziggy, don't overplay your hand. You were carrying the guns. You were handing them aboard. Lucca's dead. Who else you got to trade away?"

Ziggy listened to frogs and bugs, thought that over. Then he said, "Jeez, you caught me touching guns? Now you got me very scared. Paul Amaro, okay, you might try his hotel room."

"Hotel room?" said McCullough. "But he's supposed to be—"

"You *thought* he was supposed to be. You were mistaken."

"If you're jerking me around—"

McCullough broke off because the dark sedans were coming down the road, headlights crazily rocked and panned across the clearing. The cars stopped. An agent sprang out of one. He ran over to where Keith McCullough stood and said in a breathless whisper, "We got 'im."

"Got who?" McCullough said.

"Amaro," said the agent. "He's in the other car."

McCullough looked at Ziggy. "Hotel room, huh?"

The agent said, "We found him walking, running really, up the road."

McCullough said, "You weren't gonna cooperate, Ziggy, you shouldn't have handled the merch. That was a mistake."

"He was really winded," said the agent. "Really pushing. A man late for an appointment."

McCullough said, "Bring him over here." He smirked at Ziggy. Ziggy tried to smirk back but he couldn't. He was scared. Scared for Angelina. He'd given her a gun. The gun was supposed to keep Paul Amaro away. Bad things sometimes happened when guns were brandished by people who weren't prepared to use them.

A moment passed. Doves mumbled, mosquitos darted in and out of moonlight.

A handcuffed man was led through the shadow of the mangroves. It was Uncle Louie.

Keith McCullough said, "That's not Paul Amaro."

The agent looked confused. "We I.D.'d 'im, everything. Amaro."

McCullough looked disgusted. He said to Louie, "Fuck you doing here?"

Uncle Louie didn't answer right away. His thin hair was plastered down with sweat. He was a little bitten up and nervous but also sort of proud. He'd never been handcuffed before. He'd never been interrogated. He glanced at Ziggy. Then he said, "Just out for a walk."

Ziggy smirked.

McCullough grimaced. He said, "Where's your brother?"

Louie thought a moment, then said, "My brother Joe? Or my brother Al?"

McCullough pawed the ground, pulled in a deep, damp breath of air that smelled of rot and sulfur.

Ziggy said, "If you mean Paul, I told you, Buckwheat, he's in his room."

"I'm gonna bring him in," McCullough said.

"Bring him in for what?" said Louie. "Staying in his room?"

"For questioning. Suspicion."

"Questioning," said Ziggy. "Suspicion. That's just perfect."

"Perfect?" said McCullough.

"You'll keep 'im just long enough for me to propose to his daughter."

* * *

When they had a moment alone, Ziggy whispered to Louie, "What the hell were you doing walking down that road?"

"The cabbie," Uncle Louie said, "he wouldn't bring me off the highway. God knows what he thought I had in mind."

"Yeah, yeah," said Ziggy. "But why were you out there in the first place?"

Louie didn't answer, he chewed his lower lip.

"Didn't trust me, did you?" Ziggy said.

"Family's family."

"And if I'd gone against your brother—what?"

Louie shrugged. He didn't know what would have happened or what he would have done. "I just felt I oughta be there."

Ziggy shook his head. "Louie, you're a piece a work."

Angelina's uncle smiled inwardly, took it as a compliment. Which it was. The kind of thing that people only said to someone that they'd really noticed, to someone whose being there, or not, made a difference in the world.

* * *

Later, as the sinking moon was going from yellow to orange and painting a russet stripe across the flat waters of the Florida Straits, Ziggy and Angelina walked without touching along the trucked-in sand that imperfectly covered the nubbly rock of Smathers Beach. There were no waves; the ocean made the softest hiss as a line of foam, thinner than the head on beer, dissolved between the stones.

Ziggy was shaking his head, impressed, amused. He said, "You bowled him over?"

"I didn't plan it," Angelina said. "Didn't have time. He stood up very fast. But then there was a hesitation, he sort of swayed, his eyes went out of focus."

"Like faint?" said Ziggy.

"Light-headed, whatever. Blood pressure. Arms just hanging."

"So you decided—"

"I didn't decide," she corrected. "I just found myself springing toward him, shoulder down."

They walked, coral pieces crunched under their feet. Ziggy said, "And the gun?"

"I guess I just dropped it, found it later underneath the bed. I hated having it, it felt disgusting in my lap."

"So you hit him with your shoulder—"

"Shoulder, head, everything," said Angelina. "Hard as I could. His hands never came up. He fell back across the bed. I landed on top of him, bounced off, and then I got really terrified."

"That he'd hurt you?"

"That I hurt him. He didn't move. His eyes were closed. I thought . . . I didn't know what to think. Stroke? Heart attack? An awful idea grabbed hold of me: What if he died and the last thing he carried into death was this feeling that I hated him? It made me start to cry. From one second to the next I was crying like I haven't cried in years and years. I touched his hair, his face. I thought, all growing up I had this lie, he was the greatest daddy in the world, he was perfect, and nothing got around that lie, I couldn't see anything wrong with him. Then when I saw it I got so mad that I couldn't see he was still my father, couldn't see I loved him anyway. Now finally I felt it all at once, all sides of it together."

Ziggy said, "And then he came around?"

Angelina nodded, soft red moonlight played across her skin as her face turned up then down. "Was only out a few seconds, I guess. Maybe fainted. Maybe I just knocked the wind out. I was stroking his cheek and his eyes popped open."

"He try to leave again?"

"No," said Angelina. "The fight was out of him. Out of both of us, I guess. Call it a draw. We just sat and talked and cried until the cops showed up."

Ziggy was silent, respectful of a daughter talking alone with her father. They walked, felt the peaceful heaviness of footsteps over sand, the odd relief of knowing you could not go very fast or very far. Then he said, "The cops, there's nothing they can do to him this time."

"Thank you for that," said Angelina.

There was nothing pointed in the way she said it but the words made Ziggy wince, the eyebrows pulled together along his remade forehead. He said, "Jesus, don't thank me."

She said nothing. The russet line of moonlight on the water tracked them as they strolled.

He went on, "There's something I have to tell you, Angelina, I've never come right out and said it. What happened with me and your father, what I did, I've always been ashamed of it."

Looking down at softly gleaming sand she said, "My father did bad things. He got punished for them. They call that justice, right?"

"Yeah, but what I did, it wasn't about justice, it wasn't about believing in the law or any crap like that. I just tried to make things easy for myself."

She didn't answer, just watched her feet churn through the beach.

"And the fear," he said, "the looking over your shoulder all the time—it's not only fear of the guy you sent away. It's shame. That's what keeps your skin feeling wrong, makes your face seem unfamiliar. Shame."

They walked. A south breeze carried smells of iodine and spice; on the land side palm fronds rustled dryly, the sound was like maracas. Angelina said, "I'm glad you told me that. You feel better, telling me?"

Ziggy's hand came up against his chest, he rubbed himself like he was checking for wounds. "Yeah," he said, sounding a little bit surprised. "I do."

The moon slouched toward the horizon, its orange color dimmed and warped toward powdery pink, a gentle, used-up shade. They walked, their footsteps crunched. Their legs were weary as the moon but they kept on walking, they were on their way to some end or some beginning and it seemed they couldn't stop until they'd reached it. Ziggy said, "What we've been through, you and me, it's been pretty crazy."

Angelina crossed her arms against her midriff, squeezed herself a little. She remembered kissing Sal Martucci in the shadows in her father's hallways, his fingers putting goose bumps on her neck. She thought about the fallow years, years she'd mostly believed were exalted by their dedication to a secret passion. "Yeah," she said, "it has been pretty crazy."

"I was thinking," Ziggy said, "that maybe the crazy part is over."

Angelina feared to answer that, just walked and watched the pocked face of the slipping moon. Ziggy reached out, took her hand, tried to stop her walking. She left her hand in his but pulled him onward, something was preventing her from standing still.

Ziggy tagged along, a little flustered. He was ready to propose, and it seemed odd to be proposing on the march, and it did not occur to him that Angelina knew that too, and maybe she was walking to fend off the long-awaited question. He kicked a rock. He cleared his throat. He said, "Angelina, I was wondering if you'd marry me."

For all the preparation, the ten years' biding time, the question seemed abrupt, the moment clipped. It had to, being one of those divides that neatly severs history into before and after. Angelina didn't answer right away. She plodded on, looking at the moon. It was a hand's breadth above the water, it stained the ocean underneath it. At last she said, "Why?"

"Why?"

"Yeah, why? Ziggy, more and more I see we hardly know each other."

"We've known each other all our lives."

"No," she said, "we haven't. What do you know about me, Ziggy?"

He struggled not to lose heart in the unaccustomed effort to explain himself. "I know you're beautiful," he said. "I know you waited for me."

"You could be the last man in America to marry a virgin."

"Angelina, please, I'm tryin' to be romantic . . . Besides, I waited for you too."

She said, "That's a good one."

"In my way I did. I didn't fall for any—"

"It doesn't matter," Angelina interrupted. "But Ziggy, doesn't it feel, I don't know, like kid stuff, like something from a life that's finished now?"

He looked off at the ocean. Everybody wrestled with the same few questions in life, but people asked them at different times in different ways; kept asking them even after they'd been answered; and Ziggy vaguely realized that he and Angelina had gradually swapped positions on almost everything. He asked her. "How many lives you think you got?"

"More than I've lived so far," she said.

They walked. The moon sank toward the water, in its final moments it changed from something that was falling to something that was melting, its contours going soft and edgeless as its red reflection climbed up off the sea to join it.

Ziggy said, "Those other lives, maybe we could live them together."

Angelina stopped at last. Without the steady crunch and squeak of footsteps the world seemed very quiet. She looked at him, at the black eyes she remembered, in the changed face that by now challenged memory as the true face.

She said, "I don't think so, Ziggy. It's what I've wanted for the longest time, but I don't think so."

The last red rays fell across her cheek, her neck. Ziggy said, "So now I have to wait for you?"

"You said you were waiting before. In your way."

"But then I didn't know it."

She managed half a smile, said, "Waiting isn't that much fun."

The moon touched the horizon, seemed to balance there a moment, then began to slide into the ocean, serene and stately as a queen entering her bath.

Angelina watched it being slowly swallowed up, said, "One fantasy, Ziggy? One fantasy at least? Hold me till the moon is gone."

He reached across the tiny swath of beach between them and took her in his arms, they stood like lovers until the moon was covered up in ocean, and the stars got bluer as the red gleam was extinguished and the russet arrow on the water disappeared. Then she walked away from him, her footsteps crunching on the coral underneath the sand.

EPILOGUE

Ziggy was right about the cops and Paul Amaro.

The guns could not be traced. The seafood truck led back no farther than Tommy Lucca's chop shop. Neither Carmen Salazar nor Johnny Castro nor Carlos Mendez chose to say a word that would implicate the mobster from New York. It took one phone call from his lawyer to get him released.

As for the other would-be smugglers, they followed Carlos Mendez's lead and played the Cuba card; the U.S. government chose to regard them not as common criminals but misguided patriots. In quiet plea bargains, Johnny Castro agreed to the forfeiture of his boat and six months minimum security; Carlos Mendez paid a fifty-thousand-dollar fine and received a two-year sentence, suspended in light of his standing in the Miami charitable community.

Carmen Salazar, who was, after all, only a middle man, got off with three years' probation, a settlement he cheerfully accepted, once he'd bargained for wording that would allow him to hold a liquor license. He painted the candy store turquoise, put a kitchen at the rear, and opened up a funky-stylish

Cuban bistro where people paid twelve dollars for a plate of rice and beans. La Bodega was a triumph for its owner, who had lost his taste for rackets anyway, and really wanted nothing more than to make a living without having to leave his garden very often.

Less of a victory fell to Keith McCullough and Terry Sykes, who received private congratulations for their work, but no official recognition. Politically, that would have been awkward. No one was doing real jail time for a conspiracy to smuggle weapons, and a suspect had been shot through the heart when a wound in the arm might have been sufficient to subdue him. Even so, Sykes was miffed. "You said I'd get a citation," he groused. McCullough just shrugged. For him, the value of the undercover posting to Key West lay elsewhere. Not without anguish, he'd tardily examined his range of disguises and ploys, traced out the scarred seam where the masks ended and the person began. He decided on a trial separation from his wife and started discreetly keeping company with a cute town cop from Boca.

Michael, a connoisseur of romantic disappointments, got over Keith/David quickly, and, in the calm of retrospect, put him far down on the B list of significant attachments. Still, he swore to himself, as he had a hundred times before, that next time, he'd fall in love less hard, less fast. He managed to remain uninfatuated until he left Key West, but on the plane back to New York he sat across the aisle from a handsome guy named Ted. When Michael wrote to Angelina, as he'd promised he would, he told her he and Ted were trying to take it slow and easy, but his eye kept wandering around his fourth floor walk-up, trying to find room enough for two.

Louie and Rose also went back to New York, but only to put their affairs in order. Enough was enough with the plumbing business and enough was enough with the Bronx. Louie closed the store, but not before he'd tracked down Eddie the Dominican kid, hired him to help pack up the apartment, and given him a generous severance. Then Angelina's aunt and uncle moved back to Key West and started looking for a house. Their retirement would be a very modest one, but neither of them cared. After a life of feeling small, Louie had found a town where he felt big, where he'd found the bigness that was in him all the time; in the same town, a mild and tender contentment had sneaked up and surprised the hell out of Rose.

Paul Amaro went back to his quiet mansion and silent wife as a man who'd realized he was old. The world no longer matched the things he thought he knew about it, and while he might perhaps still have the strength to learn things over, he wasn't sure he cared to. There was peace in becoming archaic, serenity in lack of interest. Most mornings he still went to the Gatto Bianco Social Club, but he went there now as an obsolete executive, politely consulted but seldom obeyed. He drank coffee, watched Funzie Gallo get fatter and fatter. Sometimes he thought about his daughter. She would never again live at home, he knew; he wouldn't see her very often. Yet the loss he felt was tempered by the memory of their talk at Flagler House. She loved him for what he'd tried to do; forgave him for what he'd done. How many fathers could expect more?

Ziggy was both surprised and not surprised that Angelina wouldn't have him. How could a decade of devotion go so suddenly thumbs-down? Then again, how could a flesh and blood man, sloppy and selfish and sulky and real, measure up to the daydreams of such a passionate virgin? He would have disappointed her; just as well she dumped him. Secretly he was relieved. He'd flirted with the terrifying prospect of having a life, and he was off the hook again.

He was even more off the hook when word came, through intermediaries in Tampa, that Paul Amaro had absolved him, he was no longer under threat.

For the first time he could remember, he was free, and the freedom nearly wrecked him. The low roof was lifted from his world, he panicked at first at the lack of dark corners. Then he grew manic at the thought of his options. Exotic destinations whose names he'd evoked as impossible havens now in fact seemed real to him; they beckoned. He flew to Mexico, bummed around Belize, Honduras, sleeping in hammocks slung between palms. He told himself he'd come back to the States when he was ready, but ready for what, he did not know.

Angelina stayed in Key West for the summer. Having decided to live no longer on her father's money, she moved out of Coral Shores, found a small apartment and a job waiting tables. Quite often, she visited her aunt and uncle, ate Rose's lousy cooking. Once, they watched that first vacation video again, and laughed, a little smugly, at how different the town looked to a tourist, how little the tourists saw.

As April passed, then May, the weather got hotter and hotter, the breezes sputtered and died. Sometimes, after work, late, Angelina walked on the beach, to watch the moon and maybe find some scraps of moving air. One night she passed a man whose crunching footsteps were moving in the opposite direction. They smiled at each other. He had a nice smile, shy, and Angelina felt something that amazed her, felt in the ripeness of her body that her heart was also free. She sensed that they would meet again.

Key West 1996

978-0-595-46913-0
0-595-46913-2

Made in the USA
Lexington, KY
07 September 2011